romancing the workplace series

I0748078

The Midnight Meet-Up

alia smith

BAL
KON
media

ALSO BY ALIA SMITH

ROMANCING THE WORKPLACE SERIES

THE MIDNIGHT MEET-UP

Published by Balkon Media

Paperback edition ISBN: 978-1-916970-14-4
Also available as an E-book

A CIP catalogue record for this title is available from the British Library.

Edited by Hanna Elizabeth

Cover Design: graphichouse123

www.balkon.media

To the optimists and dreamers,
the coffee-fueled overthinkers...
and everyone who's ever accidentally fallen in love
when they least expected it.

ONE

♥

LILY

"BP's crashing, Dr. Harper," Patty states with all the urgency of someone reciting a grocery list.

My pulse is the only thing in this room that's not flatlining. Blood pools on the table. Monitors screech like they're mocking us. The only thing louder is the buzzing in my skull.

"Then let's stop wasting time," I reply, my voice firm. A clamp waits in my outstretched hand. There's a splash of scarlet, a tremble, and a surgical resident ready to crumble like stale cake. "If you hesitate again, you're out. Focus." If I say it enough, maybe one of us will actually do it.

The resident falters. My instincts kick in before he has a chance to fumble anything else. I snatch the instrument and take control. Methodical. Unforgiving.

"Suction," I snap, shifting my focus to the next step. Hours blur in my mind. Minutes turn into blood-soaked seconds. The patient's chest is open wide—I stare into the wound and wonder which will kill me first, the pressure or the sleep deprivation.

"Clamp, clamp, clamp," I repeat. My vision tunnels as I ignore the chaos around me. The monitors, the blood, the failure, all fade into the background. I locate the source of the bleed, pinpoint its weakness. Hands steady. Mind sharp. Five more seconds and it's over.

The patient's vitals crash lower.

"This should have been done ten minutes ago." Patty, again, as if I'm not aware.

As if I haven't been hyper-aware since I walked into this room. The buzzing in my head is a chainsaw now, drowning out everything but my pulse. No anesthesia needed; I've gone entirely numb on my own.

"We're losing him." A voice, a tremor, a doubt in my ability.

No.

"We are not losing him!"

Focus. Clamp. Focus. Clamp.

My hands blur through a dozen instruments. Scalpel. Forceps. Suture. I don't stop to figure out which. No time for a blood transfusion. No time for their second guessing. I can't lose another patient this week. Not like this. Not because of a surgical resident who can't keep up. I feel my exhaustion taunting me, daring me to fail, and I silence it with precision.

"BP's coming back," Patty says, softer this time.

I stitch a closure, count out three steady breaths, wait for the chest to rise on its own. It does.

"Nice work, Doc."

The silence should be comforting, but it's a reminder of how loud my failures were a minute ago. I survey the bloody battlefield around me, noting the carnage on the operating table and especially on the floor.

"Lucky he didn't bleed out," Patty adds, handing me the chart, calling it like she sees it. "That was a hell of a mess."

"We controlled it," I reply. Her eyes say we both know what "it" is. The word hovers between us like a question.

One crisis down, a hundred more to go. I strip off my gloves and toss them in the trash. "It won't happen again."

'More patients coming in from the same accident. It's gonna be a long one," Patty warns. "You planning to take a break, or you gonna keep working like you've got a death wish?"

I ignore the comment, the concern, the past twenty hours. "If you see an open OR, let me know." I catch the surgical resident's eye. Let him know with a single look that his card is marked. "Don't hesitate again," I remind him as we scrub out.

The hallway is cold and bright, which makes it easier to pretend I'm awake. I can't remember the last time I slept. My feet take me in two directions, toward the family waiting area and toward another twelve-hour shift.

The family sits in a cluster of panic, half-collapsed into chairs with soggy tissues and tear-stained faces. I know the type. The hysterics. The over-thankers. The ones who take and take and take until there's nothing left but sleep deprivation and regret. The patient's wife clutches her daughter's arm, using it as a handkerchief. Her sobs fill the entire room. Her breathing labored.

"He's going to be okay, Mom," the daughter says. She looks sixteen, and not at all convinced by her own words. "They've got this. Right?"

I'm five feet away and they're already fishing for hope.

"Mrs. Martin?" I ask, glancing down at the chart like I didn't memorize it hours ago. Like I don't have every detail tattooed behind my eyes.

The woman lifts her head, puffy and raw, eyes leaking relief. "Oh, God," she says, clutching the daughter harder, searching my face for answers. For more than answers. For reassurance and things I don't have. "Is he okay?"

"The surgery went well," I say instead, falling into a chair across from them. Mrs. Martin scoots closer, ignoring my attempt to keep this clinical. "We found the source of the bleeding and stabilized him." My voice is even. "He's stable in the ICU."

Tears form anew, pooling at the corners of the wife's eyes like the blood on my OR table. "Thank you. Thank you, thank you, thank you." Each word sounds like a sob. Like she's used to disappointment. Like she expected me to fail.

They start to tumble, a dam bursting, a river of relief. The woman throws herself at me with the reckless desperation of a patient in V-fib.

I'm quick to suture. I'm slow to react.

My limbs stiffen. Breathing tightens. I stand like an idiot with her arms squeezing me.

My heart knows exactly how many beats per minute this discomfort is. I don't move. I don't breathe. I don't acknowledge the tightness in my chest. She holds me as if I'm saving her life, but all I feel is failure creeping up my spine.

This is the worst I've done since the appendix incident of 2018. I could never have anticipated how hard the hit would be.

I swallow thickly, run through an emotional checklist and come up blank. I need to say something. Anything. A whole sentence. But all that comes out is, "It's my job."

I'm the least-human human they've ever seen.

Mrs. Martin releases me and collapses into the daughter's arms, where the gratitude feels a little more earned. I retreat instead, rubbing my neck where I still feel the contact. The warmth. The failure.

"You're sure he's okay?" The daughter this time, hopeful and sad and two seconds away from finding out I have nothing to give but medical updates.

"We controlled the bleeding," I repeat, turning clinical on

autopilot. "You can check in with the ICU." The words fill the silence.

"He's stable," I assure them. The subtext: I'm not.

Mrs. Martin cries into the daughter's hair. It's a tender, quiet scene that makes my stomach flip like I've swallowed a virus. It's the kind of connection I can't process, so I dissect it instead. Break it into tiny, manageable parts. I know how close I came to failing them. They don't.

"Thank you," the daughter says. "So much."

I rise and back away, stiff, aware of the mess I've left behind. My spine has more rigor than a cadaver. The family is a blur as I make my exit. Their relief is too loud. It makes me uncomfortable. It makes me feel.

I pretend not to hear.

I pause in the stairwell and let the cold wall bite into my spine, let it remind me that I'm a surgeon, not a failure. There's a small voice in my head that sounds suspiciously like my father, telling me that the difference between the two is paper thin. I shut him out, shut everything out. Echoes from the past twenty-four hours bounce off the walls, wrap around my neck. The uncertainty of everything except my exhaustion.

My body aches like an overworked muscle. My mind is worse, churning with static and blood loss. The adrenaline is gone and I feel every single second of the last shift, twenty hours stacked on top of one another. I let myself slide down the wall, as far as my pride allows, until I'm sitting on the stairs with my head in my hands and the exhaustion catches up with me.

Laughter echoes down the stairwell, muffled and distant and meant for people with lives outside these walls. It's a conversation I'll never be a part of, voices from another world. My mind is heavy, but it never shuts off. It whirs and hums and tells me that rest is for people who don't have anything to prove.

If my parents could see me now, collapsed on the stairs, they'd say I was a disappointment. They'd say I didn't have the grit or the drive. And they'd be right. I don't. Not today. Not like this.

The chill of the concrete floor seeps through my scrubs and into my bones. I close my eyes, but it's a mistake, because all I see are the images I've tried to bury deep: the car accident, the blood, the kid who nearly lost his dad because I'd hesitated.

It won't happen again.

My eyes snap open. The sterile white walls close in. My pulse thuds in my ears.

The wife. The hug. The awkward, strangled words that made me feel more helpless than a failed procedure. Why do people have to make things so damn messy? My chest tightens and I want to bolt, but the fatigue has other plans.

This is why I don't let myself think.

When you hold yourself together with stitches, you start to unravel the moment you stop moving.

The stairwell door creaks open and lets in two junior residents, chipper and laughing like the last shift was a walk in the park. Maybe for them it was. Maybe it always will be. They breeze past me without noticing I'm there. I should be thankful. If they saw me slouched on the stairs, they'd know how close I came to cracking.

I lean my head back and stare at the ceiling, ignoring the throbbing in my skull and the tiny, persistent part of me that says this isn't sustainable.

"Pancakes and waffles?" one of them says, as if he can't believe such things exist.

"Breakfast of champions," the other replies. "Count me in."

I try not to be bitter. I try to convince myself that I don't want that kind of freedom, that kind of detachment. That I've chosen this, and I'd choose it again.

"You coming, Dr. Harper?" One of the residents stops and peers down at me. He must not know me very well. He must not know I'm a ghost, haunting this place without even knowing why anymore.

I'm tempted to snap. I'm tempted to say something cruel, like, "If you have time for breakfast, you're not a real doctor."

But I surprise myself. The hesitation is a foreign feeling, an unfamiliar twinge in my chest.

"Maybe next time," I say. I'm not sure who I am for a moment.

The residents leave and I listen to their footsteps fade, listen to their easy laughter as they push open the stairwell door on a lower floor and disappear into the world. Their happiness is an echo, a hollow sound that rings in my ears and makes me more tired than ever.

I catch my breath, my pulse, my composure. I square my shoulders, push myself to my feet, and shove the fatigue away. This is the way it has to be. This is what it takes.

It's not pretty, but it's stable.

I push open the door and let it close with a decisive clang.

TWO

♥

NOAH

Blood pours like a bad horror flick, an over-the-top fountain of gore. I count six heartbeats on the monitor—each slower than the last—before the guy's done for, and I don't plan on wasting a single one. Not today.

"Noah, we're losing him," shouts Nurse Patty. She's all grit and tough love, which explains why I like her so much.

I cut a glance at the newbie, who's about five seconds away from ruining his scrubs.

"Shouldn't we wait for Dr. Patel?" he says, voice cracking, but I'm already snapping on gloves. "If we wait, he's dead." I'm not the waiting type.

This guy's artery is slashed, his blood forming little red lakes around the wheels of the gurney. We haven't seen a bleeder like this since New Year's Eve—the wound you'd get from whiskey bottles and pool cues, not the more pedestrian stabbings.

Nurse Patty yanks a fresh packet of gauze and shoots me a look that says both, 'you're insane' and 'hurry up.'

"He's crashing, Noah!" she shouts, barking out orders and elbowing the resident to suction.

The monitors tell me I have no room for error. No room for anything but an unsteady pulse and dropping BP. A heart rate that's only memorable because it's tanking fast. It's why I don't think twice about the thoracotomy or how much trouble I'll be in for it. You can't teach instincts like mine, but you can get your ass handed to you for using them. I slice the blade cleanly into his chest and feel a slight shudder as my hand hits the rib cage. Rookie loses more color.

"We're really doing this?" he asks, mostly to himself, while Patty already has her hands over the wound, keeping it steady, keeping it real.

I know better than to answer. I focus. The guy's lungs are in the way, his tissue and muscle resistant and fleshy and fighting. It's like an anatomy textbook come to life in a very R-rated fashion, and the kid looks ready to hurl. I pry the ribs apart. My gloved hand fishes inside like it's searching for the world's worst piñata prize.

It's been a few seconds now. Way too many.

"Nine-zero over forty," calls Patty.

The resident's still holding his breath, and I'm about to punch the air out of him if he doesn't catch it soon. "What now, doc?" Patty prods, no fear, just steel.

"I've got this," I insist. I hope.

The organ's a limp, purplish mass of nothing, and I thumb the artery, feeling where it's knotted and tearing and wanting to give up.

But I'm not the giving-up type.

Then: life.

It flutters under my fingers like a newborn bird. One kick. Two. Then full rhythm, and I swear it's the sweetest damn sound I've ever heard. Better than vinyl. Better than old guitars. A steady *lub-dub* from the ECG that wipes the horror-show clean, and for a moment, there's nothing else but this. The win.

"Pulse is one-ten. Pressure's coming up." The monitor pings alive. Patty's mouth quirks into what passes for a grin, and her satisfaction's almost as good as a thank-you note. "Not bad, doc. For a guy working solo."

I wipe my brow with a bloody wrist, feel the tension and adrenaline in every molecule of my body. "You know me—big on happy endings."

Patty snorts. "Big on something."

Resident regains some color. He's still more frightened than awed, but he'll come around. The rest of the team exhales. The room shifts from panic to relief, collective fear shedding like an old skin. Only the suction unit still wheezes, the wet splatter of blood underfoot like rain. They all saw it. They all saw what happens when I get in too deep and too fast and actually pull it off.

"He's stable. Let's get him to the OR." Patty takes charge, shoving the gurney out the door while the rest of the staff stand around, like we just caught the last ten seconds of the Super Bowl. Most of them still don't know what to say when Noah Carter hijacks a trauma case, and that's just the way I like it.

For now, anyway.

Because my celebrations last about as long as it takes for Dr. Patel to breeze in, take a sweeping glance around the carnage, and fix his stare on me. He's crisp. Unhurried. Puts together the whole situation before I even get a chance to bask.

"Dr. Carter," he says. "A word."

Dr. Ajay Patel's office AC is set so low I can feel it chilling my blood. If my talk with him lasts longer than five minutes, I'm suing for frostbite. The desk is a barren wasteland, and Patel's expressions aren't any better. He doesn't bother with hellos or have-a-seats, just straight to business.

"Dr. Carter," he starts, without preamble, "you do not make that call without an attending present."

He's the king of rule-following, and I can practically feel the protocol manual hurling itself at my head.

"He would have died," I counter, but not loud enough to sound like I have a leg to stand on.

"That's not your decision to make," Patel insists, voice clipped and sterile, like the rest of his damn office. He sits back, arms crossed in a way that makes me cross mine too, purely out of spite. "You are a resident, not a hero."

My jaw twitches. I hope it doesn't look too obvious. "With respect, I did what I thought was necessary."

His eyes bore into me, relentless, like a particularly exhausting CT scan. I'm still trying to thaw out from the frosty reception when he delivers the next blow.

"This is the last time we will have this conversation," he states.

The unsaid—*or else*—floats between us like an iceberg, and I know when I'm about to hit something hard. It takes every ounce of self-control not to roll my eyes or laugh out loud. Not because I don't believe him, but because I do. Patel isn't the kind to bluff. If anything, he's probably insulted that I don't take him more seriously.

"Understood," I say, my words as short and sharp as I can make them.

Patel doesn't respond. His silence speaks volumes, most of which are titled *You Are on Thin Fucking Ice*. I'm out the door and into the corridor before the walls start closing in. My pulse is still racing, still wired from the thrill of diving in headfirst and getting away with it. Almost. The only thing I hate more than getting called out is getting called out when I know I'm right, and it's eating me alive.

"Patel looks pissed," comes a voice from the nurses' station. Marcus Young. My partner in crime, except he never gets caught and never breaks a sweat. He's leaning against the counter, all casual-like, grinning in that way that tells me I'm about to be made fun of. "How bad was it?"

I pull up beside him, trying to match his breezy air, trying to forget the crack in my façade that Patel must have seen.

"Could've been worse."

He shakes his head in mock dismay. "Could've been better. So that's, what, your third warning?"

"Fourth," I correct, like it's a point of pride. "But who's counting?"

Marcus laughs, and it's a solid, reassuring sound, like a warm blanket over all this cold, clinical shit. He hands me a chart to review and claps me on the shoulder.

"You are," he says. "At least, you should be."

I snort, pretending not to care but caring more than I'd ever admit. It's the same argument every time, and Marcus has seen me through enough of them to have the script memorized.

"Patel doesn't want a repeat of last year, man. You're not in New York anymore. Just keep your head down for a while, okay?"

"Where's the fun in that?" I fire back, scanning the chart, scanning his face. He's the only one who ever dares to tell me the truth straight up, even if he knows I won't listen. Especially if he knows I won't listen.

We're in the eye of the storm, nurses running in every direction, clipboards flying, cases stacked up like overdue bills, but Marcus and I stand still in the chaos, anchored.

I shrug it off, or try to. "As long as the patients live, does it really matter?"

Marcus's eyes are sympathetic, but unyielding. He's got the whole perceptive-best-friend thing down to an art.

"Maybe not to you," he replies, "but this place isn't Emerald City, and you're not the Wizard. They play by different rules here."

"Rules, *shmrules*," I retort, feigning bravado, ignoring the tight knot in my chest, the one I never quite shake when someone calls me out on my shit. The one Marcus can see plain as day. "It'll be fine."

He arches an eyebrow. "It always is until it isn't."

I know he means well, but it's more than I can deal with right now. Too much truth, too much realism. I smile, a mask I've perfected over the years.

"You're right, Dad. I'll try not to embarrass the family name."

Marcus laughs again, this time louder. "Too late."

And maybe it is. Maybe it's way past too late. But at least we're still laughing about it.

The sixteen-year-old skater next on the list has the hangdog expression of a guy who's had both his bones and his pride severely broken. I'd put money on the pride being the more painful of the two.

"Dude, I think I broke it," he moans, pointing to the swollen balloon he used to call his hand.

I'm still fresh from my first scolding of the week, but I haven't lost my touch with bedside manner or sarcasm.

"What gave it away?" I ask, studying his chart. "The searing pain or the fact that your wrist looks like a pretzel?"

He glares up at me, the look every teenager saves for adults who don't immediately acknowledge how tragic their situation is. "Oh, you're funny."

"Most people think so," I shoot back, a grin breaking through despite the bruising Patel's lecture left behind. I nudge his arm gently to check the range of motion, and the kid winces in dramatic fashion.

"Am I gonna lose it?" he asks, half-concerned, half-expecting me to tell him he'll never play Xbox again.

"You'll live," I assure him, slipping on a pair of gloves. "But next time, maybe stick to Tony Hawk?"

He doesn't laugh, but I see the corners of his mouth twitch. Another hard-ass cracked, courtesy of Dr. Carter. The room's a different kind of chaos than before, still busy but humming along. This kind, I can handle with my eyes closed. I gently feel the mangled wrist again, then look him straight in the eye.

"Ready?" I say, making sure he knows what's coming.

The teen nods, an act of bravery that lasts all of one second before he shuts his eyes tight.

"Here we go," I tell him, steady hands on the fracture. "Three, two—"

A swift, precise motion. The crack sets everything back in place with a satisfying click.

"Wait, did you—?"

"All done," I confirm, grinning at his confused relief. "It'll hurt like hell for a bit, but you'll get used to it."

I unwrap my gloves, and he watches me, a strange mixture of awe and incredulity. I've seen the look a million times, but it never gets old. There's nothing like impressing a teenage boy, who has never been impressed by anything.

"You did that in, like, five seconds," he says, clearly wondering if I've been juicing.

I lean back against the counter, crossing my arms and enjoying the rare moment of being the good guy, the one no one's yelling at. "Better than spending ten weeks in a cast, huh?"

His eyes meet mine, still full of suspicion and admiration and a little bit of that leftover glare. I slap a temporary splint on and send him off for X-rays.

"Get him checked out and on his way," I tell the nurse,

handing over the chart. "This kid's got a story to tell, and it's not gonna sound believable if we keep him here all day."

The nurse nods, and the teen shoots me a last look as he's wheeled out.

"Thanks, doc," he mumbles, embarrassed and relieved, like most of my patients. Like most of the people in my life.

"No problem," I call after him, even though he's already out of earshot. I don't expect a parade in my honor, but I'd settle for a quiet cup of coffee, just me and the chaos and the dull roar of a trauma ward that never stops being loud.

The desk is stacked with more cases. An elderly woman with hip pain, a middle-aged guy with chest tightness, a toddler with a Lego where Legos should never be. Routine. Comfortable.

It's a fine line, what we do here. Walking the tightrope between urgency and ease, crisis and calm. One minute, I'm literally holding someone's heart in my hands, squeezing it like I want to restart the world, and the next I'm setting bones and cracking jokes and pretending like nothing gets under my skin. Not the work. Not the warnings. Not the way I run from one to the next, hoping this place can keep up with me, hoping I can keep up with myself.

"Dr. Carter, we need you in bay four," calls the nurse, and the respite vanishes, a puff of smoke. A pretty illusion.

"On my way," I say, grabbing the next chart and getting ready to jump back in.

By the time I get to the break room, my entire day has been caffeine-deprived, sarcasm-reliant, and desperately in need of a quiet five minutes. I crack open a drink and find Dr. Lily Harper, an incredible surgeon and reigning ice queen of Emerald Bay, standing by the coffee pot like it just insulted her entire family.

"Of course," she mutters, in that way that tells me I'm about to get way more enjoyment out of this encounter than she will.

"You seem surprised," I say, leaning casually against the counter. "Night shift coffee is a gamble at best."

Lily's sharp features are drawn in focused irritation, the kind she usually reserves for uncooperative interns. "And yet, somehow, I always lose."

There's a hum of broken air conditioning in the background. I sip my drink, let her think she's ignoring me, which is exactly the opposite of what she's doing.

"Rough night?" I ask, my voice as innocent as I can make it.

She finally looks at me, brown eyes flicking with the intensity of a thousand derailed plans. "I spent the last five hours stitching organs back together. And now, the one thing keeping me going is gone."

"The work or the caffeine?" I quip, knowing full well what she means.

"The caffeine," she states flatly, not missing a beat. I have to admire her dedication. And her stubbornness. It's almost as strong as mine.

"Poor Lily," I say, the mock sympathy dripping from my words as I hold up my half-empty energy drink. "You want half?"

"I'd rather die," she retorts, so fast and deadpan that it nearly knocks me over.

I have to laugh, because it's exactly what I expect from her. Everything I say, she's got a comeback twice as quick, twice as dismissive.

"All right, Doctor," I declare, enjoying the game, enjoying how much it bugs her that she's playing. "Let's make a deal. I'll refill the pot if you admit I'm your favorite ER doc."

She stares at me, unimpressed. "That's a bold assumption."

"I like my odds." I grin, and it's her turn to ignore me, except we both know she can't. I watch, amused, as she finally grabs the coffee canister and sets to work.

Lily Harper doesn't know how to lose, even at this. She doesn't know how to back down. Not when I corner her like this, and maybe that's why I do it. To see the cracks in her armor, the flashes of real, human irritation.

I'm still smiling as she turns her back, the universal signal for *I'm done with you*, which means it's only a matter of time before she gets pulled back in.

The pot gurgles to life, and she gives it more attention than it deserves, like if she just ignores me enough I'll leave, like she doesn't know I'm staying until she blinks first.

"That all you've got?" I press, loving the stubborn set of her shoulders. Loving the challenge.

"Pretty sure you're late for another heroic rescue," she counters, without looking, without losing the smugness in her tone.

I chuckle, raising my drink in a mock salute. "Catch you later, Lily."

The use of her first name earns me a frown, but it's worth it. Every time. I walk out of the room, energy drink still in hand, and already I'm wondering what she'll say next. Already counting the minutes until I get to bait her again, see that look she saves just for me.

The woman is infuriating. The woman is brilliant. The woman is never, ever going to admit I'm her favorite. But one day, she might. She might even mean it.

THREE

♥

LILY

It's almost a disappointment when the door swings open, and the expected silence of the break room isn't silent at all. The industrial coffee machine, which usually sputters and gags like a geriatric cat, is brewing a fresh pot, filling the air with what could be mistaken for real Arabica.

I pause in the doorway, the moment stretched out in caffeinated possibility, until my eyes land on Noah, leaning against the counter. *Not again.* His mouth curves into a slow, self-satisfied smirk, and I realize the bastard's been waiting for me.

I hover at the threshold, suspicion creeping in. This is an unusual situation, one that doesn't compute with the standard variables of a night shift. I've mentally prepared for a midnight caffeine injection, already gearing myself up to face another eight-hour stretch fueled solely by grit and sarcasm. Instead, I'm faced with this—this smug, scruffy, coffee-making apparition—and I can't decide whether to turn around or charge forward.

Noah is too calm for his own good, always inappropriately relaxed in the middle of whatever chaos the ER throws at him. Here outside the trauma ward, he looks almost domestic. The coffee pot finishes its cycle with a cheerful ding, and he reaches to switch it off, glancing up to meet my gaze with a casual nod.

"Lily," he says, stretching out my name like it's a question and an answer all at once.

The space between us is about the length of a heart transplant incision. I shouldn't be surprised he's here—if there's anything I've learned over the past few weeks, it's that Noah Carter is like hospital gossip. Just when you think you've gotten rid of him, he shows up in the most unexpected places.

"Doctor Carter," I say, trying for crisp formality but sounding more like I've got a frog in my throat. I can't help but follow the aromatic trail as it winds toward the counter. "Is that... coffee?"

"No, it's actually a new cardio drug," he replies, looking infuriatingly pleased with himself. "Didn't expect a refill, did you?"

I let his sarcasm drip for a moment, mirroring the coffee as it pools in the pot.

"I thought I smelled something suspicious."

I let my eyes narrow in on Noah, trying to gauge his intent like I would a particularly cryptic chest X-ray. He doesn't move, just watches me with a gaze that's both infuriatingly knowing and frustratingly attractive. This whole scenario—the dim lights, the surprise caffeine, his way-too-relaxed posture—feels engineered for maximum effect.

I clear my throat and raise an eyebrow, playing the role of a woman whose carefully scheduled night has not just been thrown off balance.

"Didn't realize you were working my shift. Or is this how

you get your kicks now? Sitting in empty break rooms and surprising unsuspecting surgeons?"

He grins. "Thought I'd do the night shift a favor and refill the pot. Better than your usual sludge, right?"

He knows too well how predictable I am, counting on the fact that I'd end up here at exactly this time. I cross my arms, trying to look unimpressed by both his presence and the aroma that's making it increasingly hard to stick to the charade.

"Why are you here?" I demand, doing my best to sound annoyed rather than intrigued. "The ER too boring for you?"

Noah shrugs, his expression so infuriatingly casual I want to shake him. "Had a couple hours free, thought I'd swing by. You know, remind you what real coffee tastes like."

"Should have known it was you. Who else has this much free time on their hands?"

Despite my best efforts to remain aloof, I walk straight over to the counter and the enticing aroma. I hate how transparent I am when it comes to caffeine. I hate how well Noah seems to know it.

He watches with amusement as I approach, like a cat watching a very stubborn mouse. I glance from him to the coffee and back again, deciding how best to navigate this mine-field of banter and beans. His smirk widens, and I'm struck by the ridiculousness of the situation—a hardened, dedicated, exhausted resident getting flustered over a goddamn cup of coffee and a laid-back ER doctor.

"Didn't realize my coffee would make this much of an impression," Noah says, his voice full of mock wonder. "If I'd known, I'd have started brewing it sooner."

"Is this the part where I'm supposed to thank you?" I ask, arching an eyebrow.

"Only if you really mean it," he teases.

I make a show of considering the steaming pot before me. "Hmmm. No."

"Fair enough," Noah chuckles. "But I saw that look in your eyes, Doctor Harper. You can't hide your feelings forever."

His words linger longer than I expect, layering on meanings he might not even intend. I'm suddenly aware of how easy it is to talk to him, how these little exchanges have started to feel like some warped version of a break.

He leans against the table now, close enough that I can see the faint scruff on his jawline. The intimacy of the space between us is unsettling.

Determined to keep this interaction within the realm of predictable sarcasm, I nod toward the door. "Don't you have something better to do?"

"Honestly?" he says, leaning back with exaggerated thoughtfulness. "No. This is kind of the highlight of my night."

The bastard. I let out a sigh, more resigned than exasperated, and finally give in to the temptation I've been resisting.

The coffee is just as amazing as I imagined.

"That good, huh?" Noah's voice cuts through my caffeine haze, and I shoot him a glare over the rim of my cup.

"Let's just say I'm surprised," I admit, unwilling to give him more.

"I'll take that as a compliment."

He would. And somehow, despite my better judgment, I find myself sitting down, a reluctant participant in this impromptu coffee date.

I take another sip, letting the taste linger before I grudgingly concede, "It's not bad."

"Not bad? Wow, now I'm really flattered."

I narrow my eyes, trying to project more skepticism than his coffee deserves. "This is a one-time thing, right? I don't want you getting any ideas."

He feigns shock, a hand to his chest. "Lily, I'm offended. You think I don't have anything better to do than supply caffeine to overworked residents?"

It's exactly what I think, and he knows it. I settle into a chair, fighting the gravitational pull of our banter and finding myself slipping in deeper anyway.

"So," he says, stretching the word out like it's an invitation. "Is this the first time you've sat down all night?"

The shift in topic is subtle, but I catch it. I know where this is going. I brace myself for his inevitable attempt to dissect my life choices, like they're an interesting case study.

"We can't all hang out in break rooms waiting to ambush unsuspecting colleagues," I reply.

"Come on," he nudges. "Don't tell me you haven't taken a break since you clocked in."

"I don't take breaks, Dr. Carter. I work."

"Why am I not surprised?"

The words hang in the air. There's no judgment in his voice, just curiosity. It bothers me more than I care to admit.

I try to deflect, going for sarcasm. "You mean, unlike you?"

He shrugs. "Somebody's gotta show you how it's done."

I'm not used to this kind of attention—this insistent, focused attempt to get under my skin. I thrive in ORs, where the only things I need to worry about are stats and sutures, where no one cares what I do in my nonexistent spare time. This, with Noah's watchful gaze and infuriating patience, is a different battlefield entirely.

"Seriously, though," he presses, his tone light but his gaze unrelenting. "What do you do when you're not here?"

"Try not to think about being here,"

"So, never?"

"Exactly."

"You're missing out, Harper. You're telling me you've never blown off steam? Never played hooky, even once?" he asks.

"Not everyone has the luxury."

Noah's silent for a beat too long, just watching me with an expression I can't read. I don't know why it's suddenly so hard to hold his gaze, but it is. I look away, focusing on the cup in my hands.

"You think I don't take things seriously, don't you?" he says.

"You don't. You float through the hospital like none of it matters."

"That's one way to look at it."

"It's the way I look at it," I insist.

"You don't have to," he says, so quietly I almost miss it. "But I've learned it helps if you can let go."

I've spent my whole life holding on, working harder, being the best, because what else is there? I don't know how to let go. I'm not even sure I want to learn.

"Is that what you call it?"

"What would you call it?"

I search for the right comeback, something that will end this conversation before it veers any closer to an inconvenient truth. But before I can speak, the break room door swings open, and Nurse Patty walks in with an authoritative stride that commands instant attention.

"Is that fresh coffee I smell?" she asks, her eyes landing on us with sharp amusement. "Looks like Doctor Carter's good for something, after all."

Noah laughs, a little too loudly, like he's been caught doing something he shouldn't. "I have my moments."

"It's a miracle, alright."

Patty nods, grabbing a cup and filling it with the steaming brew. "And here I thought all he did was sweet talk the nurses." She gives us a look that's loaded with meaning, the kind that says she knows exactly what we're up to—even when we don't.

"I'm a man of many talents," Noah replies, but I can hear

the slight tension in his voice, the awareness that Patty's interrupted something. Something that's rattled me.

"Good to know," Patty says, smirking as she heads back to the chaos of the ER.

The door swings shut, and silence fills the room, pressing down with an intensity that's hard to ignore.

"Now you can get back to avoiding your feelings in peace," Noah says.

I'm halfway to the door when he calls after me, his voice a lighthearted lifeline.

"Hey, Lily," he says. "It's nice, isn't it? To know you're not alone?"

I don't respond. I leave him to his coffee and his pop psychology.

The chaos of the ER crashes over me like a welcome wave. Monitors beep their urgent soundtrack, patients bicker from behind thin curtains, and residents hustle like ants on a deadline. A fellow doctor breezes past, giving me a nod that I barely register. I let the controlled mayhem wrap around me, finding refuge in the familiar chaos of other people's emergencies.

My feet move on autopilot, navigating through the controlled disaster zone. A woman clutches her ankle in the waiting area; a kid wails like he's the first toddler to ever get stitches. This is my natural habitat, where the problems are clinical and the solutions come in neat, chart-sized boxes.

The turmoil outside should be enough to drown out what's going on inside, but my mind keeps drifting back to the break room, to Noah's earnest question: "It's nice, isn't it? To know you're not alone?"

The din of the ER is preferable to the unexpected intimacy of his words. I cut a sharp path through the commotion, pretending not to hear the echoes of our conversation ricocheting off the antiseptic walls. A paramedic hustles by, followed by a nurse shouting orders to no one in particular. My heart is a little too in sync with the beeping machines.

I round a corner and spot Nurse Patty, stationed like a general surveying her troops. She barks instructions, dispatching nurses with the efficiency of an air traffic controller, until her eyes land on me. Her gaze is piercing, knowing. I feel exposed before she even opens her mouth.

"Doctor Harper," she says, but the way she smirks at my name makes me brace for the follow-up. "That didn't take long. Coffee date over already?"

I'm suddenly seventeen again, being caught sneaking back into the house by my very disappointed mother.

"It wasn't a date," I insist, but my voice sounds flimsy even to me.

"Could've fooled me," Patty replies.

Her sarcasm has an edge I usually find reassuring. Today, it's unsettling.

I cross my arms, trying to look busy and unbothered. "Shouldn't you be patching up one of those people who made the excellent life choice to crash their motorcycles into oncoming traffic?"

She waves a hand, dismissing my deflection with a seasoned nurse's ease. "Oh, they're fine. We've got bigger emergencies, like Doctor Carter—"

"Noah and I—" I start, but Patty cuts me off.

"Are just friends?" she supplies.

"We're colleagues," I correct.

"Sure, honey." She chuckles, a sound that manages to be both warm and cutting. "Keep telling yourself that."

I should walk away. I should go update charts or examine X-rays or do literally anything that involves avoiding this conversation.

Patty's gaze softens, her tone shifting from mockery to genuine concern. "Look, Lily, the way I see it? You could use a little fun."

"Fun," I echo, as if it's a foreign word I can't quite pronounce.

"Yeah, you know. That thing people do when they're not at work."

I have no idea how to respond. The truth is, I can't remember the last time I did anything for the hell of it. My entire life has been a tightrope walk of achievements and expectations, and the thought of throwing balance to the wind for the sake of "fun" is as appealing as elective surgery.

"Just think about it," Patty says, laying a hand on my shoulder. "And maybe cut yourself a little slack."

She returns to her post with a final, pointed look that follows me like a specter as I make my way down the hall. I push through the swinging doors, back into the bedlam of the ER, trying to shake off the feeling of being known too well. The faster I move, the less room there is for Noah and Patty to take up real estate in my brain.

I spend the next couple of hours drowning out my thoughts with work, but the chaos isn't as consuming as I'd hoped. The ER thins out around two a.m., leaving me alone with my thoughts and a particularly stubborn nosebleed patient.

As I sign the final chart and step back from the bustle, I realize something I'm not ready to admit. I want the connection I've spent so long pretending not to need. The thought unsettles me more than any emergency ever could.

By the time I finally head out, Noah's words and Patty's observations are firmly lodged in my mind. I'm not used to feeling this exposed, this raw, this human. I've spent years building an identity around being unshakeable, untouchable, but this? This is new. And I don't know what to do about it.

FOUR

♥

NOAH

A grown man should not look that proud over seven stitches. It's embarrassing. He's flexing like he just won a gold medal, but the shaky grin and twitchy knee tell me that, despite his claims, he's definitely not a needle guy. I slap a waterproof bandage over the handiwork and use the excuse to bump his knee. Just once, just a little. That sets him off with a jump and a string of surprised laughter that borders on maniacal. At least he's not screaming. There's been enough of that today, even for a Monday.

I give him the basics on what not to do if he wants the stitches to hold. Mainly avoiding chainsaws and not wrestling porcupines, since those seem to be the real dangers. He nods a lot and keeps blinking, so either he's touched by my concern or concussed. I start looking for the discharge papers when I spot Marcus across the room, washing his hands at the sink.

He's grinning in that I've-got-something-to-say way, so I pretend I don't see him, and that lasts a whole thirty seconds.

"Okay, what did you do?" Marcus is trying to sound all casual, but there's a glint in his eyes that suggests he already knows the answer.

I play dumb, hands in my pockets. I'm aiming for innocence but probably landing closer to misdemeanor.

"Nothing," I say. "Just made a new friend."

He raises an eyebrow like, *You really want to do this?* And I'm not about to lose the upper hand, so I just shrug. He crosses his arms.

"A friend or another person who wants to kill you?" he asks, pushing away from the sink. The floor is still wet where he was standing, but Marcus doesn't believe in health and safety when there's gossip at stake.

"Bit of both, probably," I tell him. "Keeps life exciting."

"Who was it?"

I walk backwards, making him follow me like a very nosy duck. "Dr. Harper."

Marcus stops and nearly drops his scrub brush. The laughter that comes out of him is loud enough to draw looks from the nurses, but he doesn't care.

"Lily Harper?" he says. "The Ice Queen?" Marcus smirks. The expression on his face is priceless. It's equal parts impressed and oh-you-are-so-dead.

"She prefers Dr. Ice Queen," I say.

Marcus shakes his head, the grin still there, like it's been glued in place. "Since when do you go for the overachieving types?" he asks. "I thought you liked your women a little more fun and a lot less likely to stab you."

"Well, you've been wrong before," I remind him. It was over a decade ago, but I can pretend otherwise.

"Never on this scale," Marcus says. "The only thing Lily Harper loves is surgery. She's like a robot. Or a vampire. Or a vampire robot."

He's not wrong. Which is probably why she drives me insane. She's smart, quick, terrifying—like an expensive sports car that I really shouldn't try to steal.

"I can handle Lily," I say, with a casualness I almost believe.

Marcus rolls his eyes and bumps his shoulder against mine. "Yeah, you say that now."

We pass the nurse's station and narrowly avoid getting caught in the crossfire of a three-way argument about bed assignments. At Emerald Bay Hospital, this is the grown-up version of recess, complete with shouting and people giving up in tears. I snag a pile of discharge forms from the counter and watch Marcus fish his vibrating pager out of his pocket. He checks it and groans.

"Damn it," he says. "Looks like they found me. Let's grab a beer after this shift. I want to hear all about how you plan to piss off the entire surgery department."

"Sure," I say. "Maybe I'll take notes from you, since you've been doing it since day one."

Marcus flashes me one more smile, the kind that says *I know what you're up to*, before vanishing into the ER chaos.

I don't miss the commotion in the exam room I'm walking by. It's hard to when the guy inside is loudly begging his wife for an epidural. "Or a gun, honey, just get me something!"

I laugh to myself and mentally count the minutes until this shift is over, when I get to torture Marcus with even more stories. But for now, I focus on the paperwork and finishing this shift without further drama, even if there is some small part of me that's disappointed Marcus didn't take more convincing. He's right about Lily. That should worry me more than it does.

Dr. Hale's office smells like hospital-grade success. Everything is sharp corners and polished wood, no-nonsense and sterile. It's the kind of place that makes you want to confess your sins and promise never to repeat them, just in case you're one of the germs he's trying to disinfect.

Hale stands behind his desk with arms folded, staring me down like he caught me sticking gum under one of those shiny chairs. He's going for intimidating, and it probably works on most people. But I'm not most people, and I know what to expect.

"Dr. Carter," he says, coolly. "We need to discuss your involvement in the cardiac trauma case from earlier."

Here we go.

"I heard you inserted yourself into a situation you were neither assigned to nor qualified for." Hale pauses, like he's waiting for me to admit to murder.

"I was in the ER when they brought him in," I say, not taking the bait. "His pressure was bottoming out. Thought I'd lend a hand before we lost him on the table. I'm sure Dr. Patel would have done exactly the same, under the circumstances."

"You thought." Hale unfolds his arms and leans forward. The glare from his desk lamp makes his glasses look like they're about to shoot lasers. "And now I'm hearing reports of recklessness?"

I let the word hang between us and pretend it's an interesting medical mystery.

"I wouldn't say that," I answer slowly, and watch him watch me.

"But others would."

"They'd say alive," I offer, half under my breath.

Hale's mouth twitches. He makes it sound like a curse. "Dr. Carter."

He's got the whole I'm-disappointed-in-you look perfected. It's a talent, really. I wonder if he teaches it in those continuing education seminars, right between *How to Conquer Your Enemies* and *The Care Profession and Keeping Your Giant Ego.*

"You keep blurring the lines between cavalier and responsible," he tells me. "And I can't have that. Not in this hospital."

I let that hang, too. It's one of his favorite speeches.

"Understood," I say.

Hale narrows his eyes. He doesn't like it when people fold too fast. He'd have done better in law school, where everyone puts up a fight.

"One day, that overconfidence is going to cost someone." He sounds almost mournful, but I know he's just trying to scare me. Like I haven't heard that one before.

I nod as if I've been humbled, and Hale takes it as a victory. "That will be all, Dr. Carter."

I exit the office with my imaginary tail between my legs. I don't slow down until I hit the break room and see Marcus leaning against the fridge.

"And a spanking from Dr. Hale to add to the collection. Two in one day... Good work." Marcus quips. He looks amused, which was exactly the point of the exercise.

"He's a kind and considerate disciplinarian," I say. "Could work on his foreplay a bit though."

Marcus hands me a mug. "Coffee with two sugars, extra political warfare?" he asks.

I roll my eyes and take the cup.

"Same lecture, different day. Apparently, saving lives isn't enough. I have to play nice, too."

I open the fridge and freeze. My milk carton is half-empty. I squint to make sure it's not my imagination.

"She actually did it," I say.

Marcus raises an eyebrow. "Did what?"

"Declared war." Maybe it's just milk, but it's the principle of the thing. Also, I don't like black coffee and this could prove catastrophic at about four in the morning.

"You're going to marry that woman," Marcus jokes.

"Not if she kills me first," I tell him, watching him leave. I mutter a "Thanks for the coffee," but he's already gone. I spend the next few minutes waiting for my pager to go off, wondering how Lily manages to steal my focus even when she's not in the room.

FIVE

♥

LILY

It's seven a.m., I've been on shift for eight hours, and I'm rushing from one examination bay to another. Someone barely gets out of my way before I flatten them with a stack of patient files. No time for apologies, no time for niceties, no time for—

"What, no hello?" Noah's across the hall, and then he's there, right there, his strides long and easy next to my surgical power walk. He matches my pace without breaking a sweat, infuriatingly athletic.

"Good morning, Lily," he says with a grin that could start a cult.

"It's Dr. Harper," I reply, knowing he's immune to correction. "And no time for greetings."

"Guessing you've already read the morning updates. Twice."

"Three times," I say, hoping to leave him in the dust.

The corridor is an obstacle course of people and gurneys and Noah. He moves like it's all a game, weaving through the chaos with that lazy, unruffled charm that somehow draws every eye in the room. His too-cool-to-care attitude is a siren song I refuse to hear.

"So, what's the rush today?" he asks, falling back into step. "Late for a trophy ceremony?"

"And what are you doing here? I didn't think the ER even needed clocks."

"Guess that's the difference between us," he says, hands tucked into his scrubs' pockets. "I'm not too concerned about deadlines."

"No, your specialty is crisis management," I say. "Never planning ahead, always swooping in at the last minute."

He nods like I've just paid him a compliment. "Exactly. You should try it sometime."

"I like having my life in order, thank you."

"Sure it's your life you're talking about? Sounds more like a meticulously organized library."

I aim a sharp look at him, though it only seems to encourage his persistent proximity. The air hums with overlapping conversations and Noah's voice cutting through it all.

"You seem very certain," I say, "that your 'wing it' method is sustainable."

"Hey, it's gotten me this far."

"Exactly my point."

"Nice. You've got a sense of humor buried somewhere in that schedule of yours," he says. "Knew I'd find it eventually."

We dodge a huddle of nurses, our shoulders almost touching. His presence is gravitational, pulling at me no matter how I angle myself away.

He looks over, his eyes daring me to admit I enjoy the chase.

"You know, I like this," he says, barely out of breath. "Little morning workout. Clears the mind."

"It's not a workout," I say, maneuvering around a lost-looking intern. "It's a head start."

"Still trying to outrun me?"

"Trying and succeeding," I say, managing to pull half a step ahead.

We're nearing the surgical wing, and I can almost see the look on his face—part admiration, part mischief—as I disappear through the double doors. But when I risk a glance back, he's still there, still maddeningly Noah, still entirely unshakable.

He gives a mock salute. "Catch you later, Dr. Harper."

At eleven in the morning, I'm in the surgical board room when everyone else shuffles in like they've got nowhere better to be. Noah takes the seat across from me.

"Congrats on the new project," someone whispers.

I frown. The department head hasn't even announced anything yet. That happens two minutes later, and then the world collapses.

"Dr. Harper, Dr. Carter, we're counting on you two for this." Emergency surgical protocols, joint effort, ER and Surgical departments. Noah, already shining with unearned victory. Me, swallowing back a carefully composed expression of horror. *It can't be true.*

The room shifts around me, people leaning in to discuss the news like we've been given a gift instead of a ticking bomb. I keep my gaze fixed on the notes I'm pretending to take, the words swimming on the page. Joint project. Emergency protocols. Unavoidable interaction.

"I'd like to echo that congratulations," Noah says, entirely too pleased.

I shoot him a look meant to incinerate.

"Come on, Lily, it'll be fun," he adds, stretching back like he's already completed the task.

I turn my attention to the department head, whose expression suggests he's satisfied with the minor explosion he's set off. This isn't a mistake; this is a deliberate pairing. They actually want us to work together. To collaborate.

"I expect everyone to fully support Drs. Harper and Carter," he says. "This project is a priority."

The room eventually clears out, leaving only the words "joint effort" echoing like a taunt.

Noah doesn't move, just sits there, the last person I want to deal with but somehow the only person in the room.

"I'm serious," he says. "Congratulations."

"What did you do?" I demand, setting my pen down with a sharp click.

"Nothing. I'm guessing someone finally realized what a dream team we'd be."

"This is not a dream," I say. "It's a potential nightmare."

"Only if you insist on overplanning," he says, not at all fazed by my rising irritation.

"That's called preparation, Noah. You should try it sometime."

"And miss out on all your brilliantly panicked reactions? Not a chance."

"I am not panicked," I lie, gathering my things with a precision that should register as fury.

"You just don't like sharing the spotlight," he says, not unkindly. "You think I'll drag you down."

"No," I counter, "I know you'll drag me down."

"Sounds like you're a little scared of some healthy competition."

"We're supposed to be on the same team," I say, though I don't even sound convinced.

"Then you've got nothing to worry about," he says.

He stands up, smooth and confident, like this has been the plan all along.

My response is a brisk nod, an about-face, and an exit as fast as humanly possible. He's following me, I'm sure, but this time I manage to escape before he catches up.

The break room is an incubator, and I'm about to overheat. It's early afternoon, and Noah's sitting across from me at a small table buried in research journals and laptops. He's as loose and uncontained as ever. Me, I'm the opposite, frayed nerves barely bound together by highlighters and discipline.

I push a meticulously structured outline in his direction, loaded with hard data on post-ER surgery survival rates. "This should guide us," I say.

"Love that you can twist the numbers to fit our needs," he responds.

"That's not how research works," I snap.

"If you say so," he grins.

I think I might implode.

We've been at this for an hour, maybe more. Noah seems unfazed, but I can feel the beginnings of a stress migraine.

"We need a clear plan," I insist, shoving another printout across the table. It's color-coded, comprehensive, and perfect.

"We need room to breathe," he says, like this is a yoga class.

My fingers tap a staccato rhythm against the tabletop. "You can't just wing a research project."

"Says who?" He runs a hand through his hair, scruffy and reckless. "Maybe we'll discover something unexpected."

"And maybe we'll waste weeks chasing our tails."

"It's called innovation."

"It's called chaos."

He leans in, too close for my comfort. "Is it physically painful for you to let go a little?"

"Yes," I say, only half-joking.

"Look, I respect your method," he says. "But we need flexibility. Real life isn't a controlled environment."

"This project can be."

"Don't you get bored, Lily? Doing everything by the book?"

"I get results," I say, as though that's the end of it. It never is with him.

"Sure, but do you get any fun?"

He lifts a document from the pile, skimming it with infuriating casualness. "This is good," he admits. "Detailed. We can work with it."

"It's what I've been saying," I mutter, refusing to be mollified by his approval.

"Okay, let's split the work," he suggests. "You do the heavy lifting; I'll fill in the blanks."

"There shouldn't be blanks," I say, pinching the bridge of my nose.

"I think you're convinced the world will end unless you control every second of it."

"Only because you're determined to do the opposite," I reply, giving him a hard stare.

"It's what makes us such a good team," he says.

I pause, unsure if I want to disagree.

"This isn't going to be easy," I say, softer now.

"No," he agrees. "But it's going to be interesting."

He holds my gaze a moment longer than necessary.

"We should get back to work," I say.

"Yeah," he replies, stretching like a cat. "Let's get to it."

Someone screams, "Incoming!" and then the world blurs, adrenaline and urgency overriding every other sense. The emergency room fills with a tsunami of trauma victims from a multi-car accident. Gurneys are flooding in, the noise sharp and jarring against my focus. The space rearranges itself around critical mass and bloody chaos. Noah's voice cuts through it all, louder than the sirens and shouts. He's in command, a lighthouse in the storm.

"Collapsed lung in Room Three," he orders. "Dr. Harper, let's go."

A resident fumbles, his hands slick with sweat or blood.

"If we wait, he's dead," Noah says.

I'm right there, scalpel in hand, the steady to his instinct. We don't even look at each other, but it's like we share the same heartbeat.

We're moving through a sea of noise and desperation. Noah shouts instructions, every word purposeful and clear.

"Get the bleeders clamped!" I command, my voice slicing through the noise as we push through the crowded hallway.

"Prioritize the crush victims!" Noah directs, and the team shifts like a well-oiled machine.

This is where we clash and blend. This is where I'm most alive.

Room Three is a war zone. The patient's chest is a battlefield of trauma, every second critical.

"He needs a chest tube now," Noah says, hands moving swiftly over the man's broken ribs. "Lily, you ready?"

I'm already scrubbed and masked, anticipation pulsing like a second heartbeat. "Always," I reply.

A nurse suctions blood, red and visceral against the sterile white. The lights are blinding; the tension electric.

"Let's do this," Noah says, as if it's a dare.

We move together, a two-person assault on death itself. The room fades away until it's just us and the trauma, our skills fusing like a new alloy.

"Rib spreader," I demand, as precise as a conductor with an orchestra.

"Suction!" Noah follows, not missing a beat.

He's bold, aggressive, exactly what the situation demands.

"Needle and wire," he says, sealing the last bleeder with confidence and a hint of panache.

"Pressure's dropping!" a nurse calls, eyes wide and uncertain.

"Start compressions," Noah commands. "Lily, internal massage. Now."

I plunge my hand into the chest cavity, feeling the rhythm of life and death under my fingertips. It's gruesome. It's vital. It's everything I've trained for.

"Got it," I say, the heartbeat strengthening with every second.

Our eyes meet for a brief, charged moment over the mask's edge, and in that flicker of time, everything else disappears.

"Nice work, Dr. Harper," Noah says as the monitors stabilize, his voice tinged with the smallest note of admiration.

"Team effort, Dr. Carter," I reply, trying to keep my own respect buried deep under professionalism.

We step back, letting the nurses finish, our clothes spattered with the evidence of success.

The tension shifts from frantic to relieved. I feel the adrenaline begin to fade.

"So," he says, "are you still worried I'll drag you down?"

I give him a sidelong glance. "We'll see," I say, and for the first time, I actually mean it.

I'm caffeinating. It's the late-evening ritual of running on fumes and making plans to run on more fumes. The break room is a shrine to artificial energy, scattered with Styrofoam cups and bad intentions.

I sit across from Noah, case notes and adrenaline still buzzing in our heads. The day's trauma looms between us, half-intensity, half-triumph.

"Your decision-making in there saved lives," I mutter, staring into my coffee like it might offer me something stronger.

Noah lifts his cup in mock-toast. "And your precision stopped us from falling apart."

His tone is less teasing now, almost sincere.

Neither of us knows what to say next.

The silence is comfortable in a way I'm not used to, like a blanket I can't decide if I want to pull around me or throw off. We're both still catching our breath from the insanity of the day, exhaustion seeping into our bones, the sharp edges of competition worn down to something closer to camaraderie.

I risk a glance at him. He looks different, stripped of his usual bravado. Tired but not defeated. Human.

"You really think it was the right call?" I ask, though I already know his answer.

"Yeah," he says. "But I didn't expect you to jump in like that."

"It's what I do."

"It's what we did," he corrects, and there's no arrogance in his voice this time. Just fact.

"I meant what I said," he adds, his voice lower. "About us being a good team."

"Don't get used to it."

He smirks. "I think you liked it."

I roll my eyes, the old habit of pushing him away more reflex than anything else. "What I like is a clear outcome."

"And what do you call today?" he asks, genuinely curious.

"A mess," I say, then a beat later, "A win."

"I'll take it," he says.

Noah taps his fingers against his cup, a muted rhythm in the quiet room.

"Don't know about you," he says, finally standing up, "but I might try to sleep tonight."

"Don't know about you," I reply, mirroring his words, "but I might work."

We pause, suspended in a moment neither of us expected to have.

He nods. "Good night, Dr. Harper," he says, leaving with the quiet confidence of someone who's not worried about what happens next.

It takes me a full minute to realize I'm smiling into my coffee.

SIX

NOAH

The pager's shriek rips a hole in my sleep cycle and probably my eardrum. There's something singular about the sound: it's not like a normal alarm, which nags and pleads; it's a banshee wail, demanding attention and promising blood. I glance at the display: "PED EMERG—CODE RED."

That's how you start a morning in the ER. No warm-up, no stretching. Just a straight sprint from break room to trauma bay, coffee sloshing in my veins, half a sandwich dead on the table behind me.

The ER is already in tilt mode. One of the rotating glass doors is stuck open, and it's pouring down and cold, drenching the entrance with a streak of Seattle rain. Inside, the trauma team's prepping for impact, shifting supplies and rolling carts like a pit crew on meth. I catch Nurse Patty's eye as I push through. She's already got the gloves out and the trauma kit cracked open.

"Talk to me, Patty," I say. My hands are in gloves before I reach the kid.

"Eight-year-old male. Fell from the top of a jungle gym at school. Unresponsive on arrival. Suspected internal. Mom's a mess." She jerks her head toward a woman pacing a three-foot line near the gurney, mouthing prayers into her knuckles.

The kid on the table is small, which somehow makes it worse. Dried blood fans out across his T-shirt like a war wound, and his legs are too still, splayed the way only unconscious kids and dead bugs land. He's pale with a ghostly tinge, lips too blue, breath a shallow flutter under the oxygen mask.

"Okay, people, let's get a line in and start a cross-match. I want scans lined up in the next five, not ten," I bark.

A resident tries to hook up the IV and fails, shaking more than he should. "Hand," I say, and he gives up the spot on the kid's arm, skin so thin you could trace the vein with your fingernail.

The mother is up in my face before I can say anything else, mascara making black runoff creeks down both cheeks. "He just—he was just playing, he—"

"He's in good hands," I say, using my calm voice. The one I reserve for parents, high-strung patients, and sometimes Lily when she's circling the sun too fast. "You did everything right getting him here. We're going to fix this."

There's a flicker of trust, or maybe it's just exhaustion. Either way, she collapses into a chair, one eye glued to the chaos, the other glazing over with dread.

Kids are the one thing I can't compartmentalize. Adults, sure—everyone has a number in the actuarial table, and you get what you get. But kids? They haven't even had a chance to screw up their lives yet. Everything feels like it's stolen, not just lost.

A whiff of memory: Lucy, six years old, blood on her knees, me patting her head with a paper towel, telling her it's fine, she's fine, but she's not breathing now, and neither am I.

"Pulse is dropping," calls one of the nurses.

I'm already on it. The room tightens around my focus; everyone's waiting on my next move, like I'm the only adult left in the building.

"Get a crash cart ready. I want trauma surgery paged now."

Patty reads my mind. "Already did."

"Let's get him stabilized for imaging," I say, then to the kid: "Hang in there, buddy. You're not allowed to bail this early. House rules."

His eyelids flicker, or maybe I just want them to.

The team works the protocol like it's gospel, but I'm improvising, rewriting the verses in real-time. He's losing too much, too fast. There's a burst of action as we load him onto the gurney, the kind where every second ticks louder than the last.

As they wheel him away, I catch the mother's eye again. She's clutching the chair so hard her fingers have gone white.

"He's strong," I say, because sometimes a lie is better medicine than hope.

She nods, shaking, and I get the feeling she hears me anyway.

The trauma bay empties out, leaving behind only the mess —bloody gauze, a toy truck someone yanked out of the kid's pocket, and the afterimage of a disaster narrowly postponed.

I take a breath, counting down from ten. The world snaps back into its usual shade of mayhem. I toss my gloves in the bin and look for something, anything, to do with my hands.

"He's lucky you were here," says Patty, coming up with a clipboard.

I shrug, but my heartbeat hasn't let up. "We'll see how lucky he is after the knife."

She gives me a look that says she knows more than she lets on. "You want me to keep the mother updated?"

"I'll do it." The words come out before I can think better of it. "Just... give her a minute."

Patty nods, drifting away, and I stand in the ruins of the trauma bay, watching rain streak the windows and trying not to picture the kid's face in every shadow.

The OR is its own universe, bright and cold and utterly indifferent. The kid is on the table, chest prepped and draped, a single star in the middle of a field of green. Everything else falls away—the wet shoes, the sticky floors, the mother's rabbit-thumping heart out in the hall. Here, it's just flesh and blood and time.

I run the checklist. Instruments: accounted for. Scrub nurse: triple-checked. Anaesthesiologist: eyes never leaving the monitors. The residents are in position, hands up, faces blanched and goggled. The attending surgeon—technically my superior—gives a tight nod and says, "You're lead, Dr. Carter."

I nod back, and the scalpel's in my hand like it never left. "Let's make this look easy," I say, and the team laughs, nervous and thin.

The first cut is clean, textbook. I let the residents suction and clamp, watching their hands and feeling the old rhythm take over. The kid's heart is steady but faint on the monitor, something I'm not going to stop watching.

I'm halfway through the dissection when I spot it—an arterial nick, just shy of disaster. The bleeder is buried, sneaky, and it takes a microsecond to decide: go deep and risk more trauma, or work the margins and pray. I opt for door three: grip it, clamp it, and hope my hands are as steady as my voice.

They are.

Right as I'm threading the suture, I glance up at the scrub nurse and catch a flash of red above her mask—a dry, raw patch just below her eye, obvious even under the stadium lighting.

"Hey, Collins, your cheek," I say, not looking away from

the stitch, "you should try calendula ointment for that. Prescription strength. Works better than the hospital stuff."

She blinks, surprised. "Noted, Doctor."

"Sorry, I just can't stand inefficiency. Especially in skin."

The room chuckles, and the tension drops five degrees. Even the attending cracks a smile.

Back to the kid. The vessel holds, the blood flow eases. The next steps are by the book—clean, close, hope. Every move is muscle memory, but the difference is in the stakes. This is a person who might be drawing stick figures on a thank you card to the nurses by next week, if we get this right.

The final closure goes smoothly. Monitors brighten, lines stabilize. The team exhales in chorus.

"That was... damn good," says one of the residents, voice reverent.

"Teamwork," I say. "And next time, someone else gets to be the hero. I'm due for a nap."

As we clear the field, I glance up at Nurse Collins. She's eyeing me like I just guessed her Social Security number.

"Thanks for the tip," she says.

"Anytime," I reply, and for a second, I let myself feel a tiny bloom of pride. Then I remember the mother in the hallway and the mountain I have to climb to get back to baseline.

I strip the gloves, toss them, and trade the OR for the hallway's recycled air, leaving behind the world's most expensive version of hope stitched up in three layers.

In the waiting area, the mother is a fixture—no one else could look that hollow and still animate. Her knee bounces in a panic rhythm, and she jumps when I say her name.

"Mrs. Jacobs?"

She stands, tries to look braver than she is, and fails. I motion for her to sit, then crouch down so we're eye-level, like I'm not the same guy who just fished a pint of blood out of her kid.

"He's okay," I say, skipping the pleasantries. "We fixed the bleed. There's going to be a scar, but he's a tough kid. He'll be running around again in a week or two."

It's like turning off a power grid. Her shoulders collapse, chin hits chest, and for a second all she can do is sob, fists pressed into her eyes like she could hide in her own bones.

I let her cry it out. The best medicine sometimes is silence, or at least not making it worse.

"Can I see him?" she says finally, voice shredded.

"He's in recovery, still asleep. But yeah, you can."

I lead her through the maze of recovery rooms, the air heavy with disinfectant and whispered prayers. The boy is there, small and bandaged, chest rising slow and steady. She stands at the doorway, afraid to touch him, as if he's made of glass.

"You can go closer," I say.

She does, and when she brushes his hair back from his forehead, her hands are shaking so badly she nearly misses.

I hand the mother a box of tissues, because it's easier than dealing with tears.

"The team here is the best, he's in good hands," I say.

She thanks me a thousand times, words tumbling out too fast to catch. I nod, say it was a team effort, and duck out before I start to care too much.

In the on-call room, the lights are dim, the couch lumpy and broken. My sandwich is right where I left it, and so is my appetite. I stare at the wall for a good five minutes, letting the exhaustion claw its way in.

This is the part no one talks about: not the surgery, not the saving, but the empty echo that follows. You win a round, but the fight never ends. And no one is ever really off the clock.

The couch in the on-call room is the closest thing I have to a bed. It's a repurposed relic from someone's living room, stuffing bleeding out the sides, and probably a vector for several strains of MRSA. I sprawl across it, staring at the ceiling tiles, each one a slightly different shade of nicotine yellow. My brain won't shut up, cycling through the trauma, the win, the impossible odds, and back again.

My phone buzzes against my thigh. I half expect it to be a page from the ER, another disaster inbound. But no, it's just a text—no, not just a text. It's from Ava.

Ava is—was—an ER nurse before she left for a year of "finding herself" in Mexico. She's back now. I know this because she announced it in all-caps the moment her plane landed, followed by a sequence of winking emojis that made my skin itch.

Her message is short, but not subtle:

I'm bored. Want to come over and fix that? 😏

I stare at it, thumb hovering over the reply. We both know what this is. She wants a hook-up, not someone to talk to. That used to be enough for me—hell, sometimes it was preferred. No complications, no feelings, no maintenance. Like ordering takeout for the soul.

But now, all I can think of is the last time I was with Ava. Post-coital, both of us on opposite ends of her bed, scrolling through our phones. The silence was so absolute, it felt engineered. She was right there, but a million miles away. There's a word for it—ennui. French for "This is fine, but why bother?"

Another buzz:

You there?

Yeah, I'm here. Just not the same "here" as before.

I thumb back through our old messages, searching for something real. There's a lot of flirting, a lot of innuendo, but nothing that survives the moment. Even our fights were boring —scripted, almost. I scroll further, as if I'll find the missing piece somewhere in the feed, but it's all the same: disposable, temporary, a high with no half-life.

I think about Lily, and it pisses me off. She's nothing like Ava. She's sharper, meaner, more alive. She calls me on my bullshit, cuts through my defenses like they're made of rice paper. With her, every conversation is a duel; every silence, an armistice. I don't know what I want from her, or what she wants from me, but I know I've never been bored.

Ava sends another text:

> It's okay if you're seeing someone. Just
> say so.

I'm not, but the idea doesn't bother me. Maybe I should be. Maybe I want to be.

I close the thread and, after a moment's hesitation, delete the whole thing. It's weirdly satisfying, like yanking out a loose tooth. It hurts for a second, and then it's gone.

The silence in the room is still there, but it doesn't feel as empty. If anything, it feels cleaner.

I toss my phone onto the armrest, close my eyes, and wait for whatever comes next.

The new section of the trauma protocol I've been working on is right where I left it—centered on the break room table, half-buried under a pile of abandoned journals and an empty energy drink. I flip it open, expecting the same cold bureaucrat c jargon that's haunted every hospital since the dawn of time.

Instead, it's a forensic masterpiece. Lily's handwriting is a force of nature—tiny, all-caps, each word compressed to its absolute limit, but razor-sharp and perfectly aligned. Every margin is full of notes, corrections, tweaks. She's cross-referenced studies, flagged protocols, even color-coded highlighters like she's building a bomb and the slightest error might blow the whole floor sky-high.

I find myself smiling, which is a new and alarming development. She's circled a stat in the second section—thrice, just in case I missed the point—and written, in bold black ink: "THIS IS WHY YOU PLAN AHEAD, MORON."

I trace the line with my finger, and for a second, I wonder what she'd do if I just showed up at her door and said I wanted her—not the file, not the project, but... her. The idea is so insane, so completely off-script, that I laugh out loud.

I work through her comments one by one, revising and expanding, trying to match her relentless logic. It takes longer than I'd like, but when I'm done, the document is the best damn version of itself I've ever seen. I scribble my own notes in red, just to leave a mark. Not to compete, just to... exist next to hers.

When I finish, it's dark outside, and the clock says I've been at this for two hours. I look at the finished draft and feel the strangest urge to show it to her, see her reaction, make her proud, or at least less annoyed.

I could just leave it in her office, but that feels cheap. Instead, I gather the papers, stack them with surgical precision, and promise myself I'll hand it to her tomorrow. In person.

It's a weak excuse to see her again. But it's better than nothing. And right now, that's enough.

SEVEN

♥

LILY

The break room is empty except for Noah and me. He sits close, his presence a constant, easy reminder that I have better things to do than indulge his careless spontaneity.

I present our revised outline—neatly typed, stapled, color-coded. I'm sure I hear him stifle a laugh when I reveal the Gantt chart I added this morning, but I keep talking over him, ensuring he knows how serious this is.

He listens, arms crossed, eyes not as dismissive as usual. "A bit ambitious, don't you think?" he says, flipping through my hard work like it's yesterday's newspaper. "Might be worth letting people breathe between tasks."

I remind myself to be civil, that professionalism is key to surviving this collaboration. We debate the merits of structured timelines versus flexible, patient-centered approaches, and I almost get whiplash from the unanticipated moment when we agree on something.

This isn't going to be easy.

"Seriously, Lily. It looks like you robbed an office supply store." Noah grins, leaning back in his chair, impossibly casual.

"This is a project, not improv night at the comedy club," I snap, wishing my annoyance would wipe that smile off his face. "Organization is key to success."

He picks up a copy of the outline and waves it like a flag. "You think one of these for each person, or do we save paper and share?"

"I can make more." I glance at my watch, indicating I have better things to do than listen to his jokes. "This is important, Noah. I want it done right."

"And doing it right means breathing," he says, catching my eye. "Something we're big on in the ER."

I'm tempted to remind him that in the ER, they have to page actual surgeons when things get complicated, but I hold back. Instead, I take a breath myself. I can handle this. Noah may not respect schedules or structure, but he's good at his job, and I can use that.

"So, where do you want to start?" I ask, steering us back on course. "My outline suggests beginning with establishing clear protocols."

His eyebrows shoot up. "Really? I thought it said, 'Here's a six-month sentence for anyone with a life outside the hospital.'"

"It's an efficient timeline," I insist, though I can't help noticing how he makes everything sound so simple. *Too simple.* "We'll get better results if we have a concrete plan. Something adaptable leads to chaos."

"Or to innovation," he counters. He taps the table with a finger, annoyingly rhythmic, but at least he's focusing. "Let's think bigger than just ticking boxes. What's really going to help patients?"

"Protocols help patients," I insist. "It's what keeps them safe. You don't just 'wing it' in surgery, Noah."

He shrugs, too relaxed for someone who's arguing with me. "But we don't always know what we're dealing with until we see it. Especially in trauma. We need room to adjust."

He's wrong, but he's not as wrong as I expected him to be. I tap my pen, consider what he's saying. "Adjustments," I concede, though the word tastes bitter. "Fine. We can build in some flexibility. But there needs to be a foundation."

"Agreed." Noah's nod is more serious, his teasing finally dialed down. "But if it's all foundation, nothing gets built."

It's more cooperative than he's been all day. I allow myself a small smile. "That sounds like something a motivational poster would say."

He points at me. "See? You're loosening up already."

As the hours pass, the room shifts. My irritation with him melts into a surprising kind of respect. Noah watches me organize our chaos into a workable plan, and I watch him turn rigid lines into flexible, dynamic paths. We're building something new, and it's not at all what I thought it would be.

"So this is how you operate," he says as I pin our final chart to the wall. "Who knew a control freak could be so open to suggestion?"

I roll my eyes, but there's no bite left in it. "And who knew Mr. Laidback could actually focus long enough to contribute?"

He laughs, a sound that resonates in the room and between us, filling the spaces I didn't know were there.

"We should call it a day," I say, packing up but not rushing out the door.

"Or a truce," Noah suggests, leaning against the table. "If we keep agreeing like this, people will talk."

I shoot him a look, half-warning, half-amused. "If we keep agreeing, we might actually finish this."

"Where's the fun in that?"

I look up after another hour or so of protocol planning, and realize that we're the only two people left in the break room, surrounded by coffee cups, scattered notes, and too many words. My eyes burn from lack of sleep, my fingers are ink-stained from rewriting protocols Noah insists aren't necessary.

He watches me make sense of our mess, his mind too sharp for someone who should be exhausted.

"We really should leave," I say, though it comes out more as a question than I'd like.

He doesn't answer, just smirks in that infuriating way that means he's nowhere near done. I should hate that we're still here, but for some reason, I don't.

"You make sense of chaos better than anyone I've ever met," he says, gesturing to our tangled web of papers. "I'd still be trying to find the first page."

"Obviously, I'm a genius," I reply, though I'm more proud of his admission than I let on.

"A genius who needs sleep." He glances at his watch. "Think they'll kick us out?"

I shake my head. "Nah. We practically own this place."

He leans back, surveys our progress with a satisfied nod. "Never thought I'd see the day. You actually getting along with me?"

"Don't get used to it."

"You know," Noah says, leaning forward, "I always wanted to be a veterinarian."

I raise an eyebrow. "Another of your famous jokes?"

"Not this time." He's smiling, but it's more memory than amusement. "Then I fainted the first time I saw a dog with a broken leg."

"Fainted?"

"Passed out cold. Total disgrace." He shrugs, and I can see the kid he used to be—the one who was fearless until he wasn't.

"Should have known then you weren't cut out for real medicine," I tease.

"Should have," he agrees, eyes meeting mine. "But I never know when to quit."

"I performed surgeries on my stuffed animals," I admit, the sudden turn surprising even me. "With actual scissors. My parents confiscated my toys."

He laughs. "What were you, five?"

"Three."

"You win. You always win.

"Okay then. Med school stories?" Noah asks, raising an eyebrow. "Bet you were at the top of your class."

I feign shock. "Who told you? That's confidential information."

"Wild guess."

"Can you guess the worst moment of my internship?"

"Not even gonna try," he says. "Tell me."

I take a breath, dive into the memory. "ER rotation. First week. Car crash. The doctors who witnessed it call me Dr. Loses-It to this day."

He chuckles, the sound unexpectedly kind. "Didn't peg you as the kind who panics."

"I don't," I insist. "Anymore."

"I had a lot of worse moments." Noah looks past me, to the window or somewhere beyond it. "Lost a kid. Probably should have quit then too, but I'm stubborn."

The room shifts with the weight of his words, the air charged with shared histories.

"You didn't quit," I say.

"Neither did you."

It's clear we've done all we can do for today. I gather my things with practiced efficiency, a ritual as precise as it is empty.

'Do you ever think we work so much because it's easier than dealing with the rest of life?" he asks.

The question echoes. I focus on my packing rather than looking at him. Laptop into bag, notes stacked, pens aligned. "I work because I'm good at it," I say, the words too mechanical, even to my ears.

'That's a given," Noah replies, his voice closer. "Doesn't answer the question, though."

I look up, caught in the calm intensity of his gaze. He's waiting for something more, something real, something human.

'What else is there?" I deflect. "Outside of this?"

He doesn't respond immediately, just watches me with an understanding that's almost unbearable.

'Life," he finally says.

I shove a pen into my bag, annoyed at its refusal to stay put, annoyed at everything.

'Maybe for some people."

Noah doesn't let up. "You're one of those people, Lily."

The quiet conviction in his voice is infuriating, and for a second, I consider walking out, leaving him there with his uncomfortable truths and unwavering eyes. But I can't. Something roots me in place, holds me to this conversation like gravity.

'You're wrong," I insist, a last-ditch effort to reclaim some semblance of control. "Work isn't easier. It's just better."

'Sure about that?"

I have to break this connection, this understanding that threatens to unravel everything I've built. "What about you, then?" I shoot back. "Always here. Always working. Maybe you're the one avoiding something."

He nods slightly, the movement slow and accepting. "Maybe," he admits, but there's no defensiveness in it. Just a reflection of what he sees in me.

"I have to go," I say, my voice sharper than I mean it to be.

Noah doesn't try to stop me. He just looks at me with that same knowing expression, and I hate how exposed it makes me feel.

"See you tomorrow?" His words are gentle, a reminder that he'll still be here.

I nod, unable to trust my voice, and turn to leave.

The door closes behind me, but the distance doesn't mute the question that's now lodged in my mind. *Do I really work so much to avoid everything else?* I don't know. I thought I didn't, but now, with Noah's insight uncomfortably lodged inside me, I'm not sure of anything.

I walk down the corridor, the sound of my footsteps hollow in the empty hall. Each step takes me farther from the break room, but closer to the realization that maybe Noah isn't wrong. Maybe I'm just too scared to admit it.

EIGHT

NOAH

Lily scrubs her hands like she's trying to wash the skin off. The sink's steel surface is a war zone of blood and water, and her shoulders are drawn so tight I'm amazed they haven't snapped. From across the doorway, I can see how mechanical it is—how she forces the motions even when her arms start to falter. She's just stepped out of a six-hour surgery, but there she is, washing up as if another heart will land on the table any second.

Watching her, I remember why I can never quite decide if I'm impressed or terrified. I lean against the wall, arms crossed, trying not to look like I'm waiting to catch her when she collapses.

Six hours in surgery and she's barely flinching. It's impressive, sure, but the relentlessness of it—the way she can't stop—is what gives me pause. Even when she's spent, she keeps pushing, keeps scrubbing, like if she just works hard enough, she'll get what she wants. I wonder, not for the first time, what it would take to make her stop.

As Lily turns off the faucet, I see the way her hands shake

for just a moment before she clutches a towel, drying her fingers like she's counting each one—checking they're all still there. Still optimal.

It's moments like this that make me consider stepping in, but then I remember: she's a force. A hurricane. The kind of natural disaster they name after women, and when you stand in the middle of it, you either learn to hold on or get blown away.

I think I get her. But right now, I'm wondering if this whole "work until your hands fall off" thing is her version of a cry for help. There's a tiny, microscopic part of me that wants to run over and tell her it's okay to take a break. But a larger, more self-preserving part knows it'd be like throwing myself into a volcano. Maybe she's just waiting for someone to call her on it. Or maybe she's just that convinced that there's no other way.

It doesn't help that there's no denying what she's afraid of. Failure. Weakness. She treats them like diseases she's got to eradicate from her system. I get why she does it, the pressure she's under, but I wish she'd see what the rest of us see: a surgeon so talented that it hurts just watching her try to be more.

More perfect. More prepared. More in control.

She dries her hands, discards the towel, and doesn't miss a beat as she strides back toward the chaos that keeps her ticking.

There's admiration, sure, but now? Now, it's starting to feel a lot like worry.

I remember when she used to look a little more relaxed, less likely to pop a blood vessel in pursuit of perfection. These days, though, the ambition's wound her up so tight I'm not sure where she ends and the pressure begins.

Watching her now, it's clear she doesn't know either. She grabs the nearest case file, eyes blazing with the same intensity she's had since day one, and charges into her next procedure. No sign of slowing down.

The break room light buzzes like a mosquito and gives off about as much warmth. I sit in the half-darkness with an empty cup and too much on my mind, so when I see Lily pass the door, it's like a lifeline.

"Coffee?" I call out, watching her slow to a stop.

For a moment, she looks like she's weighing the risks, like a caffeine hit might be a gateway drug to something more terrifying, like actual human contact. She steps inside anyway, and I'm up in a flash, pouring her a cup that's miraculously not three days old. As I hand it over, I throw in a lopsided grin for free.

She takes the mug like she's expecting it to burn. I'm not surprised. Most of the time, Lily treats my attempts at friendliness the way she'd treat an unfamiliar bacteria strain: approach with caution and prepare for the worst. But today, something's different. Her eyes meet mine for a second, and there's a flicker of uncertainty, a hesitation that makes me think maybe, just maybe, she's as tired as I am of pretending we don't affect each other.

I watch her as she settles into a chair, the silence between us not quite as awkward as it should be. It's a game of chicken, this thing we do. She's half-convinced that letting her guard down will lead to catastrophe, and I'm half-terrified that she'll realize she doesn't have to settle for the mess that is me. The way she sits, with that little extra bit of space between her and the table, is like a reminder that she's only here on a trial basis.

"Miracle you could even spot the break room," I say, disturbing the silence with what I hope is the right mix of teasing and sincere. "Didn't think it'd show up on your radar without a giant heart attached."

She's quiet for a beat too long, long enough that I'm not sure if I've pushed the joke too far. But then the corners of her mouth turn up just slightly, the closest thing to a smile that Dr. Lily Harper might risk at work.

"I got lost," she replies, deadpan. "Thought I'd stop by for directions."

I feel something like relief and lean back in my chair, letting the tension slip away. This is the moment—the pause, the flicker, the brief chance to sit across from each other and pretend there's no history, no expectations, no tangled mess of feelings just waiting to get in the way.

"Should I give you the tour?" I ask, my voice a bit lighter, my hope a bit higher. "Or just send you off with a map?"

"Depends," she says. "Is this where you tell me I should spend more time relaxing?"

"It's the first stop on the tour," I assure her, "right after the coffee station."

We're both quiet again, but this time the silence is easy, filled with the hum of the vending machine and the distant sounds of hospital life that feel like they belong to someone else. I've seen Lily in every possible crisis, watched her conquer a dozen emergencies with nothing but her mind and her will, but this—sitting across from her, feeling the gap between us shrink—is a victory all its own.

"Next time, just give me the map," she says, and I can't help but grin.

The world outside can wait. Surgery can wait. For a moment, the only thing that matters is the space between us and how it keeps getting smaller.

The room settles into a quieter mood as I see Lily's expression shift, her bravado thinning into something more real. Her voice is almost a whisper, each word heavy with unspoken fears.

'I can't risk a single error." It's a confession, stripped bare and vulnerable, the truth she never lets anyone see. I stay quiet, giving her the space to speak and the chance to back away, but the words hang between us, a fragile testament to everything she tries to hide.

In the pause that follows, I watch her, unsure if she regrets saying it, if she's about to pull back into her shell. But she doesn't. Instead, there's a rawness in her eyes, an uncertainty that's so different from the confident, unflappable Lily I've come to expect.

I want to reach across the table and hold her hand, to show her that I understand, but I know better. She'd probably bolt if I so much as moved.

"You don't have to risk it," I say gently, knowing how much those words cost her. "Not alone, anyway."

She doesn't flinch, doesn't shut down like I expect. It's a tiny miracle. Instead, she looks at me with something close to disbelief, like she's still waiting for the punchline. But I'm serious. More than she realizes. Her mouth opens slightly, but no words come out, and for a moment, I see the Lily that no one else gets to see.

Vulnerable. Unsure. Human.

"Maybe you don't need to carry the whole hospital on your shoulders," I continue, my voice barely more than a murmur, trying not to spook her.

Lily's fingers tremble against the coffee mug, and I wonder if she'll break the silence with more honesty or if she'll hide behind her usual defenses.

"You think I'm too serious," she says finally, a note of challenge in her voice. I can tell she's fighting it, the urge to retreat into sarcasm and dry wit, but the effort leaves her softer, almost resigned.

"I think you're amazing," I reply, and her eyes widen like she didn't expect me to say it. Hell, I didn't expect to say it, but there it is, out in the open. "But I also think it's okay not to be perfect."

"Hard habits to break," she mutters, almost to herself. She glances away.

"It's late," she says abruptly, the old Lily resurfacing, determined to change the subject before it gets too real.

The break room door swings open and Marcus enters abruptly, shattering the fragile intimacy of the moment.

"Am I interrupting?" he asks with his trademark smirk, the one that says he already knows the answer. He looks between us, taking in the charged atmosphere and the way Lily's still standing like she's not sure whether to sit back down or run. "Sorry, lovebirds, but I need to steal Noah for a consult."

The room's tension pops like a soap bubble, leaving behind a different kind of air, one that's lighter but just as full. I catch the flash of confusion in Lily's eyes, the way Marcus's presence throws her off balance, and I can't decide if I want to thank him or punch him.

"Let's go, Romeo," Marcus urges, clearly enjoying the disruption more than is decent.

Lily stays quiet, and I know she's processing, recalibrating, figuring out what just happened. It's not just the interruption that catches her off guard—it's how close we were, how real it got before we were forced back to reality.

"Sorry about that," Marcus says, but the gleam in his eye suggests he's anything but. "Didn't realize you two were having a moment."

I'm almost at the door when I stop, half-tempted to tell Marcus where to shove his apology, but I settle for giving Lily one last, lingering look.

"Next coffee's on you, Harper," I call out, making sure she knows I'm not backing off.

She doesn't answer, doesn't have to.

Marcus doesn't miss a beat as we leave. "Thought I'd find you napping in here, not wooing Dr. Harper."

"It's called having a conversation."

"Conversation," Marcus repeats, amused. "That what the kids are calling it these days?"

I glance back, hoping to see Lily leave the breakroom, but I just see the closed door before Marcus pulls me along and around the corner.

"You gonna make a move, or are you just going to sit around with your coffee and your unresolved feelings?" Marcus asks.

"Maybe both," I reply, half serious, half playing along. "Multitasking.

"So, what's the diagnosis?" I ask Marcus, deflecting, but not fully. My mind's still in that break room, still with Lily.

"That you're hopeless," he replies, and it's all I can do not to laugh.

Maybe he's right. Maybe I am.

NINE

♥

LILY

I am spectacularly bad at social events, and this is the Mount Everest of them all. The Emerald Bay Medical Center Charity Gala. Complete with the smell of expensive perfume and desperation. I hover near the entrance, considering a mad dash for freedom, but a wealthy donor zeroes in before I can escape.

"Dr. Harper!" he gushes.

"Yes. Hello."

"I saw you at that awards ceremony," he continues, oblivious. "Top surgical resident! I said to my wife, 'Now there's a young woman who's going places.'"

"Very kind of you to say." I wonder if it's worth finding a potted plant to hide behind. He doesn't let me move an inch.

He looks pleased, like I've just agreed to do a live demo of open-heart surgery in his living room. "How does it feel to be so accomplished at your age?" He pauses to give me a congratulatory pat on the shoulder, his cufflinks glinting under the ballroom lights.

I use the age-old wave to a fictitious friend just arriving, and make my excuses.

The entranceway is my safe zone. One well-timed move, and I'm gone before anyone notices. I tug at my dress—black, practical, something I can wear again if I ever get dragged to another one of these events. It makes me look like I'm headed to a board meeting, but at least it doesn't scream "Look at me!" like everything else in the room. I'd give anything to disappear, but my conscience won't let me skip it. Surgical resident wins prestigious award, blows off charity gala to drink wine alone in sweatpants. It would haunt me all night. Not that it's better being here, but at least now I'm haunted and have free champagne.

I survey the room, noting exit points and likely obstacles. The clink of glasses and forced laughter ricochets off the high ceilings, filling the air with noise and unwanted cheer. A sea of expensive suits and sequined dresses blur together, each more garish than the last. Sixty hours this week, I tell myself. Sixty hours, and this is my reward. Even my feet hurt, and I'm not wearing heels. One of my few good decisions.

Before I can find a quiet corner to hide in, a woman swoops in and locks me in place. Late fifties, perfect makeup, wearing what appears to be a defrosted wedding cake. I recognize her as the wife of one of the senior physicians. More importantly, I recognize her as an old acquaintance of my mother's.

"Lily Harper," she says, like she's uncovering a buried treasure. "I thought I saw you in the program." Her eyes sparkle with curiosity, like she's about to ask me if I've landed a very eligible husband yet. "I hear you're making quite the name for yourself."

I give her the same tight smile I've been perfecting all night. "Just working hard and trying to stay afloat."

She winks like we're sharing a dirty joke. "Oh, I'm sure you're doing better than that." Then, in a lower voice, "How's your father? Still setting impossible standards for the rest of us?"

"He's well." *Relentless, emotionally unavailable, probably at home reading a medical journal with a glass of scotch.* "He'll be sorry he missed this."

"I doubt that very much," she says, just as the donor seizes the conversation again. Her advice cuts through his chatter.

"Keep an eye out for a certain ER doctor. Dr. Carter." Her tone is all ominous implication. "Terrible influence."

I almost laugh. *Noah Carter. Terrible influence?* It's true enough, but hearing it from the wife of one of the senior staff takes me by surprise.

My stunned look only encourages her. "You're very driven," she tells me. "I admire that."

"Thank you." The back of my neck itches. Her hand, heavy with diamonds, settles on my arm, and the donor starts again.

"This hospital's lucky to have someone like you," he beams. "All these young, attractive doctors working such long hours together. How nice for you."

My smile freezes in place. I can already tell I'll have sore cheeks tomorrow.

"Too bad my husband retired," the wife jokes, eyeing me like I'm a decadent dessert she's saving for later. "You'd be a much better influence."

"Quite the combination," the donor chimes in. "Your determination, and such good genes!"

"Bet you've got an eligible boyfriend too," she says.

"I don't," I say, glancing away. "My schedule doesn't allow for one." I offer a saccharine smile, the kind that used to get me grounded for disrespect when I was younger. "Medicine is my one and only commitment."

"Well," she sighs. "At least you don't have to worry about being distracted."

They might be unbearable, but they've got that much right. The room's getting stuffy, like everyone's crowding around to see who can land the most socially acceptable punch.

She gives me a long, pitying look. "We heard about your friend in Boston."

My friend? I'm too tired to process what she means, then I realize. Sarah—my father's former resident. She left cardiothoracics for a teaching position last year. Scandalous.

'It must have been a blow to lose your mentor," she simpers. "But then, you've always been the self-sufficient one, haven't you?"

More like the disposable one, I think, but don't say. "You know me," I manage.

A server passes with a tray of champagne flutes. I grab one and drain half of it before I can talk myself out of it. The woman's still rattling off her medical drama and social gossip as my eyes scan the room again.

I spot Noah across the ballroom. The unmistakable swoop of dark blond hair, the easy smile. The scruffy ER doctor, the terrible influence, the thorn in my side. Somehow, he even manages to look like he belongs here. Probably because he doesn't care that he doesn't. His navy suit hangs casually, like he threw it on at the last minute, which he probably did. He's surrounded by a group of colleagues, all talking at once. Marcus, his trusty sidekick, slaps him on the back and makes a joke I can't hear. I doubt it's funny.

Noah breaks away from his group and starts toward me. I feel the attention shift as he approaches, the donors keen to see what might unfold. He's close enough now that I can read the annoyingly confident look on his face, the same look he has when he takes over my trauma cases, like he's doing me a favor.

He stops beside me, hands in his pockets, like he has all the time in the world. His presence draws a new set of questions.

"Are you two working on an exciting project together?" the donor wants to know.

His wife nods along. "Yes, please."

"Only if that project involves an open bar," Noah replies, with a smirk that could be charming if I didn't know better. He lets them off easy, joking about the gala, the cheap fizz, the horrible speeches. It's almost impressive how quickly he defuses their attention. "We'll catch up later," he tells them. "Maybe I'll even let her have some fun."

Before I can protest, he steers me away, grinning as the band strikes up another song.

"You hate these things, don't you?"

"Desperately."

He gestures toward the dance floor, where couples sway in their designer tuxedos and gowns. "Then dance with me."

I almost choke on my drink. "Excuse me?"

"Come on. One dance. Get away from the donors for five minutes."

The jazz tune lures couples onto the dance floor, where they sway with insufferable elegance. I sip my drink and weigh my options. It's tempting, but admitting that would be admitting weakness. Then again, it's only five minutes.

"That, and you looked like you needed to be rescued," he adds.

I'm about to say no, to tell him he's ridiculous, but the alternative is heading back to the interrogation squad. Instead, I grab his hand and let him lead me to the dance floor.

Noah slides his hand to my waist. His touch is casual but deliberate. I'm irritated and not sure why. Maybe because he's right about how much I want to be anywhere but socializing with wealthy donors. Maybe because he looks too good in a suit for someone who I only ever see wearing scrubs.

"Relax, Harper," he murmurs. "I'm not going to step on your feet."

"I'm more concerned about you stepping on my last nerve."

"You should be flattered," he says. "I don't make this kind of effort for just anyone."

"Hardly any effort at all," I say. "It's almost like you're not even trying."

He draws me closer. "Who says I'm not?"

The question hangs between us. I can't let him win this one.

"I can't believe I'm doing this," I say, deflecting.

His eyes meet mine, unwavering. "Dancing?"

"Dancing with you."

He laughs, low and warm. "My gift to you," he says. "Being stuck with me for five whole minutes."

"You know I'll make you pay for this later."

"I'm counting on it." He pulls me even closer, and I can feel the steady beat of his heart against my chest. It matches the rhythm of the music, the sway of our bodies, the things we're not saying.

"You're an incredible surgeon, Harper." He says it like he knows the weight of every word. "But you really need to start enjoying life once in a while."

"That's... incredibly condescending."

I want to accuse him of being a know-it-all, of being reckless with his career and with this dance. But the words don't come out, and my pager gives me the excuse I need.

"You're enjoying this, aren't you?" I mutter, and I don't wait for a response. I pull away as the song reaches its last, excruciating note, and Noah is left standing in the middle of the dance floor.

He watches me go, his expression a mix of amusement and

something I can't quite place. It unnerves me, and I pretend I don't notice.

I can't believe I let him get to me like this. My chest tightens with irritation and it doesn't loosen, even as I push through the crowd and finally make it to the door. I tell myself I'm not bothered by the way he looked at me, or by the fact that he's not running after me.

TEN

♥

NOAH

The fizz in my champagne is long gone, but I'm still standing at the edge of the dance floor, still holding it like Lily might somehow materialize back into the gala. Back into the near-moment when she was here, her hand on my shoulder, her eyes on mine. Now it's just me and the glitzy crowd and the echo of music, me and a reminder that the hospital owns more of her than I'd like. I know I should let this go, that I know exactly what it means to be paged, but the empty spot she left pulls at me more than it should.

What's strange is how close it felt, like I was about to see the real Lily, the one she keeps under lock and key, behind a whole tower of pagers and excuses. It's like there was an actual human heartbeat beneath all that ambition, a heartbeat that almost matched my own before it disappeared into the surgical wing of Emerald Bay. She actually stayed for a full twenty minutes this time—and it seemed like she might have even been having fun dancing with me.

There was this second—this nanosecond—where it felt like

we were the only two people here. Her eyes said something that the rest of her wouldn't dare to. *Vulnerability, maybe? A flicker of uncertainty?* Before I could figure it out, she was gone, leaving me with nothing but a champagne glass that's as flat as my chances.

She apologized. I'm sure she meant it, in that sharp, direct way of hers. But that doesn't change how fast she ran. Doesn't change how every damn time we get close, she bolts for the OR like there's a contest for who can die from overwork the fastest.

The thing is, I don't blame her for leaving. Emergency surgery trumps whatever the hell this is between us. I get that. It's not like I haven't been called away in the middle of something. But damn if the timing doesn't suck. She couldn't have known that I've never waited around for anyone before. That she'd be the first.

The emptiness of the dance floor mirrors the emptiness she left behind. It's all suits and sequins and laughter and chatter, the entire department having a grand old time pretending they have lives outside the hospital. The music echoes off the walls and the edges of my own indecision, not quite reaching me. Without her here, everything else feels like background noise. The party feels just as flat as the bottle of Dom they opened an hour ago.

I wonder how she'd react if she knew the state she'd left me in. Would she feel guilty about the interruption? Relieved? I don't want to imagine the smirk on her face, the one that says *I told you so* without ever opening her mouth. Lily Harper, queen of unavailability, always disappearing, always proving she's got better things to do. Yet somehow, she matters in a way I can't just shrug off, can't ignore.

When the hell did I become this guy? The guy who's hung up on a woman who can't even stay for one stupid dance?

I don't do strings. At least, I didn't. Lily's a different story. She's all strings, like a tangled ball of them, and I'm trying to find the start, the end, anything to hold on to. It's ironic as hell, being left stranded at my own emotional party. Normally, I'd be halfway to forgetting by now, erasing it over whiskey at a dive bar with Marcus or losing it somewhere between the sheets with a woman who doesn't require the Jaws of Life to pry open.

But the space she left is too big to ignore, the silence too loud. I have to remind myself to breathe, to stay anchored, or else I'll float off into the same oblivion she did. The fact that she even came to this gala is something. It's got to be something, right? For Lily, committing to five minutes of small talk is practically marriage. So what does it mean that she stayed long enough to tell me she had to go?

It's not just about her leaving. It's about how she left me, standing on the edge of the whole damn ballroom, watching and hoping like an idiot that she'd come back. This is a new feeling, being the one left behind. New, and frankly, a bit fucked. It's almost enough to make me give up.

Almost.

She'd like that, wouldn't she? She'd like me to throw my hands up and say I tried, Lily, but you're a lost cause. She'd like me to play the role of the jilted lover so she can pretend she doesn't care. I finish my champagne in one go, finally tasting the flat bitterness that's been hanging around in my hand for too long. It's a reminder of what I'll do to keep this from ending, like the start of some crappy sob story.

This isn't just a challenge. It's the challenge, the only one that's ever made me reconsider my game plan. Even if I don't know what my next move is, I know this isn't it. I set down my glass on the edge of the nearest table and let the music fade around me, one stupid, hopeful note at a time.

Marcus appears from behind me, arms crossed, like he's been waiting all night to ambush me.

"Slow dancing with the Ice Queen, huh?" He's barely able

to hold back a grin. "Thought you were allergic to women who wear both flats and ambition." I roll my eyes, but don't even try to deny it. "Didn't expect to see you all starry-eyed at the gala,"

"I like her," I admit, as much to myself as to him.

He shakes his head with a knowing look.

"You realize she's not the hit-it-and-quit-it type, right?"

"I know," I say, more serious than I intend to sound. "I didn't plan on this."

"No shit. Your usual plan involves far fewer surgical residents and a lot less groveling." He's right, and we both know it. That doesn't stop me from pretending he isn't.

"I'm full of surprises, Marcus. You, of all people, should know that."

He studies me like I'm one of our trauma cases, the kind that takes some real unraveling. "So, what's the plan? You gonna wait around until she decides she likes you back? Hope she fits you into her surgical schedule?"

"You done?"

"Didn't realize you were such a masochist, Carter," he says, shaking his head. "Just don't come crying to me when she cuts you loose for a coronary artery bypass."

"I can handle it." It's a reflex, but not a lie.

"Seriously, man. Lily's different. She's not like the others."

"Good," I say, and I mean it.

"Well, for the record, I think you might be in over your head."

Lily moves through the hospital corridor like last night's dance didn't happen. She has her walls so high this morning I'm surprised they don't violate the building code. Gone is the woman from the gala, the one who almost let me see her. Now it's all Dr. Harper, all brisk and professional and entirely too focused on the triage board to notice me.

I hang back, not wanting to scare her off. Instead, I stand back to watch the way she works, the way she avoids. Her eyes flicker to me for half a second before she's off to her next patient, pretending she doesn't know I'm still here.

That's the thing about Lily. She's damn good at pretending, at shifting from vulnerable to invincible in a way that almost makes me question if last night was real. But I know it was. I saw the way she hesitated, the feeling she would have stayed, had it not been for a surgical emergency.

The interns are terrified of her, and even the attendings are keeping a safe distance. I catch bits and pieces of conversation as I follow her through the corridor, words like "acute" and "resect" and "is that Dr. Harper's case?" They tumble into the white noise of a normal morning at Emerald Bay, background chatter that can't compete with the only question I'm interested in: where did last night's Lily go?

I move closer, hoping for an opening, but she's sealed tighter than the OR she ditched me for. It's impressive, really. Her ability to compartmentalize is on par with her ability to perform open-heart surgery. Both are infuriating and kind of brilliant.

I wait until there's no one else around; until the noise and bustle fade enough that she can't ignore me. "Lily," I say, as casually as I can.

She looks up, surprised to see me. Her professionalism wavers for a split second before snapping back into place. "Dr. Carter," she says, all business, all efficiency.

"You disappeared on me," I say, trying to lighten the air between us.

Her eyes linger on mine for a second too long, a fraction of a fraction of a second that tells me I'm not the only one thinking about last night. "There was a ruptured aneurysm," she says. "Life-threatening."

"So that's it? I don't see you until the next gala?"

"We have very different priorities, Noah," she says, turning back to the triage board. "We always have."

"It's too bad," I say, softer now. "I liked where our priorities were heading."

She freezes, a glitch in her usually flawless efficiency, before continuing to scan the board. I let her, knowing the look she'll have if I push too hard. I've seen it before, on other women's faces. But not like this. Not like it matters.

We move down the corridor, side by side, but miles apart. She doesn't give me much, just the barest of hesitations, but it's enough.

Our paths intersect with a group of residents, and I can tell by their expressions that they're terrified of her.

"Dr. Harper," one of them says, breathless and eager. "We need your opinion on a consult."

She nods, efficient and in control, but before she follows them she gives me a look. It's half a warning, half something else, something that almost makes me think Marcus is right and I'm in over my head.

I shrug, as casual as I can muster, and she shakes her head with exasperation and marches off.

Marcus catches my eye as I pass him in the trauma bay. He raises an eyebrow, an unspoken, *how's that going for you?* that makes me wish he wasn't so good at this.

I flash him a grin and don't slow down.

Let him think what he wants.

I lose myself in rounds, in consults and charts and patients, but she's there, always there. In the back of my mind, in the space she left behind, the space that's less empty than it was last night.

We pass each other again later, both moving too quickly to

stop, but not so quickly we can't share a look. It's a careful dance, proximity and distance, and it makes me want to change the song, change the rules.

I get a brief, sideways smile as she speeds by, a glimmer of the Lily I knew was in there somewhere, and it's more than I thought I'd get this soon. I watch her until she disappears around a corner, until I'm the one standing still while everything else moves around me.

Marcus is wrong. This is good. Better than good. It's exactly what I'm here for, exactly why I haven't bailed yet.

I make a split-second decision to play this her way, to wait her out, but not because I don't know what to do next. Because I do.

She doesn't look back again, but she doesn't need to. I've got all the time in the world.

I walk into the staff break room with two shop-bought coffees, a timing miracle I pretend is coincidence. "What are the odds?" I say, handing her the cup with the perfect amount of sugar and a not-so-perfect amount of distance.

Lily raises an eyebrow but takes it. She's skeptical, and I don't blame her.

"You're supposed to be in the ER," she says, not quite accusing, more of an observation. A test. I pass it by sitting down.

"Marcus thinks he's got it under control. I'm inclined to agree," I say. "Until the real disasters come in, anyway."

She almost smiles. Almost.

"I think he meant you."

"See? He knows everything."

Lily takes a sip, looks away. I can see her considering her next move, her next words, and I know I've got to make this easy for her or she'll bolt faster than her cup can cool. "I'm surprised you haven't asked more about last night," she says finally, cautiously.

"Why would I? I know exactly how it went," I say. I don't push, don't even mention the dance.

She gives me a look, not buying it but willing to let it slide. For now. "You do, huh?"

"Of course. We were both there," I say, then pause. "Well, until you weren't."

It's out before I can stop it, and I brace myself for her to shut down, shut me out, but she doesn't. She just shakes her head and laughs, a small, barely audible sound that might be the best thing I've heard all week.

"You're impossible, Noah."

"So they tell me," I reply. "Frequently."

Finally, she nods to herself, decision made. "How are you getting on with your sections of the trauma protocols?" she asks, changing the subject to something safer, something less like a live grenade.

"Going well," I say. "Could use some Harper-level input, though."

I follow her lead, talking cases and hospital politics, dropping the pretense that I'm here for anything other than exactly this. Her. Us.

It's different from last time, from every time before. The tension's still there, but it's not so sharp, not so impossible. She's letting it be easier, letting me be closer.

I keep the conversation going, letting it flow from charts to rivalries to the vending machine that's been out of Diet Coke for three days. Each new topic, each new moment where she doesn't shut down, feels like a victory.

By the time our coffees are done, she's talking more freely, more openly. Frustratingly, I have to get back. She does too.

"Same time tomorrow?" I ask, knowing I'll be here whether she is or not, knowing that she knows it too.

"We'll see," she says, getting up and heading for the door.

But I can tell by the look in her eyes, the one that flickers back to me as she leaves, that it's not a no.

Not this time.

Four long hours later, I step onto the hospital rooftop and breathe in the cold, dark night, hoping it'll clear my head as easily as the rest of the day has clouded it. The city lights blink back at me from below, like they're all in on the joke, like they know exactly how close I am to losing my cool.

I lean against the railing, steadying myself against the view and the realization that's been creeping up on me since last night. I've spent my life avoiding complications, like relationships are some kind of infection I can vaccinate against with sarcasm and charm. But then there's Lily. She's not like the rest. She's steady, brilliant, maddening, and more complicated than I've let myself admit. And for once, that's not a bad thing.

I'm not used to this, the feeling that the ground could drop out from under me at any moment. I'm used to being the one who leaves, the one who walks away with an easy shrug and a see you later. But now, with her, everything's upside down. Now I'm the one waiting, the one who doesn't know what's going to happen next. And damn if it isn't terrifying and exhilarating all at once.

I close my eyes for a second, just long enough to picture the way she looked at me in the break room, in the corridor, like she couldn't decide if I was real or a particularly stubborn hallucination. I know she's trying to figure me out, trying to see what I want, but she doesn't realize I'm trying to do the same thing. To figure out what the hell I've gotten myself into, and why I can't bring myself to get out.

The hospital hums below me, the familiar glow of fluorescent lights spilling out like a constant reminder that work never ends. Not for her. Not for us. Maybe that's why I'm here, why I'm not running in the opposite direction, like I've trained myself to do. Because even when she's knee-deep in blood and stitches and saving lives, she's never too far. Never so far that I can't reach her.

I open my eyes and look out at the city again, trying to see what she sees, trying to understand why it's worth the effort, worth the waiting.

And I do. I see it. I see all the potential she tries so hard to hide, all the connections she thinks are just complications. All the ways she pushes me to be more than I've been willing to be. It's frustrating and kind of amazing, and I don't think I can walk away from it even if I want to.

For the first time in forever, I'm not sure if I'm up to the challenge, but I'm sure as hell not backing down from it. She makes me want to stay, makes me want to find out what happens when I stop running and start trying.

I think of all the times I've talked my way out of things like this, all the ways I've sidestepped the emotional tangles and knots that people always get themselves into. It was easy, being that guy. It was uncomplicated and predictable, and nothing at all like this.

This is different. She's different. She makes me want to change my plans, to break them and rewrite them and throw them out the window. It's terrifying, the kind of terror that makes me want to see what comes next.

The air is colder than I expected, sharper and more honest than the stuff down below, where everything's muddled and rushed and artificially warm. I breathe it in, hoping it'll steel my nerves and chase away the doubts I've spent years accumulating.

An ambulance siren wails in the distance, and I know she's down there, in the thick of it, probably tearing into a medical student who had the nerve to blink too loudly. She's intense, and she's insane, and she's all the things I should be staying away from but can't bring myself to.

I grip the railing tighter, holding on to my resolve like it's the only thing keeping me from falling, the only thing I need to get through this. And maybe it is. Maybe I've never let myself get this close to someone because I didn't want to find out how far I'd fall if it didn't work.

Maybe. But that's not enough to stop me this time. That's not enough to undo the decision I've already made, the one that says I'm in this all the way.

I stay on the roof until the night gets even colder, until the hospital lights start to blur and the city feels like it's slowing down. Until I'm the only person in the world who hasn't gone home yet. And maybe I'm not going to, not anytime soon. Maybe I've finally found something worth sticking around for.

Maybe, but not maybe. Definitely.

ELEVEN

♥

LILY

I must be the only woman alive who can go from open-heart surgery to an all-night grocery store without changing out of her scrubs. The place is deserted, aisles stretching out like empty hospital corridors. Bright fluorescent lights buzz overhead, casting a familiar clinical glow. It feels almost like home.

I push my cart with a determination that says get in, get out, and for God's sake, avoid human contact. Oats, coffee, almond milk. Everything I need to sustain a life that involves nothing but work and more work. My feet drag a little—because, let's face it, I'm human—but my mind's already halfway done with this errand, calculating the quickest route to the exit.

Sterile. Efficient. Those are words I like. The air conditioning hums with the predictability of a well-tuned machine, and I know I'll be out of here in less than fifteen minutes if I plan this right. My watch ticks against my wrist, each second a reminder that there's a bed waiting for me back home—well, a mattress on the floor, if I'm being honest. Another convenience. Easy to move when I inevitably switch apartments, because who has time for anything permanent?

I reach the oats and toss a package into the cart without breaking stride. The precision of the movement would make a quarterback jealous.

People call this hour ungodly, but I'd like to inform them that God is not relevant to anything I do. Midnight is as good as noon to me. Better, even. No lines. No small talk. Just empty aisles and me, operating at maximum efficiency.

My shoes squeak against the linoleum as I make a hard left turn, aiming for the coffee next. I can almost taste it already, rich and black, a survival tool more than a beverage. I rub a knot in my shoulder, wondering for the thousandth time if maybe I should hire someone to deal with the mundane aspects of life. But the thought of surrendering even a shred of control makes my stomach turn.

Control. It's why I work harder, faster, longer than anyone else. It's how I survive. Because who wants to admit they're terrified of what happens when they're not perfect?

I reach for the almond milk, blink at it for a beat too long. Fatigue messing with my focus. My mind may be running, but my body is two steps behind. I rub at my shoulder again, absently this time, as though acknowledging the pain would be a moral defeat.

With the main essentials in my cart, I pick up speed, adjusting my plan to account for the less predictable detours. There will be coffee on my kitchen counter tomorrow morning, and that's about as close as I come to a life outside the hospital.

My father would be proud, if he even noticed. Richard Harper, esteemed cardiothoracic surgeon. I'm following in his footsteps so precisely that the ground under my feet should be wearing thin by now. But if you asked him, he'd probably say I'm moving too slow.

I haven't seen my parents in months. A dinner, once in a blue moon, is about the extent of our familial obligations. And frankly, it's easier that way. My mother lectures me on the ethics of ambition. My father stares with that cool, assessing look of his. I always leave with an inexplicable desire to run a few more laps around the track, metaphorically speaking.

The lack of sleep doesn't help. My movements are autopilot-smooth, grabbing items without thinking. But I still feel it, pulling at the edges of my mind like a slow drag.

The cart rolls over the stark white linoleum, barely any weight in it. Minimalist, my sister would say. Just the essentials. Everything I need to stay functional, and nothing more. Sometimes I wonder if that's my entire life—functioning without actually living.

An idea knocks at the door of my consciousness: *When was the last time I did something just because I wanted to, not because I had to?*

I shove the thought aside, blaming it on sleep deprivation. But it sits there, a quiet passenger on this ride, whispering that maybe I've forgotten what it's like to want anything beyond the next career milestone.

The store's emptiness presses in on me, both comforting and accusing. It's a glimpse of my life, stripped of the chaos that usually keeps me too distracted to notice how alone I am.

I turn the cart toward the coffee aisle, mind still calculating, body lagging a few seconds behind when the thought hits me: I am really, really tired.

The cart screeches to a halt, barely avoiding the emergency room doctor crouched in front of instant noodles. If Noah is surprised to see me in the wild, he recovers with astonishing speed.

"Dr. Harper," he says, eyes lighting up with a kind of smug delight. "Fancy meeting you here."

I groan internally, watching him hold up a package of sour

gummy worms like he's found the cure for cancer. A tiny, traitorous part of me almost smiles.

"Really leaning into the nutritionist lifestyle," I say, nodding at the array of artificial flavors lined up before him.

"Someone's got to represent the four main food groups," he says. "Sugar, salt, caffeine, and existential dread."

Noah stands, and I'm acutely aware of the contrast between us—his worn jeans and faded T-shirt, my surgical scrubs and exhaustion. He looks like he strolled in from a lazy Sunday morning, and I look like I just spent fifteen hours elbow-deep in someone's chest cavity. The most annoying part? He's still irritatingly attractive.

He adds a pack of gummy worms to my cart. "A thank-you for not running me over."

I pick them up with two fingers, holding them at arm's length. "Tempting. I don't know if I can handle all those calories."

Noah laughs, a sound that carries across the empty aisle and rattles around inside me. It's infuriating how easily he can shake off anything serious. Where I'm sharp edges and hard angles, he's all easy lines and no stress.

"So," he says, taking the bag of oats from my cart, "what's the occasion? You don't strike me as someone who indulges in midnight impulse buys."

He's fishing. I know he's fishing, but I still feel the pull to give him a real answer.

"Just stocking up," I say instead, shrugging with a casualness I don't quite own. "Long shift. Need coffee."

"And almond milk, oats, gluten-free soy nonsense," he recites like a grocery list savant. "Very on-brand, Harper."

"Doesn't look like I'm the only one shopping," I shoot back. I hold up the instant noodles, turning the package over with clinical disdain. "Is this even food?"

He puts a hand to his chest, feigning a dramatic wound.

"Harsh. You wouldn't last a day in the ER, Harper. No respect for the finer things in life."

"No time for a nap between cases?" I ask. "Must be rough."

Noah smirks, because he's the sort of guy who smirks instead of smiling, and it gets under my skin in all the worst, most effective ways. The store around us feels less like a fluorescent box and more like a shared secret, a moment outside the usual constraints of our professional roles. It's disarming, this sudden shift in context, like being thrown into a scene you didn't rehearse for.

Noah juggles two boxes of mac and cheese. "Organic. Free-range. Totally unprocessed," he claims, deadpan. "Perfect for the discerning surgeon."

I glance at the ingredients printed on the back of the box. "Your sodium levels must be through the roof."

"And yet, here I am. Alive and well."

"Regrettably."

He nudges my cart, still packed with my bare-bones essentials, and I watch it as though seeing my own life laid out in stark, bland relief.

In my head, I call this moment ridiculous. I remind myself that it's past midnight, I'm sleep-deprived, and running into Noah should be an inconvenience, not a distraction. But beneath all that logic, there's something else. A nagging whisper that I actually don't mind this encounter at all.

Noah takes the handles of my cart like a surgeon taking a scalpel. "I'll assist," he announces, deadpan. A box of rainbow-colored cereal sails in, then a pack of marshmallows. I don't have time to protest before he's on to the next aisle, defending each choice as though presenting a research paper.

"It's practically a vegetable," he says, holding up a frozen burrito. I roll my eyes, but I don't remove anything.

"I'll be sending you the medical bills for my sodium-induced heart attack," I say, trying to sound disapproving. The effect is ruined by the fact that I'm also trying not to laugh.

He looks entirely unbothered, tossing in a suspicious bag of neon-colored candy. "These have real fruit juice," he claims. "I'm just thinking of your health."

The efficiency of my solo mission is shot to hell, but instead of panic, I feel something else entirely. A surprising, unsettling lack of resistance. It's as if the more Noah throws my world off-kilter, the more I secretly like it. I chalk it up to delirium. Or maybe the questionable nutritional value of his company.

"I suppose the potato chips count as a salad," I say, lifting a bag as if it's hazardous waste.

"Now you're getting it." He winks.

"Do you even know what half these ingredients are?" I ask, picking up a package that requires a PhD in chemistry to understand.

He holds up a container of cheese puffs. "Pure, organic cheddar," he says, struggling to keep a straight face.

"You mean the radioactive orange ones that are basically Styrofoam?"

"That's cruel and unjust, Lily Harper. Really." He clutches the bag of cheese puffs like it's a wounded animal.

"Poor baby," I coo.

A guy pushing a cart loaded with energy drinks pauses to watch, clearly entertained by Noah's performance. I shoot him a lock that sends him scurrying.

Noah drops a second package of gummies in, eyes dancing. "Just in case you develop a sudden craving."

The absurdity of it all hits me in a way that's almost disorienting. My cart's a chaotic disaster; my heart's not far behind.

I say the words before I can think about them. "I don't remember the last time I did something unplanned."

"The *only* way I've survived is by keeping it unplanned," he says.

"Why does that not surprise me?" I ask.

"Growing up, nothing was predictable. My parents didn't know the meaning of structure."

That's the moment I realize I know nothing about him. I've seen the easygoing surface, the laid back charm that masks everything else. But here, in the hum of the freezers, he's pulling back the curtain. He's more than I gave him credit for.

"My mom," he continues, "tried to fix everything with love. Even the things that couldn't be fixed. Especially after my sister died." There's a small, almost imperceptible catch in his voice, and it hits me like a sucker punch.

"I'm sorry." The words are inadequate, but necessary. I want to reach out and touch his arm, but I'm not that person yet. I don't know how to be that person. So I let the silence hold the space between us, hoping he knows I mean it.

He shrugs, but it's not dismissive. "Losing her changed everything. Before that, I was the lazy, fun brother with no real ambition. But afterwards, nothing seemed to matter. Or maybe everything mattered too much."

The hum of the freezers fills in the gaps, a steady backdrop to his words. It should feel awkward, but it's oddly comforting, like the noise is insulating us from the rest of the world.

"And you," he says, meeting my gaze, "were never allowed to be unplanned, were you?"

His question doesn't surprise me as much as the realization that I want to answer it. I don't know what shocks me more—the truth of his words or my willingness to let them sink in.

"My parents," I say, voice more stable than I expected, "had my life mapped out before I was born. Deviating wasn't an option."

"I can't imagine," he says, genuine in a way that makes me

look away, because holding his gaze right now is too much. It's too raw, too real, and I've never been good at either.

"That's why you work so hard, isn't it? So you never have to worry about what happens when you're not perfect."

It's not a question. It's a diagnosis.

"And you," I counter, because even now I'm trying to keep us on even footing, "pretend not to care what happens, but you do. You just don't let anyone see."

His smile is soft and real, and it undoes me. "Touché, Dr. Harper."

For the first time in my life, I'm in a moment I didn't plan for, and instead of panicking, I want to let it unfold. It scares the hell out of me, but standing here with Noah, it also feels like the most sane thing I could do.

We walk the last few aisles in a comfortable silence.

At the checkout, Noah makes a last-minute grab for the ruby red shoelace candies, insisting they're "for medical research." I let him. The night air hits us as we exit, crisp and full of unsaid things. It's late, and neither of us is making a move to leave.

We walk to the cars, grocery bags in hand, the parking lot almost as empty as the store. I've always thought of late-night shopping as a necessary evil, but tonight it feels like something else—something significant and unplanned. The air is cold, our breaths forming small clouds that linger between us, like they're waiting to see what happens next.

There's a moment, a heartbeat of silence, that feels like standing at the edge of a cliff and deciding whether to jump. Noah breaks it, but his voice is softer than the crack of our earlier jokes.

"This was fun," he says, the words hanging between playful and earnest. "We should do it again."

"Yeah," I say, the word feeling like a leap into the unknown. "We should."

It's such a simple exchange, but it feels loaded with possibilities. Like saying it out loud is the first step in admitting there's more to my life than just the next surgical milestone. I expect the familiar tug of panic at the thought, but it doesn't come. Instead, there's a strange, exhilarating freedom in the admission. Like maybe I can have both.

"Good," he says, smiling in that way of his that makes me wonder if he planned this all along. I don't think I'd even mind if he did.

We finally part ways, heading to our respective cars, but neither of us moves quickly. There's a sense that we're stretching this time, elongating it like taffy, because even though we've agreed to see each other again, this is still a new kind of fragile. It feels precious and strange, like the first time I dissected a human heart and realized it was so much smaller and more delicate than I'd imagined.

I get into my car and watch as Noah opens the door to his, the outline of his figure hazy in the cold night. When he looks over, I pretend to be absorbed in buckling my seatbelt, a ridiculous attempt at nonchalance given what just transpired. But I know he sees right through me. It's both terrifying and exhilarating.

I start the engine, the headlights splash over the empty lot, illuminating the space where we stood. I glance in the rearview mirror, catching one last glimpse of him before I turn onto the street.

It's late, and I should be thinking about sleep, or the cases waiting for me in the morning. Instead, my thoughts throughout the journey home are entirely occupied with the one person who's managed to slip past all my well-fortified defenses.

TWELVE

NOAH

It's two a.m., but sleep is staging a protest somewhere across town. I lie awake, hands tucked behind my head, grinning like a teenager after a first date. The ceiling stares back at me blankly, probably judging the snacks strewn around the bed.

In the grocery store earlier, Lily had given me hell about them—disapproval for my Hot Cheetos and Oreos. I replay the scene like a movie I can't stop watching. Her in the freezer aisle, a bright contrast against frosted glass, dropping her guard and admitting that talking to me wasn't as bad as a root canal. Not exactly a confession of undying love, but coming from Lily. it was basically a sonnet. It wasn't just her smile that stuck with me; it was how strangely comfortable it felt, being there with her. Not a chase or a game, but something real.

I can't quite wrap my mind around it. It's usually not like this with women. It's definitely never like this with Lily. The whole thing replays on a loop. Her raised eyebrow as I continued to fill my cart, surveying the junk food crime scene, giving me grief about saturated fats and cholesterol levels.

"I knew it," she'd said, shaking her head like she'd just caught a kid trying to sneak out after curfew.

"Knew what?"

"That your food pyramid consists solely of refined sugars and artificial dyes."

It was supposed to be a hit-and-run, the usual light sparring, but we got stuck there.

"So, did you follow me here, or is this what you do for fun?"

Her eyes had lit up, and for once, I'd known she wasn't mocking me. How the corners of her mouth curled up when she accused me of stalking her. The way her sarcasm turned into something warm. I want to shake myself out of it, but here I am, sheets tangled around my legs, staring at the ceiling.

When she said goodbye, it took a moment longer than usual for her to turn away. She left with this smirk that was half-challenge, half-something else. It hooked into me. Now, the more I think about it, the more I realize that maybe I've been wrong. This thing between us? It's more than attraction. More than pursuit.

I roll onto my side, pull the pillow under my head, try to find a comfortable spot. It's useless. My pulse is still cranked up, thudding against the mattress. The crazy part is how comfortable it was, even in the middle of the store. Nothing forced or faked, just her and me, drifting into a rhythm that shouldn't be there.

"Infuriating," she'd called me. But there was a laugh in her voice that said otherwise. Like she'd meant it as a compliment.

I remember the way she'd looked, breath coming out in a small cloud as she stood in front of the freezer, arms crossed like she was holding herself back from something. Probably should have done the same myself, but I couldn't. Still can't.

I'm doomed. Smiling at the wall, actually doomed.

Light from the street leaks through blinds I never close, striping the room in pale gold. I squint up at it and try to imagine a scenario where this stops looping through my brain, and fail miserably. My mind keeps circling back.

I flip onto my back again, stare at the night sky pressing against the window. How is it possible for someone to throw me this far off balance? I haven't slept for hours. I haven't felt this wired since... Well, ever.

The sounds of Seattle filter in, cars whooshing through the damp streets, punctuated by the occasional siren. Usually, it's calming, the white noise of it lulling me into the kind of detachment I value most. Tonight, it's just a reminder of my own restlessness. I can feel it scratching under my skin, needling at my edges. I grab for a half-unpacked box of medical journals on the floor, thumb through one. Don't even make it past the first page before dropping it back on the pile. Not going to work.

Even my apartment feels different tonight. The snacks, the scattered textbooks, everything seems irrelevant and small. Like this tiny, too-familiar space has somehow gotten smaller. And all because I ran into her. Lily. Sharp-tongued, competitive, incredibly sexy Dr. Lily Harper.

The way she left the store, almost tentative, as if unsure whether to trust herself. And me. And what that means when we're standing two feet apart in front of the freezer section. It gnaws at me. I want to define it, put it in a box, call it something. But all I can do is lie here and stare up at the ceiling, the hint of her lingering in my head.

Attraction is one thing. I know attraction. But this is something else. It's sitting in the space between us, larger than I'd like to admit, pushing its way to the surface, daring me to acknowledge it.

I breathe out, long and slow, the sound loud in the quiet

room. I try to clear my head, push her away, but it's like trying to hold water in a net. She keeps coming back. Like a patient's case I can't quite figure out, complicated and obvious all at once.

The kettle screeches, demanding my attention like an overbearing toddler. I stand at the stove, barely awake, letting its whine shake me out of a Lily-induced stupor. Or maybe I dreamed the whole thing, all four hours of not-sleep, where my brain chased its own tail around and around her.

A sour taste coats my mouth. Reminds me of Vanessa, of the breakup talk I didn't know was a breakup talk until she called me "slippery." Like I was some kind of elusive fish, charmed everyone, committed to nothing. She'd sat across from me, candlelight making shadows on the walls, and said, "You never let anyone actually know you, Noah."

I remember thinking she was doing me a favor. Maybe I even thanked her. That part's hazy.

I pour water into the mug, watch the tea swirl in the steam. It used to be what I wanted—this ability to skate over the surface, keep things light, simple, free. Today it feels different. Heavier. And for the first time, I wonder if Vanessa had a point.

The mug warms my hands, an anchor in the storm of my head. The rest of the conversation comes back in pieces.

"Your mom says hi," she'd added, knowing it would throw me off.

We'd been over at her place for dinner. I thought we were celebrating. One year together, which felt like forever in Noah Carter time. But Vanessa was on a different calendar.

"She says she's surprised I lasted this long."

I could still smell the burned garlic on the stove, a bitter backdrop to her words.

"Come on, Vanessa, I know it's been hard, but we're good, right?"

She'd laughed, a real belly laugh that says, *I'm about to give you the world's biggest wake-up call.* "You think I don't know you're relieved, even now?"

Relieved wasn't the word. It was more like 'buoyant,' floating free of the weight I hadn't realized was dragging me down. I'd reached across the table, maybe to apologize, maybe to say thank you, maybe to eat more pasta, but she'd stood up and cleared the plates.

"Slippery," she said again. "Impossibly slippery."

Then there was Lily yesterday, laughing as she shook her head at me. "Impossibly infuriating." It echoes in the morning silence, a loop I can't escape. Was she right too?

Steam curls up from the mug, draws me back to the kitchen, to this very unfreedom-like feeling pressing on my chest. It's all so clear now. I've made a career out of getting out. Staying slippery, slippery as hell. But what if that's not what I want anymore? What if I want something more than easy, light, untangled?

I squeeze the edge of the counter, feel its solidity against my fingers, the only certain thing in a sudden sea of uncertainty. All those years, I told myself I didn't need anyone or anything to hold me down. That floating meant flying. That freedom was the best thing going. What a load of crap. Vanessa saw right through me.

It's harder to admit than I thought it would be, this truth sitting heavy in my chest. A realization lurking at the edges of my thoughts, one I've avoided so carefully until now. But there it is, written in the steam, hanging in the air: I'm not sure anymore.

I take a sip of the tea, let the heat spread through me. Lily doesn't even know she's got me thinking like this. But maybe that's why it's different. She isn't asking. I don't know if she'd even care. I just know that something shifted last night, and I'm standing in my kitchen questioning everything.

Vanessa had meant well. I see that now. It wasn't about her; it was about me. It's always been about me. How I'd rather get out clean than get in too deep. How I've always been proud of my ability to detach, to keep moving, to avoid mess and pain.

Funny thing is, it doesn't feel like pride right now. It feels like loss. Like something important got away from me while I was busy not paying attention. I don't want that to happen again. I don't want to be that guy anymore.

Vanessa—she'd moved on before I even knew she was going. Now I wonder if it's my turn to move. To change something, anything, before it's too late.

Maybe I'm done with slippery. Maybe I'm ready to be known.

"You look like someone who caught feelings at aisle six," Marcus says, side-eyeing me as he stuffs his bag into a locker. I almost drop my coffee.

"I look like someone who didn't sleep last night," I correct. "Like I'm being haunted by a very judgmental ghost." He doesn't take the bait.

"So, you ran into Lily." Not a question.

"Briefly," I admit.

Marcus chuckles, the sound reverberating against the metal. "Define briefly."

"Does it count as stalking if I showed up first?" I ask.

"Only if you followed her out," he says.

"I didn't," I say. "We left together."

"So, was it before or after she took off that you realized you're in deep?"

I open my mouth to argue, but nothing comes out. Marcus stares, and I know I've got nowhere to hide.

It's seven a.m., but the locker room is already teeming. Half-dressed doctors, the slap of shoes on the floor, the antiseptic smell that never leaves. The fluorescent lighting is doing no one any favors. I sip my coffee, trying to keep it casual. Marcus doesn't let up. He's wearing that smirk, the one that says, *This should be good.*

'We talked. For a bit," I say.

'Uh-huh." He switches his shirt for scrubs. "And what else?"

"We... laughed?" It sounds weak, even to me.

Marcus laughs too, but at me, not with me. "Man, I warned you about her."

"Lily Harper, a.k.a. the Wrath of God," I say. "I know."

"Then what are you doing?" he asks.

"I honestly don't know. It's... weird," I say, not sure how to put words to what it is.

He grins, shuts the locker door with a clang. "Welcome to being a human being."

Marcus is in rare form today, relentless, not missing a beat. We've been friends too long. He's like a mind reader. No, worse, a Noah reader.

"Look," I say, "I've never been in a slow-burn situation before. I don't know how it works."

"Shouldn't be too hard to figure out," he says. "If you don't set yourself on fire first."

A nurse rushes in, eyes scanning for an empty spot, barely noticing us as she speeds past. I lean against the lockers, stare at Marcus. "It's messing with my head."

"And yet, here you are," he says. "Staring me in the face with that lovesick expression."

"Am I that bad?"

Marcus leans back, a hand on his chin like he's studying a rare specimen. "I should start taking bets on how long until you two implode."

"We're not a thing," I say. "Not like that."

"Then what are you?" he asks. "Because I'm pretty sure this isn't your usual 'no strings attached' gig."

"I don't honestly know, but I'm going to stick around and find out," I say.

Marcus slaps me on the shoulder in a way that says, *You're an idiot, but I'm rooting for you.* "Let me know if you need a support group."

"Are you the founder?" I ask.

"Founding and only member," he says. "I've got T-shirts and everything."

He heads out, leaving me in the swirl of changing scrubs and shuffling feet. I sip my coffee again, let the chaos of the locker room fold around me.

Marcus might have a point. This isn't what I'm used to, and that's exactly why I'm in. The realization sits with me, warm and solid, and I can't stop the grin that stretches across my face.

It's the quiet kind of tired in the on-call room, the kind that settles deep in your bones after a long shift. I finish my notes, glance at the door she left through an hour ago. The old me would be scrambling to catch up, but I'm sitting here, patient as I've ever been. There's a cup of lukewarm coffee beside me, untouched, because I don't need it. Not today. I've got enough adrenaline from the sight of her to last a lifetime.

It's been one hell of a day. Long, busy, relentless. Like most shifts, it blurred by, but a single image stands out. Lily, across the corridor, not noticing me watch her. If she had, she might've seen a man who looks like he's in over his head. Might've. But probably not. I'm playing it closer now, steadier. I remember standing there, seeing her work, the realization washing over me. *I need a new approach.*

In the dim light, everything looks soft and tired. The couch with its permanent indent from countless exhausted bodies. The stack of medical journals nobody reads, like a bad joke. Usually, I'm restless in here, can't sit still for five minutes. But today, I'm calm. More settled than I've been in ages. She walked out without me an hour ago, and I didn't follow. Not like me. But maybe it's the new me.

Lily's the toughest case I've ever tried to crack. Brilliant, guarded, demanding. But that's why she's got me hooked. She doesn't need me, doesn't wait for me. I'm the one who has to catch up, to prove I can keep up.

Usually, I'd be out of here, already orchestrating the next encounter. Already trying to run into her, make her laugh, make her roll her eyes. But today, I sit back and let it happen in my head. I don't text. Don't make excuses to bump into her. Just finish my notes. It's not strategy or pressure this time. It's intention. It's patience.

The light above me flickers, a tired stutter, and I ignore it. Too focused on what I know is coming. It's the best kind of certainty, one that says, *Wait.* One that says, *It'll be worth it.*

My hand grips the pen, an anchor in the quiet. I see the shift in my own handwriting, the firmness of it. It's like looking at a stranger's script. Or maybe not a stranger. Maybe someone who's just figuring out who he is. I stack the papers, set them aside with unusual care. This is my new approach: consistency. My new game plan: be the one who stays.

I imagine her face when she realizes I'm serious. That it's not a game for me. That this time, the tables are turned, and

I'm not going anywhere. A part of me can't believe it, but a bigger part of me can't wait.

The door creaks when I push it open, the hallway lights bright. My shift might be over, but this? This thing with Lily? Just getting started. I walk out with a confidence I didn't have a day ago, a week ago, maybe ever. This is it, my final line to her.

See you soon, Dr. Harper. As many times as it takes.

THIRTEEN

♥

LILY

I close the incision on the sigmoid colon, and for one perfect moment, nothing else in the world exists. This is where I'm supposed to be—right here, tying up loose ends, both literally and metaphorically, with perfect knots.

"Running a little long, aren't we?" The scrub nurse tries to be subtle as she checks the clock, but I ignore her impatience.

Precision takes time. Excellence takes time. Unlike most people, I have all the time in the world. The final suture goes in as the doors swing open and another nurse barrels in with eyes like saucers.

"Pileup on the I-5. Mass casualties coming in hot."

The room changes with those simple but profound words. My heart rate doubles, adrenaline shifts into gear, and the world comes crashing back in with alarming clarity. I snap orders for the junior resident to close. There's a thrum in my veins as I scrub out, shedding my gloves, my mask, my identity. I should not be this excited.

"I'll take the crits in Trauma One," I say, already halfway out the door.

My brain is cataloging scenarios—crush injuries, blunt force trauma, arterial lacerations. What worries me most? That I'm excited to see Noah, to see him in charge, to see him pull this off. It's merely professional curiosity, I tell myself. Nothing more.

My world is organized chaos, every piece exactly where I need it, but a multi-vehicle accident on a rainy day is unpredictable and uncontrollable. It's also the sort of crisis that separates the competent from the brilliant.

"Don't worry, Dr. Harper," says the resident I left to finish the sutures, voice like a Labrador eager to please. "I've got this."

I don't doubt it. By the time they page the blood bank and clear the ICU, I'll have this under control. I'll have Noah under control. He's probably making jokes about fender benders and whatnot, even as the ambulances start pulling in. I bet he's already told the new staff that a real Seattleite can dodge a pileup like this with one hand on the wheel and one changing the track on their playlist. It will all be so effortless. But I know what lies beneath that calm surface—a hint of chaos. I shouldn't admire him for that.

As I swap my OR cap for an ER one, I feel the old rush, the challenge that excites me more than anything else in this world. More than anything else in this hospital. The idea that maybe Noah will falter, maybe he'll need me, is a thrilling one, as much as I hate to admit it. Maybe I don't admit it at all.

"OR 3 is free for critical overflow," I say to whomever is sitting at the nurses' station, moving faster than I've moved in weeks, adrenaline giving me speed and clarity.

The trauma bay is more mosh pit than symphony orchestra. Staff scramble to ready themselves for the tidal wave of incoming traumas, but there's no panic. They're on home turf, and it shows in their efficiency, in their rapid movements and calm voices. Monitors are prepped, gurneys arranged like dominoes ready to topple.

The only thing missing? The man in charge. But then I spot him, in the middle of it all, where he always is. He's scrubbed and ready, every inch the trauma king, already pulling on gloves before the first ambulance even arrives.

"Game time, people!" Noah yells, as bodies in scrubs fall into perfect formation.

I pretend the flush of excitement I feel is purely professional.

The gurneys start rolling in, an unholy mess of blood and bone and broken glass. Every inch of space fills with adrenaline and urgency. I jump in on a teenage patient, and it takes two seconds to realize he's coding from internal bleeding.

Noah takes one look at me, nods like we've got this, and suddenly, the symphony becomes a rock concert. His voice is steady, his commands clear, his confidence magnetic. I don't want to be impressed, but dammit, I am.

A flurry of movement surrounds us, but in my head, it's just Noah and me. He leans over the patient, fingers on the pulse, and there's no hesitation.

"He's lost pressure—might have hit the aorta," Noah says, reading the situation as fast as I do. "Get me two units of O neg."

He's good. He's really good.

Every instinct screams to take over, to put myself in control of this runaway train, but I pause. Just for a heartbeat. Noah already has them suctioning, already has a tech rushing the ultrasound over. He's watching the vitals with eyes like lasers. He's ahead of the game. I was so wrong to think he didn't have it in him.

The ultrasound shows blood in the belly. We need to open him up, stat, and my brain spins with how much time that's going to take. But then Noah flashes me that quick grin, the one that always looks like he's in on a joke nobody else knows.

"Bring him back, or I'm telling everyone you're the worst date I've ever had," he says. It cuts through my panic, and my adrenaline cranks up another notch.

"We're gonna do a clamp and run," he announces. "One, two, three, go!"

He's crazy, but the best kind of crazy. The crazy that just might work.

And then we're on the move, and I'm right there with him, rushing the patient through the hallway, pushing speed limits as well as medical ones. My hand brushes Noah's as we transfer the gurney, and there's a jolt—like a static shock, like caffeine straight to the veins. We ignore it, both of us pretending not to notice. But I feel the charge. How could I not?

We hit the OR doors, and the team is already waiting. Noah shouts instructions as I tear into the sterile gown, and there's no mistaking who's running this show. I let him. He gets first cut, and I let him. The internal bleed is even worse than we thought, and there's no room for error.

"Give me some damn good news, Dr. Harper," Noah calls from across the table, chest deep in a mess that should make him flinch, but doesn't.

I can't believe this, but I'm right there with him, fighting to get control of the bleed. Fighting to let him take the lead. My hands work, my mind races, my heart hammers like I'm sixteen and in way over my head. He makes the right calls, one after another, and I start to feel something I've never felt before. Trust.

My pulse pounds in my ears, my own voice sounds like it belongs to someone else as I shout, "That clamp is holding! Pressure's coming back up!"

The relief is sweet and immediate, and it tastes like... Well, it tastes like a lot of things I'd rather not name. Like how right it feels to do this together. Like how little I want to admit it. Like how terrifying it is that this doesn't scare me as much as it should. The bleed's under control, and I want to believe that I am, too.

Noah catches my eye over the drape, and the look we share isn't something I know how to explain. His smile says a million things. My heart says them back.

The side trauma bay is a train wreck—poor lighting, no space, blood pooling under a gurney. And then there's me and Noah, in the center of it all. They don't see us like this often. In sync. In harmony. In anything but a full-on battle for control. We've got a critical patient and a difficult chest tube placement ahead, but I'm pretty sure that by the way the entire room is watching, they think this show is about us.

There's Nurse Patty, a glint in her eye as if she's got money riding on how this turns out. There's a resident who stares like he can't decide whether to take notes or bet against us. The patient's in bad shape, but what has them all buzzing is the way we're moving. The way I'm moving with Noah. No barking, no bickering. Just this thing we're doing— together.

"This position is awful," I say, crammed against the wall, trying to get a clear angle.

Noah laughs. He actually laughs in the middle of this chaos, like a collapsed lung is just another Tuesday to him.

"Want to trade places?" he asks. "Your end looks easier."

I glare at him, or try to. It might be less effective than usual because of the way I'm almost smiling. He gets his hands where mine should be, guides the patient onto a better tilt. He reads my mind, anticipates my every move, like we've rehearsed this a thousand times and not spent four years butting heads.

"We've got one shot at this," I say, because despite the lack of competitive banter, we are still on the clock. "Are you ready?"

He hands me the scalpel with an almost infuriating ease. "Born ready," he says, and damn it if I don't believe him.

I make the incision, and the breath I've been holding since we started finally releases. It feels like the world is holding its breath, too, every eye in the room on us, on this impossibly tight space, on this thing we're doing that feels impossibly right.

"The blood," Noah says.

"Already on it," I answer, reaching for suction before the words leave his lips.

And then there's a sudden silence, a silence that vibrates with its own tension, that waits and waits and waits until we push the tube in and it slides, oh God, it slides perfectly. We both hold our breath again. And when the chest drain bubbles, it's the most wonderful sound in the world.

There's a second where we just look at each other, where we both know how big this moment is. Where we both know how much bigger it feels.

"We should do this more often," Noah says, and his grin is a mile wide.

I don't trust my own voice, so I nod and pretend I'm moving to the next patient because time is critical. But the way Patty smirks as we pass her says she's on to me. Says she knows something is shifting and I don't know how to stop it.

The resident gawks, clipboard frozen in midair. He was probably banking on me losing it, on Noah and me unraveling, but we didn't. We don't.

I keep my expression neutral. I keep everything neutral, even as I feel Noah's presence a heartbeat away, even as I feel the seismic shift of the world underneath me. Even though I know it's more than teamwork. More than a perfectly placed chest tube.

He brushes my arm on the way to the next patient. We say nothing. But maybe that's what says everything.

By the time we get the last patient stable, my adrenaline's shot. So am I.

I wash up, trying to scrub off the lingering feeling of his presence. My hands work the soap dispenser, my mind works in loops. I remember every second of the past hours, every move we made, and the memories burn hotter than anything I've ever felt. They burn right through me, and I can't deny it anymore.

It wasn't just the way he read me. It was the way I wanted him to. It was the way we did this impossible thing and made it look like breathing.

I replay the moment we got that clamp in place, the look he gave me from across the table. I don't know what the hell it was, but it wasn't nothing. I can't let it be nothing. The water runs pink and then clear. My hands work in precise, efficient circles, but my mind spins in every possible direction.

He's different from who I thought he was. From who I wanted him to be. And that's terrifying.

Someone's in the doorway, shuffling. A younger resident. He's got that green look to him, that wide-eyed I'm-exhausted-please-tell-me-I-didn't-screw-up look that every intern gets after their first trauma marathon. He's not looking me in the eye. Instead, he stares somewhere over my shoulder, but it's pretty obvious who he's thinking about. Who we're both thinking about.

"Dr. Carter's calls were unconventional," he says, trying to sound confident. "I'm surprised you went along with it."

His doubt lights a fuse inside me, and I answer without thinking. "You should be surprised you didn't think of it yourself." I turn off the faucet, take a breath that's sharper than I meant it to be. "Noah's decision—"

And that's when it hits me.

How quick I am to defend him. How my default setting has switched overnight. I haven't just let him into my OR—I've let him into something else, and I don't know how to stop it. The resident waits, eager to pounce, to learn something useful or scandalous, but I'm frozen mid-sentence, like the words themselves are traitors.

The change was sudden. He must see something on my face, something that gives me away, because his eyes widen and he practically runs from the room.

I don't blame him. I would run, too.

I stare at my reflection in the stainless steel, but all I see is a ghost, a shape I don't recognize. My hair's coming loose from my ponytail. My mask of control is slipping.

The thing that scares me most?

I liked this. I liked him. And I have no idea what to do about it.

The elevator doors close, and I finally exhale. But what comes out isn't relief. It's an admission I'm not ready to make, a surrender I'm not prepared for. My body's exhausted, but my mind is something else entirely.

Buzzing. Wired. Electric.

I lean against the wall, let it support me in a way I've never let anything or anyone. I go over the last few hours, try to make them clinical. Professional. Try to pretend that what happened with Noah was only about the medicine.

Try, and fail.

The elevator lurches, and my heart does too. I try to label it —professional respect, situational adrenaline, madness. But I've never been one to lie to myself, not really. If I'm being honest, this is the first time in my life I didn't feel alone. And that scares me more than the hours we just spent in a maze of blood and broken glass, more than the panic that didn't touch me until right this second.

I don't want to be alone.

I catch myself, a split-second before the confession slips all the way out. I'm losing it. I'm losing something. Control, maybe. I hate it, but not as much as I thought I would. Not as much as I used to.

The doors slide open, and the world waits for me to catch up. The weight of this, of everything, hangs in the air as I step into the empty hallway. I straighten my posture, as if that can fix what's coming loose inside me.

But it can't. Nothing can.

It was a day of trauma, but what scares me most is that I didn't hate it. The chaos, the connection. The not being alone. Maybe it was just an adrenaline rush. Or maybe—maybe I want it to be more.

There's no going back. Not after this. The only thing left is the one I don't want to admit. *I like him.*

I like him a lot.

FOURTEEN

NOAH

There are three of us in the room, but only two get chairs. It's fine. This way, I can keep an eye on both Dr. Patel, the hospital's risk officer, and the other one, who hasn't bothered to introduce herself. Dr. Patel has his hands clasped neatly on the table, a small, tidy man who'd probably wrinkle if you breathed on him too hard. The woman with him is cold, stone-faced, an iceberg in scrubs.

"Doctor Carter." Her voice is clipped and cold enough to freeze the blood in my veins if I let it.

"Would you like to sit?" Dr. Patel asks. He's doing that thing he always does, where he acts as if he's everyone's friend. It's meant to be disarming, and maybe it would be, if I didn't know better.

"I'm fine." I keep my posture relaxed, my grip light on the doorframe. It's a study in calculated ease, designed to give the impression that I've been here before. Which I have.

"Very well," the administrator says. She's back to business, like she's never left it in the first place. "Yesterday's incident during the multi-car pile-up..."

I nod, remembering. The ER, flooded with bodies, was a chaos of broken bones and bleating monitors.

"Yes?" I say.

"You performed an unauthorized procedure," she continues, not missing a beat.

She makes it sound so reckless, so dire, so very much like me.

"I saved a life," I remind her, my voice steady, like the air pressure before a storm.

Dr. Patel shuffles his papers but stays quiet. He's waiting to see where the wind blows.

The administrator levels her gaze at me, unblinking, unyielding. "You understand the liability this creates for the hospital, don't you? The risk to our insurance, our accreditation?"

She doesn't say my job, but we all know it's implied. It's the same threat, the same story. Only the dates and the signatures change.

"Of course," I reply, cool as a Seattle drizzle. "But when a patient is coding, I don't see the point in waiting for paperwork."

Her eyes narrow just enough to notice, a fissure in the ice. "So, you're saying you'd make the same decision again?"

"Every single time." I hold her stare, let her feel my conviction. It's real, as real as anything gets in this place.

Dr. Patel clears his throat, finally taking a stand. "While we appreciate your dedication, Noah, you need to understand the position this puts us in."

Now we have an "us." It must be serious.

"The hospital's position," I correct him, smiling. I mean it to be reassuring. I don't think it comes off that way.

The administrator taps her pen against her notepad. It's

the only sound in the room, and it echoes like a ticking clock. "This could lead to a formal review," she warns. Her voice is low, designed to unnerve, to unsettle.

"Understood." My answer is quick, deliberate, an admission without contrition. I want them to see I'm not backing down, that I mean every damn word.

"Is that all you have to say?" She leans forward, and I half expect her to slide me a piece of paper and tell me to write something down. Something apologetic, groveling.

"I'd rather be standing here with you both," I tell her, glancing at Dr. Patel to make sure he feels included, "than at someone's funeral."

Dr. Patel looks up from his notes, finally meeting my eyes. He's concerned, and that worries me more than the administrator's frost.

"If there is a review," he says, his tone softer, "it's important you have our support, Noah."

Then support me, I think.

I stay quiet, though, because I know he won't push me while I'm under investigation. He'll wait. It's his thing.

The administrator flips her folder closed, punctuating the meeting with a finality that's meant to intimidate. "I hope you realize the seriousness of the situation," she says.

"More than you know."

We hold a brief staring contest before she gives up and turns her attention to Dr. Patel. They share a glance, a whole conversation in the flick of an eye. I can't read it, but it makes me feel like they just decided not to eat me for breakfast.

I nod at them both and step out of the room, leaving the door open behind me. If they're going to hang me out to dry, at least they won't have to call me back in to do it.

The hallway outside is bright and unforgiving, like stepping out of a cave and into the midday sun. My eyes squint against the light, and I'm not sure if it's relief or exhaustion that sets in first. Probably both. I take a breath, long and deep, and let it out slowly. They may have let me off with a warning this time, but a formal review would still mean trouble.

That's when I see her, leaning against the wall.

She's there, waiting for me, arms crossed like a pair of parentheses bracketing the unlikeliest of appearances. The surprise catches in my chest, and I have to look twice to believe she's actually here. I mean, sure, this is where she works, but it's never where she waits.

Lily Harper, early and unarmed.

I must be standing there like an idiot, blinking in the fluorescent light. She's cool as always, leaning against the wall, hair pulled back tight, not a single strand or emotion out of place.

For a second, I think I must have screwed up the time or the location, or maybe even the universe. Then she pushes off the wall and closes the distance between us with a few swift strides, her eyes never leaving mine.

"They give you hell?" she asks, voice as sharp as her ponytail.

"Something like that," I manage to say, recovering from the shock of her concern. It's such a rare and delicate thing, I feel like I might break it if I'm not careful.

She nods, the hint of a smile playing at the corners of her mouth. It's more like a rare weather pattern than an actual expression, something fleeting and unexpected.

"Figured," she says, like she's known it all along, like she's always two steps ahead of the rest of us.

"And you're... waiting to say 'I told you so'?" I venture, searching her face for clues, for anything to make sense of her standing here, standing by me.

"You made the right call," she says, matter-of-factly, no hesitation, no catch. "And that's what I'll tell them in my report."

I stare at her, trying to reconcile this new reality with

everything I thought I knew. Lily Harper, high priestess of protocol, telling me I did the right thing. It's not just unusual; it's unthinkable.

"You don't agree, do you?" she asks, catching the doubt in my silence, the incredulity in my eyes.

"Honestly," I say, "I wasn't sure you would."

Her eyes are steady, direct, cutting through all my wariness and second-guessing. "If they penalize you for acting in a crisis," she continues, "it says more about hospital politics than your clinical judgment."

The words hang between us, something real, something new. It's the kind of shift that usually registers on a seismograph, but here we are, just two people in a hallway, standing closer than we've ever stood before.

I don't know what to say. Me, the guy who's always got a comeback ready, who's always deflecting with humor or sarcasm or charm.

"You don't do this, do you?" she says, watching me fumble with words and concepts like a med student on their first day. "Let someone back you."

"I'm getting used to it."

"And?"

"It's..." I look at her again, really look at her, and there's no irony, no bite, nothing but sincerity and certainty and Lily. "Different."

"Don't worry," she says. "I won't tell anyone."

"I know you didn't come down here to wait for my autograph," I say, finally finding some footing in our usual banter. "Is this a one-time offer, or can I count on your support group to have cookies next time?"

"Depends," she says. "You planning on getting written up again soon?"

"Nothing on my calendar yet, but I'll see what I can do."

The smile fades, and for a moment, she seems to reconside: everything she's just said, like maybe it was too much. But then she lifts her chin, determined, and the moment stretches between us, neither of us moving, neither of us wanting to break it.

There's a different kind of silence now, charged and unfamiliar and full of potential.

I should say something. Something clever, something definitive. But for the life of me, all I want to do is let this moment to linger, let it mean whatever it means.

This is what Lily Harper looks like when she's taking your side. And I'm starting to think I could get used to the view.

Marcus looks at me like he just got handed the full contents of a particularly juicy patient chart. He's leaning back in his chair, balancing on two legs.

The break room smells like burned coffee and disinfectant, a reminder that even here, in this sterile oasis, the hospital never really lets you forget where you are. I try to appear casual, like this is just another post-confrontation chill session, but the tension in my shoulders tells a different story.

"So," Marcus says, drawing the word out like he's unwrapping something special. "You going to tell me why Lily was pacing the hallway like an expectant father?"

"She wasn't pacing," I say, probably too quick, definitely too defensive.

"Uh-huh." He raises an eyebrow, leans in closer. "You're not even going to try for the 'How was your day, Marcus?' first?"

I rub the back of my neck, trying to work out a knot that has nothing to do with strained muscles. "How was your day, Marcus?"

"Don't worry, buddy," he says, grinning like the Cheshire cat. "We'll get to mine later."

I look at him over the rim of my cup. "We had a conversation," I say finally. "After the review."

"Oh?" He sets his cup down and steeples his fingers like he's getting ready to deliver a particularly important diagnosis. "Do tell."

"It wasn't really a review," I admit. "More of a 'Please, Noah, stop making us look bad by saving lives and breaking rules' talk."

"And where does Lily fit in all this?" His eyes light up, hungry for details, hungry for the parts I'm trying not to overthink.

"She... was there."

Marcus lets out a low whistle. "Well, shit. Sounds serious."

I glare at him, more for effect than anything else. "It's not like that."

"Not yet," he says. He takes a sip of his energy drink, savoring my discomfort like it's a rare vintage.

I shrug, feigning indifference, but we both know it's not that simple. "I didn't expect her to show up, okay? Or say what she said."

Marcus leans forward, setting all four chair legs on the ground with a definitive thump. "And what, exactly, did she say?"

"That I made the right call."

"Damn," he says, almost reverently. "A declaration of love if I ever heard one."

I can't help it; I laugh. It's half frustration, half relief, all tangled up in something else I'm not ready to name. "She took my side, Marcus. My side."

Marcus nods slowly, pretending to take notes with an invisible pen. "You do realize what this means, right?"

"Enlighten me."

"You care." He lets the words hang there, suspended in the air like a particularly tricky suture.

"Yeah, well." I rub my neck again, the knot still tight, still there. "I didn't expect to."

"But you do."

I stare into my cup, watching the coffee ripple under my breath, under my admission. "I guess I do."

"Does that mean that we're officially in 'it's complicated' territory now?"

I give him my best noncommittal shrug, the one that usually gets me out of trouble, out of having to admit what's really going on inside my head. "It's not like we're... whatever. We're not."

' But you want to be."

I don't answer right away, because honestly, I'm not sure. But the silence is its own kind of answer, and Marcus knows it.

"Dude," he says, shaking his head. "You are so screwed."

"Thanks for the vote of confidence."

"No, seriously." He points a finger at me, still amused, still knowing. "You're not even chasing chemistry anymore. You're chasing... What? Respect? Trust?"

"All the above?" I say it like it's a joke, but we both know I mean it.

"And the sad part is, you like it."

That earns him another laugh, this one not quite as hollow as before. "Yeah. I guess I do."

He smirks, drains the last of his coffee, and pushes back from the table. "You want my advice?"

"Not really."

"Tough," he says. "You're getting it anyway." He pauses for dramatic effect, makes sure I'm paying attention. "Don't screw it up."

Then he's gone, leaving me alone with my cold coffee and my thoughts.

I find her outside, near the ambulance bay, wrapped in shadows and evening chill. Her breath makes soft clouds in the cold air, and for a moment, I just watch her from a distance, trying to figure out how to approach this new version of us.

The parking lot is illuminated by security lights that stretch our shadows long and thin across the pavement. In the distance, ambulance sirens wail, a constant reminder that somewhere, someone else is running into another unknown. But here, in this small pocket of stillness, there's just us.

I take a deep breath, letting the cold air steady me, and start toward her with measured steps. She notices me when I'm halfway there, and I see her tense slightly before she relaxes, like she's been caught doing something she shouldn't but isn't about to admit it.

"Lily," I say when I reach her, the word more of a release than a greeting. "Thanks for earlier."

She looks down, brushing off my gratitude like it's snow on her shoes. "I just told the truth," she says. There's a softness to her voice that wasn't there before, a warmth that cuts through the evening chill.

We stand there, the silence between us stretching wide and strange. It's not awkward, but it's not quite comfortable either. It's something new, something charged and full of things we haven't said yet.

"I mean it," I say, breaking the silence because it's too much and not enough at the same time. "Backing me up? It means more than you know."

She meets my eyes, and there's a vulnerability there that catches me off guard. "It won't change anything," she says, almost like a warning, almost like a promise.

"Still." I take a step closer, closing some of the space that seems too big now. "It means a lot."

She shoves her hands in her coat pockets, a defensive move that somehow makes her look smaller, less like the Lily I've always known.

"I respect your choices, Noah," she says. Her words are quick and direct, as if she's afraid she'll lose them if she doesn't say them fast enough. "Even when they scare the hell out of me."

"Didn't think anything scared you," I say.

She smiles. "I'm full of surprises."

"I'd do it again," I tell her, my voice firm and unwavering. "Every time."

She doesn't flinch, doesn't look away. "I know," she replies.

The sirens fade, the night gets colder, and neither of us moves. We're like two actors in a scene who forgot to leave the stage, who forgot they even wanted to.

"I should go," she says, but she doesn't sound like she means it.

"Yeah," I say, not moving.

"See you tomorrow?"

The question is small and hesitant, like she thinks maybe I'll say no. Like she thinks, maybe this will all dissolve when the sun comes up.

"Count on it."

Her eyes stay on mine for a beat too long, and then she turns and walks toward her car. I watch her go, watch her figure shrink until it disappears into the shadows.

I reach my car and have a compelling urge to breathe hard against the glass. My breath fogs up the window, and I draw a quick circle in it with my finger, like a kid, like someone who just got handed something precious and isn't sure if it's real.

FIFTEEN

LILY

Maria flinches. It's a small thing—barely noticeable—but I've trained myself to notice everything. Especially the small things. She stands with the other residents, a wall of white coats and nervous energy, but today she's off her game.

"That's fifty milligrams, not fifteen," I correct, hearing the snap in my voice.

She's my mentee and I tell myself it's for her own good, for all their good. The hospital isn't a place for mistakes. It isn't a place for flinching, either.

Her cheeks flush, but she mutters a quiet acknowledgment and adjusts the chart, trying to look unruffled. Around us, the ward hums with its usual cacophony—machines beeping, nurses shuffling, patients groaning—but Maria's behavior throws everything off-key. My eyes narrow as I watch her, the bright-eyed optimist who usually answers before I even finish my questions. Now she's struggling to stay in tune.

Maria isn't the only one affected by my correction. I can see the other residents exchanging glances, probably relieved they're not on the receiving end today. I don't let them distract me, don't let them see the thoughts flickering behind my eyes.

"Let's move on," I say, motioning toward the next room. My tone is clipped, professional, but I can't shake the image of Maria's faltering hands.

The patient inside is a middle-aged man with a fresh abdominal scar. I look at Maria again, the weak link in today's surgical chain. The other residents expect a lecture about adhesions or infection risks, but I pivot, aim the next question squarely at her.

"What are the potential complications post-colectomy?"

Her eyes are blank for a moment—just a moment—but it's enough. "Bowel obstruction," she finally says, the words spilling out in a rush. "Abscess formation. Prolonged ileus."

"Good," I say, but it's not the full truth. The full truth is, she's only a fraction as focused as usual, and I know she knows it. My praise sounds hollow, even to me.

Rounds continue, and Maria's distraction hangs over the group like the gray Seattle sky outside. She jumps when another resident brushes past her. She's checking her phone with a frequency that borders on compulsive, like it's giving her instructions on how to get through the day. It's not hard to guess where her mind is. Harder to guess why it's there.

Another patient, another set of questions. She stumbles through a response about anticoagulation therapy, and the answer takes too long, even though it's a basic question. Something is very, very wrong.

"Dr. Alvarez?" I say, pressing her for more. I've never heard her stammer before, but there it is.

Lily: one. Maria: zero. It doesn't feel as good as it should.

The last patient of the morning is a knee arthroplasty. This time, I call on Jason, one of the other residents. He's relieved, stumbling through his own explanation of DVT prophylaxis, glancing at Maria like she's set the bar low on purpose. My presence makes him nervous, but that's not my problem. Maria's nervousness is. I pretend to listen to Jason, but all my focus is on Maria and her ridiculous phone.

When rounds finally end, the residents disperse like a flock of startled pigeons, relieved to escape. Maria lingers awkwardly, avoiding my gaze, tucking her phone back into her pocket like it's a piece of contraband. The way she moves, I can practically see the emotional bruise forming from earlier.

But more than that, I see a riddle, and it's one I intend to solve.

Maria looks guilty. It might be the lighting—dim fluorescents flickering above us—but I doubt it.

Determined to get to the bottom of it, I lead her into the supply closet, where she can't fidget away from the truth.

"Is there something going on I need to know about?" I ask, closing the door behind me.

She starts counting surgical gloves with trembling hands. "Uh, no? Why would you think that?"

The room smells like antiseptic and cardboard, cramped and confining. A place where supplies are sorted, and residents can't easily escape.

"Your focus is shot," I say, taking a step closer. "You're fumbling questions, doses—what's going on?"

Maria hesitates, her fingers stopping on a box of bandages. "I'm just tired, Lily. It won't happen again."

"That's not an answer," I tell her. We both know it's not fatigue; she works late shifts and still arrives sharper than the others. "Something's changed. Spill."

She tries to laugh it off. "You know me. I'm just a little— distracted. It's no big deal."

"Distracted isn't good enough."

Maria finally meets my eyes, and there's a flicker of fear. I know how to corner someone until the truth spills out. It's a talent and a flaw.

"Okay, okay," she says, sounding like I'm the executioner and she's choosing between methods. "There's a thing. I'm seeing someone."

"Someone?"

She stares at the floor, mumbling, "Ethan. Dr. Park."

It's like the air leaves the room, or maybe it's just my patience.

"You're dating another intern?" The question comes out sharper than intended, a reflex more than anything. I shift gears into the Lily they all know: professional, unsympathetic, unyielding. "You know hospital policy. You know the risks."

"Yes," Maria says, the word stretching with frustration. "I know all that. But it's—" She struggles, looking for the right word. "different."

"Different is a fling that turns serious," I say, not realizing I'm quoting myself. "Serious ruins careers."

I expect her to crumble. Instead, Maria's eyes spark with defiance. "I didn't mean for it to happen. But it has. I don't want to hide anymore, Lily. I also don't want to ruin my future." Her fingers twist nervously around a pen, white-knuckled and insistent.

A month ago, my answer would've been unequivocal: one passion will always compromise the other. Now, watching Maria tremble between hope and fear, I find my certainty slipping.

"You're risking a lot," I say, and it's not the lecture I intended. "This isn't like you, Maria," I say.

"It is me," she replies, eyes wide, vulnerable. "Just not the part you see every day."

Her sincerity is unnerving, and for a moment, I envy her courage.

"Think about what you're doing."

"Believe me, I have," she whispers, eyes on mine, pleading

for more than advice. Her conviction is unsettling, yet I admire it.

I open the door, letting in the sterile light of the hallway, a reminder of where we are and what's at stake. As she walks past, there's an unspoken question hanging between us—one I don't have an answer for.

It's not like me to hesitate. To pause. To question. But Maria's confession nags at me like a persistent cough.

I'm in the stairwell, a quiet place for surgical residents to think and occasionally cry, and all I can do is sit here on the cold step, my back against the wall, thinking.

It's concrete and confining, but right now it's the only space that makes sense. Maria's voice plays on repeat in my mind: "I don't want to hide anymore. I also don't want to ruin my future." She's foolish, I tell myself. Reckless. I try to cling to my initial disapproval, but the hesitation lingers like an open wound.

I force my thoughts back to professionalism, to everything I believe in. Relationships complicate careers. Careers are everything. That's been my truth, my guiding principle.

Then, Noah intruded. Uninvited, yet somehow expected.

The gala was a blur of music and awkward formalwear. I didn't want to go, didn't have any intention of staying. But there was his hand on my waist, leading me in a dance that felt like being caught in a tidal wave. For the first time in a long time, I wasn't the one in control, and the feeling was both terrifying and... exhilarating.

What scares me most is that I let it happen. I didn't push him away. Worse, I didn't want to.

I try to refocus. The stairwell door creaks open, the sound reverberating through the empty space. I half expect someone to find me here, to see through the cracks, but the door slams shut again, leaving me alone with my thoughts.

Another memory surfaces, cutting through my attempt at distraction. The trauma case. Chaos in the ER. The perfect synchronization of our hands, our minds. His steady voice, calm and reassuring.

"Nice work, Dr. Harper." He had said it with a grin that shouldn't have mattered. But it had.

I close my eyes, trying to block out the truth that's been creeping up on me since that night. I don't want to be Maria. I don't want to risk everything I've worked for. But the echo of my own advice haunts me: *Think about what you're doing.*

The café is nearly empty, a strange kind of quiet. I see Maria hesitating by the door, like she's expecting me to throw a chart at her.

"Sit down," I say, and she approaches cautiously, shoulders hunched, waiting for a reprimand.

Instead, she gets coffee. And the closest thing to real advice I've ever given.

I pretend to stir my drink, watching Maria out of the corner of my eye. Her movements are slow, deliberate, like she's crossing a minefield and expecting something to explode. I understand her surprise. I'm a little surprised too.

She sits across from me, her back straight as if bracing for impact. "You wanted to talk?" she asks, her voice careful and wary.

I nod. "A real conversation. Not just about surgery." Her eyes widen, caught off guard, and I take a sip of coffee to hide my own uncertainty. "You should hear this from me, not through hospital gossip."

Maria tenses, ready for the axe to fall. I can see the arguments building behind her eyes, the defenses she's preparing. She doesn't know I'm not here to crush them.

"I'm not going to report you," I say, my voice as even as I can manage. "But I want you to understand what you're risking." Her relief is almost comical, and I realize how unlike me this is. How unlike me it feels.

Her shoulders drop, and for the first time, she meets my gaze without flinching.

"Really? You mean—really?"

"Yes, really," I tell her. "I've been thinking about what you said. It's serious with him, isn't it?"

"It is," Maria says, her voice small but firm. "I didn't expect it to be. I didn't plan for it. But it is."

"Ethan's a good doctor. Steady. Thoughtful. But relationships... They have a way of taking over if you're not careful."

Maria leans forward, her eyes bright. "You're saying I shouldn't give up on it?"

I sigh, not quite believing my own words. "I'm saying be smart. Be careful. But don't be afraid of being human." I sound like a stranger, like someone who's starting to let the world in.

Her expression shifts from disbelief to gratitude. "I didn't expect you to understand," she admits.

I laugh, a small, wry sound. "Neither did I."

Maria studies my face, and I see the moment she realizes I'm speaking from experience. Her curiosity is palpable, but she holds back. "Has something changed for you?" she ventures, the question delicate and dangerous.

"Maybe," I reply, stirring my coffee again to avoid the truth reflected in her eyes.

"You're different," Maria says, her tone almost accusing. "Since when did Dr. Harper get so soft?"

I give her a look, half-serious, half-amused. "Don't tell the others."

She smiles, really smiles, and I feel something shift

between us. It's the beginning of trust, of understanding, that cuts deeper than the mentor-mentee roles we've played so far.

Maria leans back in her chair, the weight of uncertainty lifting from her. "Thank you," she says, and the words carry more than gratitude. They carry acceptance. Of me. Of herself.

We part with a shared, unspoken recognition. Two women navigating the same stormy sea of ambition and emotion. I watch her go, knowing she'll be okay. Maybe, just maybe, I'll be okay too.

SIXTEEN

NOAH

The smell of burned popcorn and antiseptic has its own strange harmony in the ER. I tell myself it's comforting as Jason freezes and the patient's heart rate plummets. It's not the chaos that throws him—it's the panic in the family's eyes. I recognize that, too.

Stepping in, I gently take the instruments from Jason's trembling hands and work with a steady calm that only comes from making every possible mistake once already. The room fills with the mechanical beeps of relief as the patient stabilizes. I watch Jason shrink back, vanishing into the walls, knowing I'll find him later.

The rest of the trauma team moves efficiently around me, resetting the bay for the next case. I can see Jason lingering near the door, head down, a shadow of himself. He avoids my eyes, melting into the noise of the hospital. The way he backs out is almost an art form—desperate but trying to save face.

"Close one," a nurse comments, nodding to the now-stable patient.

I give her a quick smile, more of a grimace, really.

"Too close," I say, stripping off my gloves. "Where'd they put the popcorn machine this time?"

She laughs, shaking her head. "Third floor. Don't burn the place down, Carter."

I watch the monitors beep in a steady rhythm and think about finding Jason. *We'll talk later,* I tell myself, catching sight of his retreating form one more time as I step into the hallway.

The locker room is all sharp angles and harsh lighting, the smell of sweat and bleach forming an uneasy truce. It's quieter here, but I feel the tension crackling under the surface. I open my locker and Jason is next to me, lurking like a guilty conscience.

"Noah," he says, voice tight. I can hear everything he's holding back, the way his jaw twitches, the sound of his breath catching in his throat.

"You okay?" I ask, keeping it casual. Casual is a myth in places like this.

"I froze." It comes out like a confession. "I'm sorry, I—"

"Hey," I interrupt, turning to face him. "We all do it."

He shakes his head, and I see his shoulders slump further, like he's deflating right in front of me. The posture's familiar—hauntingly so. It's the same one I've worn a thousand times.

"I don't think I'm cut out for emergency medicine." His words are so quiet, I could pretend not to hear them.

I close the locker, the clang of metal feeling final. "Let's talk after shift," I say. He doesn't look up. "It gets easier, I promise."

We stand there for a moment, a silence filled with every doubt he's ever had, every failure he thinks he can't overcome. It's too much like staring into a mirror, one that reflects all the parts of myself I don't want to see.

"Okay," he finally agrees, though it sounds more like a question.

I watch him leave, the door swinging shut with a soft, condemning thud. Alone, I sink onto the bench, trying to shake the weight of recognition that settled over me when I saw his face. When I saw my own.

I didn't expect it to hit so hard—Jason's insecurities peeling away my carefully maintained calm. Maybe it's that I'm watching history repeat itself, a cautionary tale I never thought I'd be old enough, or experienced enough, to tell. The overhead lights hum, vibrating against the silence I can't quite fill.

I shove my hands in my pockets, finding a pen cap, a receipt, nothing that feels like certainty. He sounded so fucking defeated. Just like I did.

I try to picture my mentor, Emily, imagine what she'd say to me if she were here. *You have to believe in them, Noah. Or they'll never believe in themselves.* The words hurt, an old scar tearing open. I don't know if I'm ready for that.

Jason deserves better than what I had. I think about those first months of residency, about feeling like I was constantly running on empty, constantly drowning. And here's Jason, flailing and reaching for something solid, and there's no way I'm letting him sink.

The sound of footsteps interrupts my spiral, and I look up, hoping for a second that it's him again, maybe even her. But the door stays closed, and I'm alone in the empty space, the stillness pressing in on me from all sides.

Yeah, I tell myself. *We'll talk more after shift.* I can't let him go without believing that it'll get better, that he'll get better. That we both can.

And there's still something left, something he didn't say. I could see it in the way he hesitated at the door. In the way he didn't slam it shut.

I stay on the bench a few more minutes, letting the hum

remind me I'm still here. Jason's left a textbook on the counter, and I pick it up, determined to give it back to him along with the advice he needs to hear. The advice I never received.

The staff break room feels like another planet after a shift. Quiet. Calm. Breathable. The lights are softer, the air less heavy with life-and-death consequences. Jason and I sit at a corner table with the detachment of survivors, coffee cooling between us.

"There was this cardiac arrest once," I start, watching his eyes widen, "and I stood there like a fucking idiot while everyone else ran the code."

His breath hitches, unsure whether to laugh or apologize.

I grin, putting him at ease. The lounge is safe ground, a place where our stories can exhale.

He looks at me like I'm a unicorn—a surgeon admitting to being human, letting him see behind the scrubs. I recognize the bewilderment, the part of him that's suspicious and grateful all at once.

"Then there was this one time," I continue, leaning back, "when I missed a major diagnosis. The attending had no problem announcing to everyone that I was a disgrace to modern medicine."

Jason tries to smother a laugh and fails spectacularly.

I grin, nodding. "It's okay," I assure him. "It was pretty funny. In a traumatizing kind of way."

"Seriously?" he asks. "I thought you were some kind of trauma savant."

"That's the key to looking good," I tell him, lifting my cup in a mock toast. "Don't screw up the same thing twice."

His laugh is more confident now, more real. The room around us feels expansive, a vacuum suddenly filled with the warmth of possibility. Other staff filters in and out, a background of hushed conversations and weary chuckles. But here, at our table, it's just us. It's important.

"First patient I lost was in my third month," I say, watching his reaction. He doesn't flinch this time, just listens. "It was this kid—eight years old. Came in with abdominal pain. Classic signs of appendicitis, except it wasn't. We caught it too late."

"Wow. Tough."

"I almost quit," I confess. "Marcus—that's my best friend, a charge nurse now—he had to slap some sense into me. Literally."

He smiles, imagining the scene. I think about how different it is for him. How different I can be for him.

"It's never been about screwing up, Jason. It's about learning. If you can do that, you're already ahead of the game." I tap the table with my fingertips.

He's quiet for a moment, processing. "I didn't know," he says finally. "I thought I was the only one."

"You're definitely not that special," I tease.

Jason clears his throat, eyes dropping to his coffee. "I just— I'm afraid of letting people down. My family. Everyone at the hospital. Myself."

"That never goes away," I admit. "But you learn to handle it. You learn to keep going."

"How?" His eyes are pleading, the last vestiges of desperation still clinging to the edges.

"There are things that help," I say. "For me, it was remembering why I got into this. The bigger picture. The people."

"Was that always enough?"

I think of Emily. Of the way it felt to be adrift after she was gone, like I was untethered and aimless. I think of how lost I felt without a direction, without a goal to steady me.

"Sometimes, no," I reply. "But knowing it wasn't enough—that was enough to keep going."

His expression shifts. Like he's letting himself understand.

"You're not the only one who thinks about quitting," I say, "or worries about fucking it all up. The good ones aren't the ones who never screw up. They're the ones who learn how to come back from it."

"It sounds like you're still talking yourself into it," he ventures.

He's not wrong, but he's missed something important.

I shake my head. "No. I'm talking us into it."

Jason smiles, small and shy, but there.

"I guess we'll see if I'm as good at coming back as you are," he says.

"We'll see," I agree, already knowing. Already certain.

His shoulders have dropped their burden, his eyes are brighter, and I know I've done something right today. I haven't let him fall. I haven't let him flail. And, in a way, I haven't let myself, either.

Jason leans back in his chair, the shift in his posture revealing an optimism he didn't have before. "I owe you one, Noah."

"You owe me nothing," I tell him. "Just don't burn out like I almost did."

"Promise," he says, the word almost boyish in its enthusiasm.

The conversation shifts again, this time lighter, easier. We talk about the less dire parts of the job, the parts that made us laugh even when we were too tired to stand. We talk about the patient who came in with a spoon stuck in a very inappropriate place, and the time Marcus shaved his head in solidarity with a kid who was about to lose his hair to chemo. We share stories that don't end in panic or doubt, stories that feel like redemption.

The break room fills with more staff, the ambient noise of camaraderie and commiseration. Jason doesn't shrink from it now. He seems part of it, a single point in a constellation of others just like him—trying, struggling, learning. I watch him with a satisfaction I can't quite name. He stands, finally, giving me a nod that carries more weight than any verbal thank you.

"I mean it," he says. "Thanks."

"Go home," I tell him. "Sleep. Do it all over tomorrow."

"See you, Noah."

Walking through the corridor outside the ICU, I spot her. Lily, in deep conversation with Maria, arms moving with uncharacteristic animation. Her ponytail swings as she nods. I linger near a nurses' station, pretending to study a chart but really watching the two of them with barely disguised interest. Lily is less guarded, her posture open, her smile almost fond.

The hell?

It's strange to see her like this. Soft. I don't know if I like it or if it makes me question everything I thought I knew about her. But I can't look away.

Maria's looking at Lily like she's a miracle worker. There's admiration, but it's more than that. It's an awe that comes when you see someone entirely different from how you expected. I get it. I've seen that version of Lily, too. Only now, there's a warmth I never expected. I'm not sure if I want to laugh or propose on the spot.

The interaction between them is a revelation. I watch as Lily actually touches Maria's shoulder. My jaw almost hits the floor.

I remember the first time we met four years ago, the way her eyes sliced through me like a scalpel. She was this tiny tornado of ambition and discipline, a force of nature wrapped in scrubs. That was her armor. That was her battle cry. Now, the shift in her posture, the unguarded way she listens to Maria, makes me realize just how much she's changed. Or how much she's letting herself be seen.

Maria's smile widens, and I know the words Lily says mean something. Really mean something. This is a mentor, a guide, someone more than the career-obsessed perfectionist I thought I'd figured out. I wonder if Jason looks at me the way Maria looks at her, if our talk gave him as much strength as Lily's giving now. I hope it did. I hope it does.

The whole scene is a mirror, a parallel I can't ignore. Lily is mentoring Maria, I'm mentoring Jason, and we're both finding new parts of ourselves in the process. She said I was wasting my potential. I thought she was too intense to notice anything but her own trajectory. But maybe we're not so different. Maybe she sees me better than I see myself.

I feel a rare kind of contentment watching them, seeing this unfold. It's not just a scene between two colleagues; it's an opening act of something more. I want to cross the ward, to tell Lily how much this matters, how much she matters. But I don't. I let the moment play out, let it breathe.

SEVENTEEN

♥

LILY

Home is a white box. Minimalist, not because I lack taste, but because disorder is intolerable. My apartment is on the seventh floor, high enough to avoid traffic noise, low enough that it still looks like I can touch the world, and the people in it.

I let myself in, disarm the alarm, and hang my bag and keys on their designated hooks. Next, I remove my shoes before aligning them precisely with the others. The entire process is automatic, muscle memory in staccato beats, a private ballet not performed for an audience.

The place is silent. Not just quiet—silent, like a museum after hours. Even the fridge runs in a soft, dignified murmur, as if it understands the need for restraint. There's a view of the city, but I don't look. Instead, I march straight to the kitchen and begin my decompression routine: check the mail (nothing but insurance flyers), wipe down the already clean counters, inventory the fridge. The monotony is soothing. Predictable. Nothing can go wrong if you never allow disorder to take root.

I think about Maria, about the absurdly hopeful look on her face as she confessed her secret romance. It should annoy me—the recklessness, the naïve disregard for professional consequence—but it doesn't. What annoys me is that she's happy. Or close to it. That, and the fact that I envy her.

I take out the recycling, even though there's nothing in the bin but a single Diet Coke can. I set it in the communal chute and watch it disappear, then pause in the hallway, uncertain. This is not normal. I don't hesitate. I don't pause. I execute.

Back inside, I begin checking the contents of my medicine cabinet. Band-Aids, then burn ointment, then cotton swabs, then dental floss. It's already organized, but I do it again. I try to focus on the motion—the click of plastic bottles, the gentle rasp of cardboard against Formica—but the image of Maria lingers, her smile a splinter I can't tweeze out.

I end up on my sofa, legs tucked beneath me, phone in hand The screen glows with accumulated notifications: emails from the chief resident, spam from medical journals, three new matches on a dating app I don't remember installing.

I open the app. The interface is clean, algorithmic. None of the men are worth a second look—one is a tech bro who's convinced his Peloton makes him interesting, another a would-be novelist with a chinstrap beard. There's a cardiologist from Bellevue with impressive credentials and the personality of a houseplant.

I scroll through their messages. Each is a small, hopeful gesture, a digital coin tossed into the void. I can't bring myself to answer any of them.

I toss the phone aside, then immediately pick it up again, guilt pricking at the back of my neck. I know why I downloaded the app. I know what it means. But I can't admit it, not even in the privacy of my own home, not even to myself.

I go to the kitchen. Open the freezer. Remove a single-serving tray of lasagna, homemade, labeled, and dated in block letters. I nuke it, standing in front of the microwave, arms folded. I do not eat in front of the TV. I do not eat in bed. I eat at the breakfast bar, back straight, fork in my left hand, phone in the right.

The lasagna is perfect—cheesy, salty, piping hot. I barely taste it.

I set down the fork, wipe my lips, and reload the app. I click on a profile at random. This one's a pediatrician. Brown hair, kind eyes, a dorky smile. His first message is direct: "I know we're both probably working late, but if you ever want to decompress over coffee, I'm in." I think about replying, fingers hovering over the keyboard. I could say yes. I could say no. I could ignore it, which is the path of least resistance.

Instead, I type: "You'd hate me after the first ten minutes."

I stare at the message, then delete it. I close the app, then delete that too.

I stare at the city lights, which have begun to flicker on, pixel by pixel, in the dusk outside my window. From up here, everything looks organized. There's a comfort in that, a sense that all the chaos of the world has been reduced to a grid of colored points, each one reliable, consistent, knowable.

But it isn't enough. The stillness is too complete, the silence oppressive. I wonder if this is how Maria felt before she let herself admit what she wanted.

I get up and start cleaning again, scrubbing the sink, wiping down the fridge, even though I've already done it twice. I dust the bookshelf, which has never in its existence accumulated a speck of dust.

I return to the sofa. The phone is back in my hand before I know it. This time, I don't open any apps. I just stare at my own reflection in the black glass, waiting for something to happen, some internal switch to flip.

Nothing does.

I am alone. It should feel like victory. It used to. But tonight, it feels like defeat.

I brush my teeth for exactly two minutes. Electric toothbrush, bristles worn down to half their lifespan. The timer pulses every thirty seconds; I move quadrant to quadrant, tongue to palate, never missing a spot. Somewhere in this ritual, memory creeps in, insistent as plaque.

His name was Daniel. Med student, then psych resident, then—eventually—my ex. He was the first person I dated who genuinely understood what it meant to be absorbed by work. Not just the hours or the exhaustion, but the way your mind rearranges itself around the next diagnosis, the next puzzle. I used to think that meant we'd last. In reality, it just meant our breakup was slower, more insidious.

I spit, rinse, look at myself in the mirror. There's toothpaste on my chin, which is uncharacteristic. I wipe it away and lean in, searching for traces of the woman who could be loved by someone like Daniel.

He had a way of softening the edges of things. Saturday morning bagels, crossword puzzles, half-watched movies on the couch. I can still hear the way he used to laugh when I tried to psychoanalyze him, or when I'd use medical jargon to justify why I preferred silence over conversation.

The last time I saw him, he left a note on the fridge. The memory is so clear, it's as if I'm still standing there in sweat-soaked scrubs, feet aching, mind running through surgical complications while I'm shoveling cold *Pad Thai* into my mouth.

The note was on a yellow Post-it, stuck dead center so I couldn't miss it.

I want to be a priority, not a postponement.

I read it three times before I let myself understand what he meant. My first reaction was irritation—who leaves a breakup note on a fridge? My second was guilt, sharp as lemon juice on a paper cut. The third was something I still don't have a name for.

We didn't have a spectacular blowout. No yelling, no thrown glasses, not even a dramatic exit. Just a slow reduction of text messages, an erosion of Friday nights together, a withering away that felt almost professional. After he left, I spent a week telling myself that this was how it needed to be. That sacrifice was part of the deal, and that anyone who couldn't keep up was, by definition, expendable.

It's only now, standing alone in my antiseptic bathroom, that I allow the possibility that I was wrong.

I wash my hands again, extra hard this time, as if I can scrub away the aftertaste of regret. But the mirror doesn't lie. There's a softness in my face that wasn't there before, a shadow of someone who once believed she could have both excellence and intimacy.

I turn out the light, but the memory lingers, bright and insistent. Maybe Maria isn't foolish. Maybe she's just braver than I ever was.

I get into bed, pulling the sheets over my shoulders, and let my mind drift. Not to surgical protocols, or tomorrow's rounds, but to the last time Daniel made me laugh so hard I couldn't breathe, and the way that felt like flying.

I close my eyes and pretend, for just a second, that I'm still that version of myself. The one who thought love and ambition could live in the same room.

Hospital mornings are a paradox: urgent but aimless, a marathon of waiting for disasters to happen. I make the usual rounds, scribble orders, sign forms, offer perfunctory nods to nurses and techs. The day glides past in its predictable way, until I find myself with a rare five-minute interval and nowhere to be but the nurses' station.

The place is a hive—phones ringing, monitors chirping, small knots of conversation springing up and dying out again. Most residents use the downtime to vent or trade horror stories. I usually stand apart, hovering at the edge of the counter with my coffee and a stack of unsigned charts. Today, I'm drawn to the low buzz of laughter coming from the corner.

Maria is wedged into a plastic chair, phone angled for a video call. I recognize the face on the screen—Dr. Park, her forbidden paramour. They're mid-conversation, but it's the look on her face that catches me. She's radiant. Not in the poetic sense, but literally: cheeks pink, eyes shining, every feature softened. She laughs with her entire body, as if nothing could possibly be more important than this exchange.

It's unfamiliar. The Maria I know is diligent, deferential, often nervy in my presence. This Maria is easy, open, a version of herself I didn't think existed. For a moment, I'm fascinated. For a moment, I almost resent it.

She glances up and sees me. There's a quick flash of apprehension, like she's expecting a reprimand, but I do nothing. I just nod. Maria grins and waves at me, then turns back to her phone, voice dropping to a conspiratorial murmur. I can't hear the words, but I recognize the feeling: the hush that comes with being seen by someone who actually wants to see you.

I watch longer than I should. It's unprofessional. It's borderline creepy. But I can't help it. There's a magnetic pull in watching someone be so... unburdened.

Eventually, I remember myself. I look away, pretend to review a chart, pretend the moment meant nothing. But it lingers, sharp and bright as a nerve exposed.

I tell myself I'm only concerned for her career. That I'm

just looking out for the program, for the hospital, for the well-oiled machine we both belong to.

It's a lie, but it's the kind I'm good at. I sign the chart and move on.

But something has changed. There's a fissure in the foundation, a flaw in the logic I've always used to justify my own solitude. For the rest of the day, I'm not sure what to do with it.

At two a.m., the hospital break room is a liminal space—unmoored from time, neither night nor morning, a place for the lost or the unwilling to admit defeat. I find myself here, bleary-eyed, confronting the vending machine and the ancient drip coffeemaker, its carafe burned nearly black.

In the bottom of my bag, there's a vacuum-sealed pouch of single-origin beans I brought from home. They were a gift, or maybe a bribe, from a patient's family. I told myself I'd save them for company, but company never comes. Tonight, I rip the bag open and breathe deep, letting the scent erase every clinical odor.

The noise of the grinder is harsh in the quiet, drawing a glare from a nurse folding towels at the table. I ignore her, fixated on the ritual: measuring, tamping, waiting. The rich, syrupy smell fills the cramped room, so different from the scorched bitterness that usually passes for coffee here.

As the pot gurgles and spits, I catch myself glancing at the door. It's involuntary, a reflex. I picture Noah ambling in, making some stupid joke about artisanal caffeine or accusing me of holding out on the good stuff. I brace for his entrance, the practiced smirk and the way he always leans in, just close enough to unsettle me.

But the door stays shut. The only sounds are the metallic

clink of the nurse's folding and the last sputters of the coffeemaker.

I pour a cup for myself, nothing added, and take a sip. It's objectively excellent: bold, bright, complex. I savor it, then instantly hate myself for wanting to share it. For wishing, even for a second, that someone would show up and ask for a mug.

I pour another cup anyway and set it on the counter. I stare at it, willing the universe to deliver a punchline. The cup sits, undisturbed, cooling by the minute.

Finally, I dump the second cup down the sink. I follow it with the rest of the pot, ignoring the waste, unwilling to leave evidence of this lapse.

The nurse glances up as I rinse the carafe. "Special occasion?" she asks, eyes flicking to the empty pouch on the counter.

"No," I say. "Just cleaning out the cabinets." The words come out flat, sterile, perfectly plausible. She shrugs and returns to her folding.

I dry my hands, toss the coffee bag in the trash, and leave the break room behind. I walk the corridor alone, pulse settling, the old discipline sliding back into place. The walls are as bright and clean as ever, but there's a ghost in the air: the memory of what might have happened, the longing I refuse to acknowledge.

Tomorrow will come, and I'll be ready. I always am.

EIGHTEEN

NOAH

The ER is at its manic best—nurses moving in a ballet of adrenaline, while patients compose a chorus of complaints. Inside the office, I'm somehow in charge of it all. Another sprain, another fracture, another day in paradise.

Marcus sticks his head in, mouth full of something unidentifiable from the vending machine. "You good?" he asks, chewing like a cow with gum disease.

"Just peachy," I say, knowing he can see right through me. I add a thumbprint of a signature to a consent form, ignore the ten unread emails demanding my immediate attention, and slump back in my chair. My phone vibrates, the San Francisco number flashing again. Part of me thinks *let it go*, but another part—the part that can't help itself—snatches it up like a reflex.

"Dr. Noah Carter," I answer, half expecting a wrong number, some telemarketer trying to sell me a better life.

Instead, I get Dr. Eliza Chen. My mentor after Emily retired. My favorite boss. My past, on a silver platter. She sounds the same as ever—brisk, bright, like sunshine in a bottle.

"Noah!" Dr. Chen's voice is a caffeine shot to my soul, smooth and invigorating. "I hope I'm not catching you at a bad time." Her laugh is like she knows every time is a bad time for me.

I close my eyes, letting her words spill over me like I'm twenty-five again and hearing them for the first time.

She doesn't wait for a response. "We've got an incredible opportunity at San Francisco General. Senior attending in trauma. Research funding. Flexible schedule. Your own damn parking space!" She punctuates every perk with the confidence of someone who's already won me over.

The past rushes back—coffee-fueled shifts, the golden haze of the California sun, the sense of belonging I didn't know I'd missed.

"Wow," I say, because it's the only word I can find. I lean forward, elbows on my knees, as if being physically closer to my phone will make her words feel more real. "That's—wow. Eliza, I don't know what to say." But I do, don't I? *Thank you. Yes. When do I start?*

Through the office window, I see the emergency department in full swing. Marcus is examining a kid with a kitchen knife sticking out of his foot. Nurses argue about whose turn it is to cover a missed break. And Lily—Dr. Lily Harper, surgical prodigy and the focus of my existence—barks orders at a resident, her face a masterpiece of intensity and *don't-screw-this-up*.

"We'd love to have you on board as soon as possible," Dr. Chen continues, her voice warm and eager. "Think it over, but I'd love to get your answer soon. This could be a game-changer for you, Noah."

A game-changer. My mind races ahead, filling in the blanks. Respect from colleagues who wrote me off. Financial security I've never had. Recognition of my skills and a chance to prove I'm more than just the cowboy ER doc.

"Can you give me some details?" I ask, pretending to be the calm, collected professional I'm not. I already know most of them—I can recite them like an overambitious medical student—but I need to hear her say them. Need to stretch this out, need to buy myself time.

"Of course!" Dr. Chen says, the smile audible in her words. She runs through the bullet points as if I'm not hanging on her every syllable: "Senior attending in trauma. Lots of funding for research initiatives. Competitive salary and benefits. You'd have a clear path to department leadership." She pauses, just long enough for the silence to demand an answer.

I clutch the phone tighter, my free hand tapping a frenetic rhythm against my thigh. What I should say: *This is perfect. Thank you. I'm in.* What I actually say: "I need to think about it."

Another look through the window. Lily moves with purpose, an endless loop of tenacity and caffeine. Someone I shouldn't care about, not this much, but do. Dr. Chen's words reverberate through me, echoing off all the spaces I've left deliberately empty.

"Noah?" she prompts, gently now. "I know you're not one to jump into things without considering all your options. But I want you to know how much I'd love to have you back. You're a perfect fit for this, and I'm sure we can sweeten the deal if that's what it takes."

"I really appreciate it, Eliza. I'll give it some serious thought and get back to you soon." The words sound hollow, even to me.

She says goodbye, her optimism bleeding through like an ink stain, and I end the call, staring at the typed up job description email already open on my phone screen.

The buzzing of the fluorescent lights seems louder now, a

relentless soundtrack to my unraveling. I sit there, surrounded by patient charts and the ghosts of decisions I thought I'd already made, feeling the weight of it all like a gurney dropped on my chest. Outside the office, the ER is a pressure cooker of motion and sound, a perfect storm of urgency. Right here, right now, it feels like home. I should be saying yes. But for the first time, what I should do and what I want to do are more misaligned than ever.

I watch the chaos unfold through the glass, unable to answer the one question that matters: *What's really holding me back?*

The on-call room is dark and quiet, the perfect place to wallow in self-doubt. I sink onto the sofa, holding my phone and just staring at the job offer as though it's a love letter from the universe. I let my eyes roam over the too-good-to-be-true salary, the dreamlike benefits. This should be a slam dunk, but my mind is a million miles from San Francisco.

I think of Dr. Chen's enthusiasm, the respect and stability that's always been just out of reach. But my brain has other ideas, serving up mental snapshots of Lily Harper, of midnight coffees and her rare, disarming smile. The more I try to focus on the job offer, the more she invades my thoughts. A few months ago, this would've been a no-brainer. Now, I'm trying to remember why.

The hum of the building's ancient heating system is the only sound as I sit there, tracing the words on my phone screen. Senior attending. Flexible schedule. Leadership potential. I've wanted this for so long, but my excitement has been hijacked by uncertainty. I rub a hand over my face, feel the scratch of stubble and the growing weight of what should be an easy decision. *Why is this so damn complicated?*

I switch off the phone, lie back on the bed. The ceiling tiles stare down, indifferent and unmoving. A little like Lily. My arm flops over my eyes, blocking out everything but the kaleidoscope of thoughts crashing around my skull. The hospital logo at the top of the PDF taunts me with its crispness, its assurance that this is the right move. And it is. It has to be.

I imagine showing the offer to Marcus, his eyes wide, saying: "This is huge, man. You're gonna kill it."

That's the reaction I should be having. Pure, unfiltered joy. *So why am I not?*

San Francisco. I can almost taste the sourdough and feel the fog against my skin. Everything about it screams fresh start. New city. New hospital. New chance to prove I'm more than just the class clown. It's all there, mapped out in a future I've dreamed of but never quite let myself have. So why does it feel more terrifying than thrilling?

I close my eyes, willing myself to see it. The palm trees and the sunshine and the feeling of starting over. But every time the picture comes into focus, something else creeps in. Lily's face.

My mind flickers, takes me to what-ifs I can't ignore. *What if I go and I miss this chance with her? What if I stay and it doesn't mean what I want it to mean? What if I'm wrong? What if I'm right? What if I'm overthinking, and what if I'm not? What if I don't know anything anymore?*

Marcus lounges in the staff room like a man with no worries, feet on the table and an open bag of chips in his lap. I toss a printout of the job offer in front of him, then sink into a chair, waiting for the barrage of sarcasm.

He glances at the paper, at me, then back at the paper, taking his time like a doctor savoring a long-winded diagnosis.

The room is empty except for us and the rattling of the vending machine.

"Damn, Noah." Marcus finally looks up, his expression somewhere between impressed and too smug for comfort. "You gonna take it, or are you waiting for them to add a signing bonus?" I hesitate, and Marcus raises an eyebrow, chips forgotten. "Holy shit, man. This is about Lily, isn't it?"

I fidget with my coffee cup, watch the steam curl and disappear. "Maybe." It sounds more uncertain out loud than it does in my head.

Marcus whistles low, leans back like he's got all the time in the world.

"Noah Carter, turning down the job of a lifetime for a woman." He lets out a dramatic sigh. "Never thought I'd see the day."

I frown at him, take a sip of my coffee to buy time. It's lukewarm and bitter, but I barely taste it. "I haven't turned it down."

"But you're thinking about it," Marcus presses, too quick, too perceptive.

"Yeah. So?"

Marcus grins, a knowing glint in his eyes. "So, she must be some kind of amazing." He pauses, watching me closely. "Or are you just losing your touch?"

I shake my head, trying to find the right words. *How do I explain that it's not as simple as he makes it sound? That it's not just about Lily, or just about the job, but about everything that's wrapped up in both?* "I just... I don't know, man."

The seriousness of my tone finally catches him off guard. He sets the chips aside, the paper rattling as he picks it up again. "San Francisco, Noah. The big leagues. I thought you'd be packed and gone by now."

"Thought so too," I say, more to myself than to him.

"Then what's the problem?" Marcus leans forward, elbows

on knees. "You were counting down the days until you could get back to California. You were gonna buy a surfboard and some Birkenstocks and everything."

I run a hand through my hair, feeling more uncertain than ever. "I'm not so sure anymore."

Marcus raises an eyebrow, the look on his face shifting from amusement to something else. "Because of Lily?"

"Because of everything," I say, which isn't a lie but isn't the full truth either. I avoid his gaze, pretending to be absorbed in the dregs of my coffee.

"Talk to me, man. What's going on in that overcomplicated head of yours?"

I think about the past few months, how things have changed so quickly I can barely keep up. "I didn't plan on this."

"On what? Having a life?"

"On having something to stay for." The words come out before I can stop them, raw and real. It's the first time I've said it out loud.

Marcus sits back, takes me in with a steady gaze. "Wow. You're serious."

"Yeah." I rub the back of my neck, feeling more exposed than I'd like. "I guess I am."

He's quiet for a moment, processing. Then he shakes his head, a small smile playing on his lips. "Never thought I'd see the day."

I manage a weak laugh. "Neither did I."

"So, what are you gonna do?" Marcus asks, folding the job offer like he's wrapping up the conversation with a neat little bow.

"Hell if I know."

I stare at the folded paper, having memorized the words spelling out my future, and wonder if they're as set in stone as they look.

Marcus leans back, the tension breaking as he cracks open a fresh bag of chips. "This is huge, Noah. Whatever you decide, you're gonna kill it."

Other staff enter, chattering about missed shifts and the latest ER drama. The dynamic shifts, and Marcus moves to join the conversation, his role as advisor temporarily on pause.

I linger, the weight of his words hanging over me like a cloud I can't shake. I think about Lily, about the look on her face if she knew what I was considering. Would she be surprised? Indifferent? Would she have any clue what this decision is doing to me?

I pocket the offer letter like a secret. I've got a lot to think about, and even more to say. But for now, I watch Marcus blend into the group, his laughter echoing off the walls, and realize the next conversation I have needs to be with her.

I find Lily in the quietest hallway in the hospital, eyes glued to her tablet and hair pulled back so tight it looks painful. The rest of the floor is bustling, but here it's just the two of us and the flicker of fluorescents. My footsteps echo like a countdown as I approach, and my heart decides to pound along for good measure.

"Hey," I say, too casual for the way my pulse kicks into high gear. "Got a call from my old boss. Senior attending position in San Francisco."

Her face doesn't change, but the way she's tapping the tablet screen makes me think it's dead.

"Sounds like a great opportunity," she says.

I wait, hope for a follow-up question or at least a hint that she gives a damn. But she just nods, a quick glance my way before the tablet wins her back.

I shift from one foot to the other, the silence stretching

between us like a rubber band ready to snap. *Is that it? Is that all she's going to say?*

"It is," I manage, sounding more uncertain than I'd like. I clear my throat, try again. "You think so?"

She stops tapping for a fraction of a second, then resumes. "Of course. It's what you wanted, isn't it?"

"Right," I say, nodding like an idiot. "Right." It was what I wanted. Past tense. Before things got complicated and her name started slipping into every mental pro and con list. I wait for more—a question, a comment, something that shows I'm not just another name on a white coat to her. But Lily doesn't give me anything.

"Will you be working with people you know?" she asks, not looking up.

I blink, caught off guard. It's the first thing that sounds remotely personal, and it gives me a sliver of hope.

"Yeah, Dr. Chen. She was kind of my mentor."

"Hmm." She finally lifts her eyes, but it's so brief I'm not even sure it happened. "Seems like a no-brainer."

Her words hit harder than they should. *Why does this conversation feel like a kick to the gut?*

"You think?" I ask, desperation creeping in at the edges.

"Wouldn't you agree?" Lily says, as if she's the one seeking my opinion.

I stare at her, trying to see past the calm, clinical expression. I want to say a million things. That it isn't a no-brainer. That I haven't decided. That maybe what I want isn't a job, but someone who makes everything else look pale by comparison. But the words catch in my throat, afraid to come out and find she doesn't feel the same.

"Yeah," I say instead, sounding far away, even to myself. "Guess so."

The tension is palpable, filling the space between us. I know I should keep pushing, but I'm suddenly unsure. Unsure how to break through her walls without knocking them over entirely. Unsure if I'm ready to find out that she won't ask me to stay. I hesitate, feel the moment start to slip, feel her drifting even as she stands right there.

"Hey, can you cover for Simmons later?" she asks, shifting gears quickly.

"Oh, uh, yeah. Sure," I stammer, caught off balance by how easily she transitions from what I hoped was a personal conversation to something that sounds suspiciously like a brush-off.

"He's supposed to assist on a triple-A, but they need me for handoffs," she adds, all business. Her eyes are on the OR schedule on her tablet, not on me. Not where I want them to be.

I nod, try to play it cool, try not to let on that my chest feels like it's caving in. "No problem."

"Appreciate it," she says.

I swallow, the bitter taste of disappointment lodged in my throat. She turns to leave, and I almost reach out, almost catch her by the sleeve, almost ask: *Would you care if I left?* Almost. But not quite.

Instead, I watch her retreating figure, a blur of dark hair and white coat, disappearing around the corner. Maybe Marcus was right. Maybe I'm reading this all wrong.

I stand there for a minute, maybe two, trying to convince myself that this wasn't as terrible as it felt. That maybe I wasn't as obvious as I think. But the nagging voice in my head says otherwise, and it sounds a lot like her. Like Lily, telling me to go, telling me she doesn't care if I do.

I turn back the way I came, running a hand through my hair, trying to keep my thoughts from spinning out of control. It shouldn't bother me this much. It shouldn't feel like my heart's been slammed in a door. But it does.

Maybe she's indifferent. Maybe I'm just not seeing what's

right in front of me. Or maybe, maybe, I need to make the choice before I find out for sure.

The city lights twinkle below like a thousand reminders of what I still don't know. I lean my head against the apartment window, the glass cool against my skin and my thoughts warmer than I'd like to admit. The unsigned contract sits on the counter behind me, bright white and accusing. I should be doing something with it—packing, signing, deciding—instead I'm staring into the dark, feeling the weight of everything I haven't figured out.

The apartment is quiet, too quiet, the tick of the wall clock echoing with each second I put off deciding. A car passes below, headlights sweeping across the ceiling, gone before they leave an impression. My thoughts do the same, racing ahead without sticking, without giving me anything concrete to hold on to. I turn away from the window, from the view that does nothing but remind me of how tangled up in knots I've become.

I close my eyes, the inside of my head no quieter than the city outside. I'm not used to this. Not used to caring so much, to weighing one person's opinion more heavily than anything else. *What if I'm reading her wrong? What if this is a no-brainer, like she said?*

I think of the job offer again, and the pieces fall into place —right where I left them, still without a clear picture. A way out of the chaos I'm always accused of creating. The chance to prove I'm more than the troublemaker, the rebel without a cause. A new chapter without the complications I've let my life get tangled in. All there, all perfect. Almost.

I push away from the window, my mind cycling back to where it shouldn't. To where it wants to. To where she is.

She was so unreadable today, so Lily. Her face, the way it didn't change when I told her about the offer. The way she said it was a great opportunity, like she was handing me a surgical instrument and not a future. It left me feeling more confused than ever. Confused and scared and more alive than a job offer ever could.

I let the paper fall back to the counter, not ready to sign, not ready to walk away, not ready to do anything but stand here and think and think and think. About her, and what it means to want someone this much.

It should be easier than this. Easier to know what I'm doing, easier to follow a plan I've had all along. But the plan's been derailed by someone I never saw coming, someone who's turning my world inside out.

I drop into a chair, bury my face in my hands, and see her in my mind. Her smile, the one I pretend doesn't affect me. Her sharp wit, the way it cuts through my bullshit and gets to the core of who I am. The way she makes me want to stay, even when everything else tells me to go.

The tick of the clock reminds me how long I've been sitting here, how little I've done to change things. I'm not that guy. I'm not supposed to wait around, not supposed to care this much about anyone or anything, but the next step up.

But I do.

I think about what staying means. Uncertainty. Risk. The chance to fall flat on my face. The chance to fall for her. I let it roll around my mind, each thought taking a piece of me with it. I think about the challenge of working with someone like Lily, of being with someone like her. Someone who pushes me and frustrates me and makes me want to be better. Someone who terrifies me with how much she's starting to matter.

This indecision is a new kind of chaos, one I didn't think I'd let myself want. But maybe this is what I need. To be unsure, to take a chance, to choose a life I never thought I'd have the courage to seek out.

Maybe it's time to stop avoiding, to stop waiting for the answer to come to me. Maybe it's time to take the leap and see where I land. Maybe it's time to let go of the plan and go for what I never thought I'd be bold enough to choose.

But not tonight. Not yet. I'm still me, still hanging on to the last thread of certainty. I get up, push away from the counter and the view and the decision. I know what I need to do.

NINETEEN

♥

LILY

The memo feels heavier than a single sheet of paper should. I stare at the clinical black print, skimming words I know by heart. Disciplinary board. Breach of policy. *Hearing*. Words that were just words last month, meaningless lines in an employee handbook that happen to other people. Words that now feel personal, like a scalpel nicking skin.

I expected this. Why does it still sting?

This is about Maria. I scan for the key points: Maria Alvarez and Ethan Park, a romantic relationship disclosed. My jaw sets as I read the rest. It lays out every detail, precise and dispassionate. The hearing date is set for next week. Charges include unprofessional conduct, failing to maintain workplace boundaries, risking patient care. Consequences up to and including termination.

It sounds so... final. The formal language is surgical, designed to cut deep. The rational part of me says it's exactly what I should have expected. There's no room in this field for distraction. Yet there's another part, a softer voice I don't recognize, whispering that this is unfair.

My eyes narrow as I zero in on the phrase "failure to maintain professional decorum," the words mechanical and heartless. How the hell did this escalate so fast?

I lean back in the chair and glance around the office, but it offers no answers. Just the same old fluorescent-lit sterility, as blank and emotionless as the memo. Filing cabinets stuffed with other people's mistakes, computer screens displaying sanitized patient data, chairs still tucked into empty desks. But the walls feel like they're closing in on me, and I push back against the sudden claustrophobia.

How did it come to this? I remember a week ago, seeing Maria and Ethan leaving the hospital together, her laugh echoing through the lobby, his arm a casual question mark over her shoulders. I knew someone would notice eventually. People love a scandal almost as much as they love gossip. But I thought, somehow, they'd dodge this bullet. Or maybe I just hoped they would.

I fold the memo in half, a perfect crease, and then again, until it's small enough to fit in my lab coat pocket. As I tuck it away, my hand brushes against the fabric, the texture familiar and comforting. This should feel like any other problem I can solve with logic and precision. Yet here I am, blindsided, wondering why this sterile, impersonal letter feels like an indictment of my own choices.

For a moment, I consider telling Maria before rounds, giving her a chance to brace herself. But what would I even say? There's no gentle way to deliver this kind of news. The only thing worse than hearing it from the board, which she will soon enough, would be hearing it from me.

I'll wait. She's stronger than she looks. I've taught her to be.

The sound of a distant pager jolts me back to the present,

the reality that life outside this office is continuing at its relentless pace. I get up, reach for my coffee, and pause. The mug sits cold and abandoned on the desk. It seems like a lifetime ago when that was the worst part of my morning.

Before I step out, I take another look at the room, as if something in its stark lines could explain why this feels so personal. But it's just me and my messy emotions, alone with thoughts that won't quite settle.

The memo feels like a glimpse of who I was before this started to matter, and I'm not sure which one of us is going to win.

I'm pulled into the stairwell by a pair of frantic hands. Maria's eyes are red and wide, like she's been crying for days. She paces in quick, agitated lines, and I watch her from my post against the railing, letting her words spill out in breathless waves.

"They know, Lily. They know about me and Ethan. I don't know how, I swear we were careful—"

Her voice cracks, and the echo makes it sound like she's shouting.

"We never—never—let it interfere with work, I promise. Someone must have seen us leave together, or maybe at the café— Oh God, I'm such an idiot—"

She stops, her face turned up like she's searching for divine intervention in the form of a light bulb. Her breathing is jagged, matching the tremor in her hands.

"Who would do this to us? Who would tell?"

I shrug, because saying "the entire hospital" doesn't seem helpful. Her cheeks are flushed, and I brace myself for the next onslaught.

"It was stupid. So stupid. And now they're calling us in,

and Ethan thinks we've ruined everything, and maybe we have, and we're both going to get fired, and—"

"And you're hyperventilating," I say.

She stops, just long enough to give me a wild, desperate look. "What do I do?" Her voice is small and scared, the opposite of everything I've taught her to be.

I tilt my head, assessing the situation. It's worse than I thought. "Start by breathing."

Maria resumes pacing, clutching her elbows like they're the only things holding her together. "What if they terminate us? Ethan's residency is on the line, Lily. They won't let him transfer if he has this on his record. And me—I'll never find another program that—"

"You're spiraling," I cut in, more gently this time. "Sit."

She doesn't sit, but she does stop moving, which I count as a win. Her back slides down the concrete wall until she's crouched, a small, miserable ball of panic. She looks up at me, and the hopelessness in her eyes makes my chest feel tight.

"This isn't fair, Lily," she whispers. "We were so careful."

I crouch next to her, still keeping my distance.

"You know what they say about surgeons who care, Maria. First, do no harm." I pause, choosing my words like I choose my sutures. "It's not a mistake to care about someone. The mistake is letting others write your narrative."

She looks at me like I'm speaking a language she doesn't understand, or maybe one she's never heard me use.

"You can't believe that," she says, disbelief mingling with the tiniest hint of hope.

"Believe what you want," I reply, standing up and leaning against the stair rail. "Just don't give them all the power."

Her lip trembles, and she wipes it away with the back of her hand. "But Ethan—"

"Is tougher than you think," I say. "So are you. But if you

don't want to fight, then maybe you're right. Maybe it was stupid."

The silence that follows is heavy. I can see the gears turning in her head, faster and faster, clicking into something more solid.

"Lily," she says finally, her voice steadier now, "I'm scared."

I meet her eyes, and I don't let go. "Then you're doing it right."

I watch as the words settle over her, as her frantic heartbeat slowly finds a rhythm. Her breaths are deeper now, her shoulders less hunched. The tears have stopped, and she's looking at me like she's not sure if she should be grateful or angry or both. Maybe that's because I'm not sure either.

When she stands, she seems taller.

"I should go," she says, and I can tell she doesn't want to, not really. But she's always been better at following rules than I am. I give her a short nod, and she takes it as permission to flee.

The stairwell door closes with a soft click, and I'm left in the quiet aftermath, replaying my own words and wondering when I became this person. The person who doesn't mind saying it's okay to feel something, to risk everything for it. The person I used to hate.

I push myself off the rail, ignoring the tightness in my chest that tells me I need more distance than the stairwell provides. The metal's coolness lingers against my skin as I head back into the world of things I understand.

The room feels like a courtroom and morgue combined. Leather chairs, polished wood, and enough tension to crush a lesser human. Maria and Ethan look like children in front of the looming tribunal. When I walk in uninvited, every suit at the table stares as if I've confessed to murder.

"Lily," Maria whispers, like I'm an apparition sent to haunt her.

The chairperson, a woman in a tailored navy suit with an expression to match, clears her throat. "Dr. Harper," she says, her tone icy and confused, "we weren't expecting you."

"I'm aware," I reply, taking an empty seat without asking. It scrapes against the floor with a satisfying, deliberate sound.

Ethan shifts in his chair, his back too straight to be comfortable. I catch Maria's eye and give her the smallest nod. She looks like she might burst into tears or laughter or both.

"We were just discussing Dr. Alvarez's conduct," the chairperson resumes, regaining her composure. Her voice drips with condescension. "It appears there have been... lapses in judgment."

One of the board members, a man whose tie screams 'second in command,' leans forward. "Maintaining professional boundaries is essential, Dr. Alvarez. This is a very serious matter."

Maria opens her mouth, but nothing comes out. Her panic is palpable, and I can't watch her flounder like this. I interrupt before she has the chance to drown.

"May I?" I ask, my tone less of a request and more of a statement.

The chairperson looks as if she'd like to refuse, but curiosity gets the better of her. She gestures for me to proceed.

I lean back, folding my arms. "You're questioning her professionalism based on a personal relationship. Yet Maria Alvarez has shown more dedication to her work than anyone else in this program."

"We have reason to believe—" the tie starts.

I cut him off. "You have a suspicion, nothing more. Is there a single documented case where this supposed relationship impacted patient care? A missed shift? A complaint from staff?"

The room is silent. I let it hang, giving them time to admire the lack of response.

The chairperson recovers first. "Personal relationships can lead to conflicts of interest and compromised decision-making."

"*Can* lead," I echo. "But have they?"

Ethan and Maria watch with wide eyes, like they're seeing a medical miracle unfold. It's almost enough to make me smile. Almost.

"The hospital policy is clear," she continues, trying to regain control. "These situations must be addressed before they affect performance."

"Or perhaps," I counter, my voice sharp and steady, "the policy needs reevaluation if it penalizes residents for having lives outside these walls."

The second-in-command fumbles with a stack of papers. "Dr. Harper, we appreciate your—"

"You're talking about commitment," I say, cutting him off again. "Maria Alvarez is the most committed resident I have. You should be commending her, not questioning her."

The formality of the room presses in, but I don't back down. This isn't just about Maria and Ethan. It's about everyone in the profession who's ever had to choose between their career and their heart. Everyone who thought those things were mutually exclusive.

The board members exchange glances. I can feel the shift, subtle but there. The realization that maybe—just maybe—they've underestimated their opponent.

"I understand you have procedures to follow," I say, more calmly now. "But take a moment to consider what you're really achieving here. Do you want exceptional doctors, or robots with perfect records?"

There's another pause, this one filled with the sound of my heartbeat and the knowledge that I've crossed a line I didn't even see coming. But the strange thing is, I don't regret it.

"Thank you for your perspective, Dr. Harper," the chairperson says at last, her tone grudgingly respectful.

"You're welcome," I reply, standing up. My legs feel a little shaky, but I blame it on the leather chair. "I'm sure you'll make the right decision."

I don't wait for a dismissal. I turn and leave, the door closing softly behind me. It should feel like an ending, but it doesn't. It feels like the beginning of something big and unwieldy and terrifying.

In the hallway, I let out a breath. It comes out shaky. It sounds like relief.

The on-call room is dim and quiet, a perfect match for my mental state. My white coat hangs limply over the back of a chair, abandoned like my old beliefs. I stare at the narrow cot bed, but it's not rest I need. It's something bigger, something harder to find.

I let the darkness settle around me, close and comforting, like the walls of a cave. It's the opposite of the boardroom's harsh light, the sterile office, the echoing stairwell. Here, I can breathe. Here, I don't have to pretend I'm not exhausted, not questioning everything I've ever held as true. The quiet is so thick I can almost touch it, but underneath, I hear the distant hum of hospital life continuing without me.

I should be thrilled. I just defied a room full of suits and lived to tell the tale. Maria and Ethan will get a formal warning, nothing more. They'll have to document their relationship with HR, but no one's losing their jobs. It's a victory, even if I don't quite recognize it as mine.

The outcome is good. Better than good. It's almost unbelievable, like a dream version of reality where caring doesn't equal weakness and taking a stand doesn't lead to ruin. So why do I feel like I'm falling?

The board's reactions replay in my mind, the way their expressions shifted from confident to skeptical to—almost—convinced. It was an odd thrill, watching them squirm. I didn't know I had it in me to challenge the rules, to risk so much on principle. For someone else's heart, for my own, maybe. When did I decide that love wasn't a liability?

It's been creeping up on me, this change, the way fog rolls in and blankets everything you thought you could see clearly. First Maria. Then Ethan. Now... Now I'm not sure what's left. My eyes drift to the clock on the wall, but I can't make out the time. I'm not sure I care.

I think about Maria's hug after the hearing, the way she clung to me like I was more than just a mentor. Like I was something safe. Ethan, quiet and awkward, muttering a thank you I didn't deserve. Did they know I wasn't just talking about them in there? Did they hear the truth I couldn't quite say out loud?

I pull my knees up, leaning back on the too-small bed. The mattress is stiff, but it holds me, and right now, that feels like enough. I should probably move, go home, act like a normal human with a life outside this hospital. But where would I go? Who would I be when I got there?

My thoughts turn to Noah, the one thing I can't quite reason away. The easy smile that annoys me more because I like it, the way he reads me like one of his ER patients, seeing straight through to the source of my discomfort. We've been circling each other, two sharks in different oceans, waiting to see who bleeds first—and now he's going to San Francisco.

The rules I've lived by feel like a cage now. They used to be armor, protection against uncertainty and failure, and messy things like hope. But today, in that boardroom, they seemed small and childish. I remember telling Maria not to let someone else write her narrative, and it hits me that I might have been speaking to myself all along.

The on-call room is silent, save for the distant sound of a monitor beeping, a nurse's cart squeaking. I hear each noise as if it's announcing a possibility, a reminder that I don't have to choose between being Lily Harper, the surgeon, and someone with a life. I can be both. Maybe.

My eyes feel heavy, but sleep isn't what I need. I need to get up, to move, to act on this fragile new understanding before I second-guess it away. I stand, reaching for my coat. The fabric feels like it belongs to someone else now. Someone who thought she had everything figured out.

The lamp's soft glow casts shadows against the wall, and I pause before leaving. My silhouette looks strange and new, and I'm almost afraid to claim it. The hallway is quiet when I step into it, but I don't mind. I've got enough noise inside me to fill the space.

TWENTY

NOAH

Our feet squeak in tandem as we head down the post-op hallway, and the rhythm feels about as tense as we do. We've done this dance a hundred times, but the steps are all wrong today. Too mechanical. Too stiff. I reach for the handle of a door that suddenly feels miles away.

"Great work on that consult," I say, keeping my tone strictly business to match hers. "Nice and efficient."

Lily's eyes stay glued to her notes, refusing to meet mine, and it takes everything in me not to turn this hallway into a battleground of old arguments and unfinished thoughts.

She nods, short and perfunctory. "Patient's stable," she says, like it's the only thing worth mentioning. Like we're just two people who occasionally run into each other at work and nothing more.

I swallow the urge to bring up San Francisco, shove it down deep where the rest of my frustration is building. "That new resident was lost," I offer, hoping for even the tiniest spark of our usual banter.

"New residents are always lost." She sounds distracted, but I can tell she's anything but. Every word feels deliberate, carefully designed to avoid giving me anything to hold on to.

I study her face, searching for some crack in the composure. There isn't one. She's mastered the art of looking engaged with everything except me.

We pass a patient's room, and I'm desperate enough to try humor as a Hail Mary. "Did you see the guy in 316?" I ask, forcing a grin. "He's got a tattoo that says, 'If you can read this, I'm not sedated enough.'"

Lily doesn't even glance my way. "Charming." Her voice is flat, and I'm starting to think that she's forgotten how to sound like a person instead of a medical chart.

The hallway stretches out in front of us, endless and silent. I want to shake her, force her to say anything real, anything human. But I don't. I just walk beside her, feeling more like a ghost than a person.

Her ponytail swings with each step, precise and perfect, and it reminds me of everything we aren't right now.

The farther we walk, the more I can't stand it. The distance. The pretending. The damn unflappable composure.

"Look," I say, stopping in my tracks. "You could've at least asked me to stay."

The words explode out of me, and they feel raw. Exposed. Vulnerable in a way I never wanted to be, but can't help anymore.

She stops, too, and for a second, I think I've finally caught her off guard. But when she speaks, her voice is sharp. Controlled.

"I don't ask people to stay. They stay or they don't."

I flinch like I've been hit, and maybe I have. She's not pulling punches, and now, neither am I.

"Is that really how you want to play this?"

"Play what, exactly?" She sounds genuinely curious, like

she's reading an article on how to ruin Noah Carter's life and would really love some firsthand tips.

My hands are clenched, and I try to loosen them. "Everything."

Lily looks at me, really looks, and for a split second, I think she might say what I need to hear. But she just repeats, quieter this time, "They stay or they don't."

We're staring at each other now, and it's a standoff neither of us is willing to end. I can feel the hurt in every muscle, every bone, every breath.

"Fine," I say, because there's nothing else I can say that won't make this worse. Maybe that's what I'm afraid of.

I turn and walk away, my footsteps echoing down the corridor. Each one is a little farther from her, a little closer to admitting I've lost.

The last thing I see is Lily, standing alone in the middle of the hallway. The last thing I hear is the silence swallowing us whole.

I didn't see Lily for the next two days. I wasn't avoiding her exactly—but I wasn't looking, either. Not in the break room, not in the units, and definitely not in the cafeteria, where people talk too loud and notice too much.

So when I step into the elevator and catch the back of her head—dark ponytail, stiff shoulders, gaze fixed on the floor numbers—it takes me a second to register it's her. And another to decide I'm not stepping back out. The doors close. The air gets smaller. And then the silence presses in. I count to five, the seconds dragging like hours, and then I can't take it anymore.

"You know, our last conversation didn't exactly feel great," I say, and it comes out more broken than I intended.

She turns, her eyes colder than the metal walls, and I feel every inch of the distance I swore I'd never let get between us.

"Did any of this mean anything to you?" I gesture between us, trying to sound angry instead of desperate. "The project, the coffee breaks, the damn gummy worms—was it all just passing time?"

She's silent, and I can't stand it. Not here. Not now. Not when there's no room to escape each other. I need her to say something, anything, that doesn't leave me feeling like I'm crazy for thinking this was more than a temporary distraction.

Finally, she speaks. "Of course it did. But that doesn't mean you weren't always going to leave." Her voice cracks at the end, a fissure in the armor, and for a moment, I almost believe she cares.

"That's what you think?" I demand. "That I'm just waiting for my chance to bolt?"

"But you are going."

I feel the blood drain from my face. She really believes it. "I wasn't going to leave. Not unless I had a reason to."

She laughs, but it's humorless and sharp. "And I wasn't going to be the reason someone stayed just to regret it later."

"That's not how it is," I insist, and I can hear the pleading in my voice. I hate it. Hate that I'm willing to throw myself at her feet, only to watch her step over the mess.

"Really? Because it feels a lot like it."

My hands are moving, gesturing wildly, and I know I look unhinged, but I can't stop. She's standing there like a statue, every word bouncing off her like rubber bullets.

"I told you about the offer because I thought you'd—" I break off, because admitting I need her to want me is something I can't say without falling apart.

"You thought I'd what? Ask you not to take it?"

"Something like that," I admit, my voice barely a whisper.

"Then maybe you should've told me that weeks ago," she

snaps, and there's more emotion in those words than I've ever heard from her.

We stare at each other, both of us breathing hard, the air between us thick with everything we've finally said. Everything we've left unsaid. Her eyes are wide, searching, and for a brief second, I see the person I thought I knew—the person I thought I loved—standing right in front of me.

But she's not that person. Not anymore. Maybe she never was.

The elevator jolts to a stop, and the doors slide open.

I expect her to wait, to say something, to give me one last chance to fix this. But she just walks out, her back straight and unyielding. She doesn't look back. Not even once.

The doors close, and I'm left with the silence, the cold, and the truth I didn't want to see.

There's nothing quite like a rooftop to remind you how small you are. Even smaller when the only light up here comes from a phone screen that's buzzing more than I am. I watch the city take on the bruised colors of a Seattle evening, and all I can think is that I should've asked her properly if she wanted me to stay. If I'd asked her properly, she might have answered properly. She might have even said, "*Please stay*." But I'm a coward, and I fumbled the question like I fumble life. And now we'll never know. Given I normally can't stop talking, even when I really should, I'm more shocked than anyone that I didn't have the guts to say the words when it mattered.

The air is cold, but it's not waking me up. It's just adding to the numbness. I stare at my phone, Marcus's messages piling up, his worry clear even through the screen. "Still in?" "Dude, check in!" "Don't make me send a search party!"

I ignore them, too tangled up in everything that went

wrong today. That went wrong between me and Lily. That keeps going wrong no matter how hard I try to stop it.

"I should've just said it," I mutter, like repetition will somehow turn back time and give me the chance to rewrite this day. "I should've just told her."

But I didn't. Instead, I danced around the truth, hoping she'd fill in the blanks, give me the sign I needed. I offered her half the story, expecting her to write the rest. Too afraid to be the one to take the leap.

My stomach knots with anger, but mostly at myself. This isn't me. I'm supposed to be the guy who's got it all figured out. Who doesn't let stuff like this keep him up at night, staring at city lights that won't stop blinking at him like they're mocking his indecision.

And yet, here I am. Not figured out. Not even close.

I run my hands through my hair, let out a frustrated groan that echoes across the rooftop. "I should've told her I wasn't leaving."

I should've told her everything, from the minute that offer hit my inbox. Instead, I waited, hoping she'd read my mind, hoping she'd save me the risk of saying it first.

But love isn't like that. It's not just about showing up. It's about risking it all, rejection and everything, and neither of us was brave enough to do it. Not really.

I pace along the edge, the city sprawling out below me, and I wonder how we got here. How two people who can handle the chaos of a hospital on a holiday weekend can't handle a single honest conversation.

The sadness hits me next, a wave I wasn't expecting. I sit down hard, the cold concrete grounding me just enough to keep the frustration at bay. I wasn't lying when I said I didn't want to leave. But I wasn't being honest, either, because I never admitted how much I wanted to stay.

Or why.

I let out a slow breath, watching it disappear into the evening like every word I should've said.

Maybe I was a dick for telling her the way I did. Maybe I was an even bigger dick for hoping she'd give me the reason I couldn't say out loud.

But damn, did I want that reason!

I keep hearing her voice, the way it cracked just enough to make me think this mattered to her. Just enough to make me think I wasn't the only one who needed it to.

I don't ask people to stay. They stay or they don't.

I pace again, trying to work out the knots in my head.

This was never the plan. I was never supposed to let anyone in like this. Never supposed to let it hurt this much. But here I am, hurting anyway.

And now, I'm sitting here, realizing I didn't offer her enough to make her believe in us.

Didn't risk enough.

Didn't love enough.

My voice breaks the silence again, softer this time, resigned. "I should've told her."

The city lights blink at me, and I blink back, waiting for the courage I thought I had.

The offer letter glows on my laptop screen. Fifteen-to-life in sunny California, without the possibility of parole. I stare at it from across the room, because getting any closer feels too much like committing. The only other sound in my apartment is the hum of the refrigerator, the perfect soundtrack for a life I suddenly don't know if I want anymore.

It's late, and the world outside my window is moving on like it always does. The world carries on, indifferent to my decision paralysis. I can hear the distant rumble of a train, carrying people to places they probably have more certainty about.

I need to formally reply to San Francisco, the last step in making this real. The last step in leaving.

I should feel relieved. I've always been good at this part. Change. Starting over. The easy escape when things get too close, too messy. But this time, I'm stuck.

"What the hell am I doing?" I whisper to the empty room, and the emptiness answers with silence.

My head is full of echoes—my words, her words, everything in between. *You're always going to leave.* Not unless I had a reason to. The conversation keeps replaying, a loop I can't escape.

I just keep looking at the contract, waiting for it to tell me something I don't already know.

This should be easy. It's everything I've been working toward, everything that makes sense on paper. Certainty. Advancement. A way out. But it's not enough. Not without her.

A few boxes are stacked in the corner, a physical reminder of my usual plan. To pack up, to move on. The cabinets hang open, half-empty like the rest of this apartment. Like the rest of me.

I sink down into a chair, running my hands over my face, trying to make sense of a future that feels as empty as the room.

Did I really think this was all I needed? A contract, a new city, a fresh start? Maybe I did. Until Lily. Until the stupid gummy worms and late-night coffees and the way she makes me feel like this isn't just passing time.

"You're an idiot, Carter," I say to myself, but it doesn't make me feel any smarter. It doesn't make any of this clearer.

I thought I was stronger than this, tougher, the guy who

never second-guesses a decision. But that's not who I am right now. That's not who she made me.

What the hell am I doing?

I ask again, to the apartment, to the contract, to the city.

My words hang in the air, waiting for an answer I can't give myself. I cross the room, three quick strides.

I click the button and it's done. No fanfare, no fuss. Just an immediate email notification that confirms the document has been received.

The apartment is quiet, except for my own breathing, and I let it fill the space where the certainty used to be.

TWENTY-ONE

♥

LILY

There's something Zen-like about slicing open a person's chest at five-thirty in the morning. Before the nurses start with their passive-aggressive muttering, before Dr. Hale stomps through barking his orders. It's just me, the scalpel, and an unconscious patient named Roger. He doesn't care that my eyes are rimmed with exhaustion or that my scrubs are one size too big because I was in such a hurry to get started, I grabbed the wrong set. I'm fine with it, too. It's not like I'm trying to impress anyone.

The OR is too bright for this time of day, and I like it. Every detail is clear, and the edges are all sharp. No room for mistakes. My hands move quickly, efficiently, but I'm aware of a few cracks in my performance. Most likely due to the fact I've been working fourteen hours straight and can feel the strain in my eyes. Or that I scheduled back-to-back surgeries to distract myself from the ridiculous conversation I had with Dr. Patel last week. Most of all, it's that every time I look down, I see those damn wrong-sized scrubs and can hear Noah's voice in my head: *Good thing you didn't decide to be a fashion designer.*

"You're on fire today, Dr. Harper," says Shiv, the surgical tech.

He thinks he's complimenting me, but I know his real concern. The "today" is a dead giveaway. It implies that yesterday, last week, every day since Noah's little bombshell, I've been less than blazing.

"Keep up," I reply. He does, but barely.

We finish the procedure in record time. Roger's chest is closed, and his heart is beating perfectly under my immaculate sutures. By the time they wheel him out, I'm already elbows-deep in prep for the next patient. The team lingers like they're about to stage an intervention.

"You're going again already?" One of the nurses has the nerve to ask.

I nod. "Third shift's the charm," I say with a smile that I hope looks effortless.

Their concerned glances pass between them like an airborne infection. Shiv shrugs, and they leave me to my manic devotion to surgery. The door swings shut, and I breathe in the sterile air, exhale my own fraying edges.

I grab the next chart, flipping through it with practiced indifference. The information is just familiar enough to irritate me; I've gone over it three times already, making sure I know every nuance. Nothing is a surprise, nothing is unexpected, and yet my heart does a stupid leap when I see Noah's handwriting in the margins.

Of course. It's one of our joint cases.

My eyes trace the loops and angles of his notes, and I get stuck rereading the same line over and over: *We could split this —if you ever learn to share.* I'm rethinking that statement now, since sharing apparently involves elevators and heated accusations. I should toss the file aside, instead, I just stand there, stuck in a suspended moment of pathetic indecision.

Someone clears their throat, and I look up. A nurse with sympathetic eyes.

Fantastic.

"Dr. Harper?" she says. "Everything alright?"

"Fine." I snap the file closed, set my jaw. "Why wouldn't it be?"

The nurse gives me a small, knowing smile and lets herself out. I refuse to read any further into it.

I turn back to my fortress of instruments and tasks, double-checking everything like it matters more than it does. I'm preparing for a routine gallbladder removal, but you'd think I was doing a heart transplant on the President. It's safer to pretend this is what I care about most. It's easier to bury myself in the familiar patterns of work and exhaustion, in a cocoon of productivity.

But all it takes is one tiny crack—a joint case, a stray thought of Noah, a trace of fatigue—and the whole thing comes dangerously close to unraveling.

Dr. Patel is more organized than a medical ethics seminar. I count five awards, three framed diplomas, and an entire library of medical journals—all in alphabetical order. He says it's meticulous. I say it's compulsive. I'm about to tell him this when he hands me the trauma project file, my eyes skimming over the data with a speed I hope is impressively nonchalant.

"You've been flexible, Lily," he says, studying me like I'm his next case study.

"I've been a lot of things," I reply, pretending the comment doesn't have barbs.

"Do you know what this kind of work usually takes?" He

leans back, the chair creaking with authority. "Two doctors. Four months. Less precision."

He's laying it on thick, and I'm not about to play his game. "I can always be less precise."

"That," Patel says with a smile, "I doubt." He shifts, hands clasped, as if ready for my confession. "The handover should be seamless, thanks to you."

I'm being studied, measured, examined. I'm used to being watched—patients, other residents, Dr. Hale's eagle eye—but this feels different.

"I've reviewed everything multiple times," I say. "It'll be seamless."

I sound like a goddamn parrot. I'm almost annoyed with myself.

Patel pushes the file closer to me. "This level of investment," he says, pausing like he's diagnosing a rare disease, "not many surgeons can sustain it."

"I can," I say, but it's less convincing when my mind is already dragging me back to the joint cases. My eyes catch a scribbled note in the file—instinct-driven trauma assessment. I know exactly who wrote it.

Patel doesn't miss a thing. "You've been doing an exceptional job with Maria. And with Noah."

I don't know if I want to punch him or myself. "Working with residents is part of my job."

"It's more than that," he presses. "It's collaboration. You've shown real flexibility."

There's that word again. I focus on a spot on the wall. Flexibility isn't a trait; it's a condition to avoid.

"I'm adaptable when I need to be."

"Or," he says, voice gentle but persistent, "when you let yourself."

"Did Noah tell you that?" I'm aiming for humor, but it sounds forced, even to me.

"Lily," he says, "Noah said you're as flexible as a granite slab."

I should laugh. Instead, I feel it land with more weight than I want.

Patel nods as if he sees through every single pretense. "Sometimes, being right isn't as important as being human."

I'm thrown by how much I care about his opinion. About Noah's. This isn't what I signed up for, this messy quagmire of feelings and self-doubt.

"People change," Patel says, "even those who say they won't."

His words make their way past my defenses. I try to maintain my professional facade, but the cracks are wide enough for Patel to see through.

"What if you realize that too late?"

My question hangs in the air, the confession I didn't intend to make.

He regards me with a softness I've never seen from him. I expect him to respond with one of his aphorisms, but he's quiet, letting my own words reverberate.

The silence feels different. Less of an emptiness and more of an echo chamber where I have to listen to my own doubts, my own fears. I stand to leave, taking the file with more force than necessary.

"Thank you for coming in," Patel says as I turn to the door. "And Lily?"

"Yes?"

"I'd consider making it not too late."

I nod, unsure if I've really managed to keep my composure intact or if my retreat looks as rushed as it feels. I walk out with Dr. Patel's words shadowing me, a reminder that I've spent too long pretending not to hear.

The hospital café is louder than a stampede of medical students at a free lunch, but I can still hear my thoughts over the chatter. Annoying. I can also see Maria headed my way with two coffee cups. More annoying. She slides one over to me and sits down, all wide-eyed sincerity and bleeding-heart compassion. I like her anyway. Maybe that's my problem.

"Looks like I caught you between surgeries," Maria says, nodding to the paperwork I've spread out like a defensive barrier.

"It's called multitasking. I hear some residents are good at it."

"Some mentors, too." She grins. "Which is why I'm here to say thank you. Again."

My sarcasm is ready to fire, but I can't bring myself to do it. Not when Maria looks so damned earnest. "Don't get used to it," I say instead.

"I mean it, Dr. Harper. You went to bat for me when no one else would. It meant a lot."

"I didn't do much," I say, deflecting like my life depends on it.

"You believed in me," she insists. "Not just at the hearing. The whole time."

This is edging dangerously close to heartwarming. I sip my coffee, trying to look casual and totally unmoved.

"Ethan told me I should just thank you," Maria says, laughter in her voice. "But I knew you'd try to brush it off. Like you do with everything."

"I don't brush things off," I argue. "I delegate them. Like this coffee. Delegated to you."

She leans forward, voice softening. "I almost lost him, you know. I called it all off."

"Ethan?" I ask, feigning ignorance.

"Our relationship, our jobs. Everything. I pushed him away because I was scared of ruining my career." Maria's honesty is as raw as a skinned knee. "And I nearly ruined everything instead."

The openness in her voice makes me uncomfortable, but I'm hooked. It's a car crash I can't look away from.

"But you didn't," I point out, more curious than I let on.

"Because he's the most stubborn man on the planet," Maria says, rolling her eyes. "Sound like anyone you know?"

A flash of Noah crosses my mind. His hurt expression, his words echoing like a diagnosis: *You could've asked me to stay.*

"Probably more people than you think," I admit. It's not really an answer, but Maria seems satisfied.

"I was so sure I'd lose everything if I let myself love him," she says, each word landing like a punch. "Turns out, I couldn't do it without him."

The parallel is glaring. I see myself in her story, in her fears and hesitations, and I'm struck by how familiar it all is. How different Maria and I are, and yet how similar.

"You're brave," I tell her, surprising myself with the admission.

"I learned from the best," she replies, her gratitude genuine and bright.

She stands to leave, giving my shoulder a quick, warm squeeze. I watch her go, and for once, I don't feel the need to pretend I don't care.

I stare at the papers in front of me, but they're just meaningless lines. The conversation with Maria rings loud and clear, a reminder that I'm not as different from her as I want to believe. And that maybe, I need to be as brave as she is.

The on-call room smells like antiseptic and lost hope. I sit on the edge of the bed, and the vinyl sticks to my scrubs. The walls are yellowing in a way that says, "Abandon all optimism, ye who enter here." I can't remember a time when I cared about decor. Or the ache in my chest. Both seem pressing now.

The hospital hums on the other side of the door, busy and relentless. It's comforting, usually. But right now, I'm trapped in the dim light, my thoughts playing in an endless loop. One scene, one conversation.

The elevator was brighter than this room, but the tension made it claustrophobic. It was a shared space where we finally confronted the unspoken mess between us. Now it feels like the words are carved into the walls of my brain.

You could've asked me to stay.

I never thought I'd care enough to want someone to stay. Or to be gutted when they didn't.

I bury my face in my hands, palms pressing against my eyes, but I can't shut it out. The memory is too vivid, too raw. I see Noah's hurt expression, the flicker of hope dying in his eyes, the mechanical ding as the elevator doors opened, and I let him walk out of my life.

He was waiting for me to fight for him. To show him he mattered as much as my goddamn career.

The realization is brutal. I was too afraid of needing someone to let him stay. I thought it was safer to push him away than to risk being vulnerable. I was wrong. So completely, horribly wrong.

I tell myself I'm fine alone. That I've always been fine alone. But the echo of my own heart sounds hollow, and I'm left with the certainty that this time, fine isn't enough.

Noah was willing to wait for me to figure it out. To choose him, to let myself feel more than ambition and control. I wanted him to stay, but I never said it. I never gave him a reason to believe I wanted more than my carefully guarded solitude.

The truth is painful and precise, sharper than any scalpel I wield in the OR. I didn't push him away because I didn't care.

I pushed him away because I cared too much and was too terrified to admit it.

I stare at the ceiling, the yellowing tiles blurring into each other. For once, I can't think my way out of this. I can only sit with it, letting the reality of my own fears settle over me like the dim, quiet gloom of the on-call room.

My apartment is eerily silent except for the refrigerator's low hum and the distant whisper of rain against the windows. I'm sitting at the kitchen table, staring at the laptop like it's a particularly uninspired episode of reality TV. I'm supposed to be reviewing the trauma protocol files, but my mind is as blank as the ceiling. I can almost hear Noah's voice, a mix of sarcasm and challenge: *Figure out what you want, Lily.*

The glow of the screen makes the rest of the room feel dim, shadowed. It's a stark contrast to the OR, to the constant noise and bright lights of the hospital. This should feel like a relief, but it doesn't. It feels like a vacuum, an absence of everything I've surrounded myself with to avoid this exact moment.

The files blur into meaningless data, words I can't concentrate on. I've always known what I wanted—career, success, surgical mastery. They were certainties, anchors. Now, I'm unmoored, drifting in a sea of doubts and desires I've never let myself have.

You could've asked me to stay.

Noah's words echo in the silence, reverberating in my chest like a too-loud page on the intercom. I stare at the laptop, but I'm not seeing the screen. I'm seeing him, his hurt, the way he looked at me like I was the one who made him believe in something more. The way I couldn't give him the same.

What do I want? It's the question I've been dodging, the

answer I've been too scared to admit. Not just to him, but to myself.

I told myself I'd never need anyone. I told myself I'd be fine alone. *But what if I was wrong?* What if, for once, wanting something doesn't mean sacrificing everything else?

I stare at the files until the glow of the screen feels harsh against the quiet. Until I can't pretend anymore. I close the laptop, the snap of it breaking the silence like an admission. It's the first time I haven't buried myself in work to escape. The first time I've let myself stop running from what's real.

My phone sits next to the laptop, almost taunting in its simplicity. A single tap, and I'd be reaching out. A single word, and I'd be vulnerable. My thumb hovers over Noah's contact, suspended in an indecision that's quickly becoming unbearable.

Instead of putting the phone away, hiding it like I've hidden everything I don't want to feel, I leave it on the table. Within reach. Where it can remind me of what I have to do.

"You have to want something before you can ask for it."

My voice sounds foreign in the empty room, an echo that hangs in the air like a challenge, like a promise. Like the first step toward finally letting myself feel.

TWENTY-TWO

NOAH

My fingers linger on next week's shift rota. The absence of my name really hits home. It's the department's poor excuse for a leaving party and I hate it. I let Dr. Patel tug the rota free from my grip. The congratulations and handshakes keep coming, accompanied by half-baked smiles and awkward backslaps. I watch the door instead of their faces. She's still not here, which means something I don't want it to mean.

"Well done, Dr. Carter," Dr. Patel says, flipping through the latest draft of the new Trauma Protocols. "An impressive way to conclude your work here."

There's a pop quiz lurking beneath the compliment. I'm not fooling anyone with my shitty attempt at being present.

"It's been rewarding, Dr. Patel. Emotional, but rewarding," I say, trying sincerity on for size. It doesn't fit. "Thanks for the opportunity."

He smiles, a careful arrangement of professional respect, and I wonder if it's possible to call off a goodbye at the last minute.

"You'll do well in San Francisco." It sounds suspiciously like a statement, but I catch the question underneath.

I'm about to answer when another resident charges in, full of energy and misdirected enthusiasm.

'Way to go, man!" He claps me on the shoulder, a jarring punctuation mark. "We're going to miss you around here."

More lies. More smiles. I float above them, an observer in my own life. I hear myself mutter the expected gratitude, an unconvincing soundtrack to my real thoughts.

My eyes snap to the door with every flicker of movement in the hallway. Not Lily. Not Lily. Still not Lily.

I imagine her on another floor, chasing perfection and dodging the farewells. Maybe she's scrubbed in on a case and can't be bothered. Maybe she thinks a clean break is kinder. Or maybe she just doesn't care. Each option tastes worse than the last.

I tune back into Dr. Patel, who's mid-presentation of my academic offspring. I watch him as he attempts to distill my work into sound bites, little pieces of me that he'll distribute like sugar packets.

"The ER won't be the same without you," he continues, the subtext clear: *You've achieved everything you set out to, why do you look like someone drowned your puppy?*

"Thanks," I manage, choking on the syllable. I catch the door in my peripheral vision. Still nothing. Still no one. Still the worst.

More bodies come and go, their voices blending into the ambient hum of fluorescent lights and beeping machines. There's a surreal quality to it, like I'm already a memory, like I'm being written out of the script in real-time.

One of the other docs joins the fray, and her tone is something between supportive and pitying. "You're really going to make a name for yourself, Noah."

I nod, and it feels like my head might fall off. "I'll keep you posted," I say, the biggest lie yet.

More time passes. Maybe a minute. Maybe an hour. I should pay attention to what Patel's saying about my contribution to the department, but all I can focus on is the void where Lily isn't.

"The project you've been working on with Dr. Harper really set a new standard," Patel is saying, trying to wring some engagement out of me. "The protocols you've established—"

"Happy to help," I cut him off, my gaze still glued to the entrance. It's rude, I know. But I can't shake the feeling that if I blink, I'll miss her.

"She's not coming, man," another resident jokes, following my gaze. He thinks he's being clever. "Maybe next lifetime."

I force a laugh that's too close to a wince. "Tell her to pencil me in."

He chuckles, unaware he's just pierced something vital. "Will do."

As if my heart rate is in a telemetry readout, Patel goes in for another attempt at genuine. "I'm sure your talents will be appreciated there. But remember, you always have a place at Emerald Bay."

I hear his unspoken prediction: *You'll be back.*

I imagine different scenarios. Her bursting through the door, breathless, admitting she can't believe I'm actually going. Her strolling in like it's nothing, cool as ever, with some sarcastic comment that guts me more than anything sincere. Or maybe her glancing in and out, leaving me with the echo of my own expectations.

"Dr. Carter?"

Dr. Patel's voice shakes me back to the present. It's embarrassing how far I've drifted.

"Yeah, sorry," I say, trying to hide the raw edge of my disappointment. "I'm here."

'The door's open for you anytime."

He doesn't know he's killing me with irony.

I nod and swallow hard. "Thanks. Appreciate it."

There's a pause where it's clear he's trying to decide if I'm worth reeling back in, or if he should just let me float out the door. He chooses the latter. "Good luck, Noah."

And with that, I'm alone in the crowd. More bodies, more voices. More faces telling me that this is all for the best.

I make my exit slowly, holding on to the faint, stupid hope that the minute I'm gone, Lily will show up looking for me, you know, just like in the movies. I let myself have that fantasy because it's less pathetic than the alternative: that she knew exactly what today meant, and she didn't care enough to be a part of it.

The locker room is all steel benches and bad lighting, a reflection of how I feel about my life. It's the middle ground between what just happened and what's going to happen, and I'm stuck in it. My tie is half undone, the button at my collar is open, and my determination is unraveling at about the same pace. I sit there with my head against the cold metal of my locker, waiting for a sign from the universe or maybe just from my phone.

Marcus walks in like a casual grenade.

He surveys the wreckage of my optimism, tosses his stethoscope into his locker with a nonchalant flick of the wrist, and then sits down next to me.

"Thought I'd find you here," he says, settling in like he's about to enjoy a good show.

"Where else?" I reply, staring at my shoes. They look like they're more certain of their path than I am.

Marcus leans back, one leg stretched out, the picture of

laid-back observation. "Heard the trauma protocol debrief was a real page-turner."

"Riveting," I mutter. "Almost asked for a sequel."

He nods, considering me with that calm, X-ray vision of his. "How's the big San Francisco hotshot doing?"

"Which one?" I ask. "The guy they think is excited about going, or the guy who can't find the exit?"

Marcus smiles, unbothered by my evasive maneuvers. "Probably both."

The room is silent for a beat. It's filled with the sounds of my own uncertainties echoing off the lockers. I rub a hand over my face, as if that'll wipe away the last two weeks.

"I told Patel I'd work my notice period," I say finally. The words drop like weights, and I expect the crash to be louder.

Marcus doesn't flinch. He studies my expression, or maybe the lack of it, and then nods. "When are you off?"

"Saturday. Three more shifts." I take a deep breath, more out of habit than necessity. "I thought it was the dream. Now it just feels like... momentum."

Marcus absorbs my confession with the ease of someone used to fielding curveballs. He's quiet, letting me fill in the blanks or not. He knows that sometimes just getting the words out is a miracle in itself.

"Momentum," he echoes, like he's savoring the taste of it. "Yeah, I get that."

"It's not what I expected." I hear the crack in my voice and wonder how I let it get this far.

"Life's a bitch like that," he says, with the authority of someone who knows.

I shake my head, trying to dislodge the idea that everything I'm doing is backwards. "What if I don't even want this?"

Marcus doesn't rush in with an answer. He sits with the silence, and that's when I know we're really having a conversation.

"Then don't take it," he says eventually, as if it's that simple.

"It's already in motion, the paperwork is in," I tell him. "Like a freight train, you know? It built up speed kind of without anyone really noticing, and now it just keeps going."

His eyes are on me, steady and knowing. "Doesn't mean you have to stay on it."

There's more I want to say, more I don't know how to say. Marcus waits me out, the patience of a thousand saints in one sarcastic charge nurse.

"I'm leaving because—" The words catch, like they're not supposed to be spoken.

"It's easier than staying?" Marcus finishes for me.

"Something like that."

He shrugs. "Then own it. Or change it."

"It's not that easy," I insist, even though part of me wants to believe it is. "It's not like I can just—"

"Stay?" he cuts in. "Pretty sure you could if you wanted to."

His observation lands too close to the truth. "And what the hell is staying without Lily?" I challenge, hating the sound of her name and the hold it has.

"Maybe it's harder. But maybe it's better."

We sit there for a while, neither of us willing to be the first to break the silence.

"It wasn't supposed to be like this," I say, knowing it sounds like a cliché, but needing to say it anyway.

"Things rarely are."

I try to smile, but it doesn't reach my eyes. "So what do I do now?"

Marcus gets up, casually brushing off the bench as if it's important not to leave any trace. "Only you know that, man."

I watch him walk out, leaving me alone with my half-open locker and fully open uncertainty. It strikes me that he never said anything about goodbyes. I wonder if he knows something I don't, or if he's just betting on me like he always does.

I sit there a little longer, waiting for the answers to come. I want them to arrive in clear, straightforward packages, like the test results we always wish for in the ER. Instead, all I get is the soft click of the door as it swings shut behind Marcus.

The city looks small from up here, like a toy version of itself. It's not so different from the way my future looks: something I can hold in my hands, but not necessarily something I want. I take a sip of coffee, hoping the bitterness will ground me, but all it does is remind me how far I've drifted.

The hospital's windows glow below, a reminder of everyone I'm leaving behind, whether I mean to or not. A helicopter rises into the sky, its rotors slicing through the night. I watch it disappear into the distance and whisper the words I'm not supposed to say: "Smart's not the same as right."

The air is cold, numbing my fingers and face, but I don't move. I'm rooted to the spot, a lone figure on this deserted rooftop, feeling like I'm about to jump into something bigger than I can handle.

I take another sip of coffee, its warmth not quite reaching the parts of me that need it most. It tastes like all my mornings here, all the days I've spent chasing traumas and dodging commitments. The memories of Lily blur into the memories of this place, each one harder to pack away than the last.

It wasn't supposed to be like this. I came here thinking I could get out clean, that leaving was a choice I'd already made. But it's messier than I ever imagined, tangled up in more feelings than I know what to do with.

Lily's name sits on the tip of my tongue, ready to trip me

up at any moment. I thought saying it would make things clearer, but all it does is turn everything inside out.

We were never supposed to happen. She was too driven, too focused, too much like the person I always thought I'd be, but never became. And somehow, we worked. Somehow, she made me want to be the person I always thought I'd never be.

Each window below is a different part of my life, glowing steadily while I flicker on and off. I imagine Lily somewhere down there, working a hundred-hour shift and acting like it doesn't hurt. She's the one who convinced me I had more to offer than I thought. She's the one I'm leaving because she's the one who matters most.

If I stay, what does that mean? If I go, who am I without her?

The hospital hums beneath me, full of people who are better at surviving than I am. Each light represents someone fighting, healing, saying goodbye. I thought goodbye was my strong suit, but now it feels like it might be the thing that finally does me in.

I watch the city stretch out in all directions, vast and uncaring. I tell myself I can get lost in it, lose these feelings, find new ones. But I don't want new ones. I want the old ones, the impossible ones, the ones that started when I didn't even know they had.

There's a dull roar as a medevac helicopter takes off, shattering the quiet with its urgency. I track it as it rises from the landing pad, wishing I could follow it to wherever it's going. Wishing I could just keep going, never have to land.

The helicopter disappears into the darkness, a part of someone's emergency that's more important than mine. I take a deep breath, letting the night air fill my lungs, wishing it would fill the empty places inside me too.

I tell myself that tomorrow I'll finally pack up the last of it. That I'll finish my shift on Friday and drive until the distance makes it easier. But I know, deep down, that distance isn't what I need.

My life is a disaster zone, organized into neatly labeled boxes. In a few days, the whole mess will be loaded onto a truck, destined for a future that doesn't look anything like what I imagined. I keep my hands busy, the way I always do when my head's a lost cause. Wrapping plates, packing books, checking my phone for messages that aren't there. It's like triage, except the patient is me.

I wander through the apartment, picking up random objects and deciding their fate. There's a pile of things I plan to take, a bigger pile of things I'm ready to ditch, and an enormous pile of doubts I can't shake. I drop a stack of CDs into a box marked KEEP, wondering when I last listened to any of them. I tape it shut anyway, because I'm already second-guessing enough things in my life without adding music to the list.

Books are easier. I toss them into crates, not bothering to sort by genre and author like I usually would. Even I'm not crazy enough to care if Atul Gawande ends up next to Dr. Seuss at this point. The apartment looks like a war zone, with cardboard shrapnel and packing tape strewn everywhere.

I wrap glasses in newspaper, half-assing it because I don't really care if they break on the way to my shiny new existence. As I reach for another, I see the edge of a grocery store receipt poking out from under some papers. I know exactly what it is before I even pick it up.

Lily's handwriting is unmistakable, the letters sharp and pointed like she was trying to stab her opinion into the page: "You have the palate of a twelve-year-old. This is not a compliment."

I don't remember what I bought that night, but I remember the look on her face when she said it. The mixture of disbelief and affection. The way she made me feel like being ridiculous was a skill. A reluctant smile tugs at my lips, and I hate how much power she still has over me.

I should throw the note away. That would be the smart, clean, detached thing to do. Instead, I smooth it out and set it carefully on the counter, right next to the carton of tape I plan to ignore.

I pick up another stack of dishes, but I can't shake the feeling that they're heavier than they should be. Maybe that's because I'm not just packing for San Francisco—I'm packing to forget. I drop the plates into a box with less enthusiasm than a medical conference keynote.

Everything I touch seems to have a memory attached to it. An old pair of sneakers she said looked like I'd stolen them from a middle school lost-and-found. A photo of us at the hospital fundraiser, where we were pretending to be civil, but our eyes said otherwise. I throw it into the trash pile, then fish it out and add it to KEEP.

I hear my mom's voice in my head, reminding me how to do this the way she does everything: with love and way too much concern. *One thing at a time, Noah. You'll never get it all done at once.*

One thing at a time, and none of it feels real. I used to be good at making things not feel real, but Lily ruined me for that.

My phone sits on the counter, mocking me with its silence. I check it again, hoping for a message from her, even if it's just a sarcastic jab about how much stuff I have for a guy who claims he can fit his life into a carry-on.

The screen stays empty, a digital middle finger to my denial. I set it face down, because not seeing it doesn't hurt as much as seeing nothing.

I move on to the closet, shoving clothes into suitcases with the finesse of an ER resident on their first overnight shift. Everything smells like familiarity, like comfort, like home, and none of it belongs in a city that has a year-round farmers market.

"Don't be such a cliché," Lily would say if she could see me now. "Brooding doesn't suit you." But she can't see me, and brooding is all I've got.

Eventually, the apartment is just as cluttered, but my mind is a little less so. I've been avoiding the hard part, and I know it. Marcus would call me out on it, if he were here.

"You're not ready to leave, man," he'd say.

And for once, I wouldn't have a comeback.

I sit down on the couch, surrounded by the mess I've created, and let myself imagine what it would be like if I stayed. If I told San Francisco to shove its Dungeness crab and its fog, and started unpacking instead. The thought is warm and stupid, the way all my best ones seem to be lately.

I let it linger longer than I should. Then I get up, grab some packing tape, and pretend I'm still doing this because I want to. But Lily's note stays on the counter, its presence the only thing about this move that makes any sense.

The inside of my car is silent, but I swear I can hear my brain screaming. If Marcus saw me now, he'd say it looks like I've already left. That I'm just waiting for the rest of me to catch up. My phone glows in my hand, a constant reminder of my cowardice. Lily's name is right there, taunting me.

I type: *Leaving Saturday. Didn't want to go without saying—*

I stop typing, staring at the half-sentence. The whole thing reeks of desperation, and even I'm not ready to face that.

I stare out the windshield, watching dusk swallow the city.

It's beautiful in a lonely way, the kind of view you can only appreciate when you've convinced yourself you're the only one who sees it. Seattle looks different from here, like it already knows I'm leaving and doesn't care enough to say goodbye.

My thumb taps against the steering wheel, a Morse code of hesitation. I tell myself I'm sitting here to figure things out, but it's more about how I can't figure out anything. It's like I've boxed up my entire life, and now there's no room left for words.

I glance at the phone again, the brightness too much for this half-light. There she is: Lily. Right where I always knew she'd be. Nowhere near.

It takes a stupid amount of effort to click on her name, like it's connected to all the things I've tried to unplug. I scroll through old messages, the familiar exchanges of sarcasm and near-affection. Each one is a jab to the heart I thought I'd numbed.

Leaving Saturday. Didn't want to go without saying—

The sentence mocks me with its insufficiency.

The car feels smaller, like it's folding in on itself. Like I'm stuck in a place I'm trying to escape, both on the map and in my mind. I want to throw open the door and run back inside, find Lily, make her see. But my feet are glued to the floor mat, and the only thing I'm running from is what I really want.

I try a new message. Same beginning, same emptiness. Same outcome.

Leaving Saturday. Didn't want to go without saying—

A few more characters and I could finish it. But then it would be real, and she might not reply, and that would probably break me in two.

The unfinished thought sits there, like it's daring me to press send or delete or even just breathe.

I hit backspace. It's almost harder than not hitting send. Each letter disappears in a cowardly puff of smoke.

The inside of the car grows darker, the phone screen my only light. Maybe I'll sit here until the battery dies. Maybe I'll sit here until I die. Anything feels easier than what I'm supposed to do.

My phone lands on the passenger seat with more force than it deserves. I tighten my grip on the steering wheel, like that'll keep me from unraveling completely. It doesn't.

"Goddamn it, Noah," I say to the empty car.

I tighten my grip on the wheel again, wondering if I'm holding on or holding back.

The city outside the window glitters with indifference, each light a reminder of something I'll miss. I used to think I wouldn't miss anything, and now I think I'm going to miss it all. But most of all, I'm going to miss her, and she's the one thing I have no right to hold on to.

I stare at the blank screen, waiting for it to fill itself with better ideas than the ones I've got. Instead, it fades to black, mirroring the inside of my head.

If she wanted to stop me, she would've.

If she wanted to stop me—

I turn the key in the ignition, and the car sputters to life, breaking the silence with a mechanical cough. It's a cold sound, a lonely sound, like the soundtrack of all my worst fears. I pull away from the curb, and drive.

TWENTY-THREE

LILY

I wake up at four thirty-seven a.m. because I have things to do, and I'm someone who gets things done. Or maybe because I haven't really slept, and no amount of getting things done can fix the fact that he's as good as gone.

It's been one week since Noah handed in his resignation. One week of me staring at surgical reports and pretending I care more about hemoglobin than him. One week of me not saying anything to him and now today will be his last shift at Emerald Bay.

I shove my pillow over my head, but his words are still there, clear as day and impossible to ignore: *"You're the one who let me leave."* It turns out you can be the best surgical resident in the hospital and still have no clue how to stitch yourself back together.

I peel myself out of bed. It's too early for anything but regret. Maybe coffee, if I'm being generous. But when you're emotionally compromised and ninety percent caffeine, it's a thin line between generous and pathetic. The hardwood is cold against my feet, the whole apartment silent except for the sound of my own unravelling.

There's a stack of medical journals on the kitchen table, the top one turned to an article I haven't actually read. "Advancements in Cardiothoracic Surgery." It was supposed to be my mantra, my reason for existing. Now it's just an accusation. I flip it closed and turn on the coffeemaker, watching as the pot fills with watery promises of alertness.

I stare at the drip, drip, drip of the coffee. For once, it feels too slow. My thoughts jump between the exact moment I knew I'd lose him (when he asked me whether he should go) and the moment I lost him (in the elevator, where I could have said something, anything). The memories hurt, but I can't stop poking at them. I run my hands through my hair, yank the tie out of my ponytail, and try to breathe.

My phone buzzes, cutting through the fog of indecision. Probably a surgery alert. Someone else needing something only I can do. I glance at the screen, and my own reflection looks back, sleep-deprived and angry. *"You're the one who let me leave,"* it whispers, again and again until I want to smash the damn thing.

He gave me every opportunity to stop him. *"Tell me not to go,"* he'd said, his eyes too steady, too patient. I'd frozen. Of course I froze. I'm Dr. Lily Harper, Ice Queen of Emerald Bay, so professional I might as well have a stick up my perfectly pressed scrubs.

I grab the phone, fingers tight enough to crack the case. It doesn't feel like it belongs in my hand. Too awkward. Too unsure. But I know I'm going to make the call, even if I don't know what I'm going to say.

First, coffee. I fill a mug and burn my tongue on the first sip, then immediately take another. Self-punishment is one of my specialties.

Maria picks up on the second ring. "Lily?" She sounds

groggy, probably wrapped in some sappy, romantic sleep that I'm about to ruin.

"I need a favor," I say, words spilling out before I can reel them back. "And a little help making a scene."

There's a pause. She's wondering if she's still dreaming or if I've truly, finally, lost my mind. "Are you okay?"

"I'm great," I lie, because it's what I do. "Can we meet later? I'll explain then."

"Of course," she says, voice softening. "See you at eight. I'll bring coffee."

I hang up and stand there, gripping my empty mug like it's the only thing keeping me from collapsing. A favor. A scene. It's drastic, and I know it. But so is waking up to an empty bed and realizing I can't fix this alone.

The minutes tick by in silence, each one a countdown to something I haven't yet defined. I think about what Maria will say, about the ridiculous lengths she'll go to just to see me admit I need help. I imagine her showing up with a thermos the size of my ego and an insufferably knowing smile.

But none of that matters. Not really. What matters is that I've made a decision. A wild, terrifying, utterly necessary decision. I place my mug on the counter, stand taller than I have in days, and let the last words Noah said to me ricochet through my mind until resolve takes the place of fear: "You're the one who let me leave."

I sit across from Maria in the Emerald Bay cafeteria, clutching a stale muffin like it's a surgical instrument.

"I need to make a scene," I repeat, because I'm still not sure I believe it myself.

But Maria believes it. I can tell by the way her eyes light

up, like I've handed her a golden ticket to my emotional breakdown.

"I knew you'd come to your senses," she says, beaming at me like the unrepentant romantic she is.

I try not to scowl. "I haven't come to anything. I just need to talk to him before he—" I stop myself. Admitting it will make it real.

"Before he leaves," she finishes for me, no hesitation. It's like watching someone wield a scalpel with absolute precision.

It takes five seconds for her to recruit Ethan, six for him to join us, and seven for my insides to twist into the world's tightest knot. This must be what having friends feels like.

"We're throwing a farewell for Noah," Maria announces, and Ethan's eyes widen.

"Does he know?" Ethan asks, a hint of panic in his voice. He's heard about my need for control, how I've steamrolled over many an unsuspecting colleague.

"He will," Maria says, grinning. "That's the point."

Ethen shakes his head. "If this goes wrong—"

"It won't," Maria interrupts, so certain that I almost believe her.

Ethan nods, getting into the spirit. "Marcus can get him there. We'll make it seem like a last-minute wrap-up."

They're both looking at me now, Maria's eyes filled with expectation, Ethan's with gentle support. I take a deep breath.

"Okay," I concede. "Let's make a scene."

We move to the admin wing, a quiet corner where Maria and Ethan whisper logistics while I pretend to supervise.

"We'll need to reserve a room," Maria says, flipping through a clipboard with alarming efficiency.

"And food," Ethan adds. "You know how Noah is about snacks."

"I'll order something," I offer, trying to regain a semblance of control.

Maria raises an eyebrow. "Maybe let us handle it?" She's gentle but firm, a reminder that I've asked for their help, and I need to let them give it.

I sit at a desk with a blank sheet of paper and a pen that feels too heavy in my hand. Words are supposed to be my specialty. Concise. Clear. But nothing about this feels surgical.

"I used to think professionalism meant distance," I scribble, then immediately scratch it out. "No. Too clinical."

I try again. "I've learned connection isn't a liability." Another line through it, the ink smudging like the betrayal of my own intentions. I crumple the paper and toss it aside.

Maria watches from across the room, her sympathy palpable. "It's okay, you know," she says. "To not have it all planned."

"I'm not good at not planning," I mutter, more to myself than to her.

She laughs softly. "Then you're going to have to practice."

They plan around me, Maria and Ethan, exchanging hushed words that float in and out of my awareness. I'm not used to this, the feeling of people rallying around me for something other than a medical miracle.

"The room's booked," Ethan announces.

Maria hands me a piece of paper. "Here's the timeline."

I stare at it, then at them, then back to the scribbled schedule. They've thought of everything. I think of how differently I'd have done this on my own. Sterile. Cold. Nothing like this... collaborative chaos.

"Okay," I say, voice stronger. "This might actually work."

Maria nods, her smile the kind that insists on optimism. "It will."

I hear the door open behind me, but I don't turn. I know it's him. I feel it before I see it—the subtle shift in the air, the pause in the quiet shuffling of papers and polite murmurs. The room reacts to his arrival before I do. My heart kicks like it's been shocked awake.

I steal a glance over my shoulder. There he is. Noah, standing in the doorway, like he wasn't sure whether to walk in or walk away. For a second, he just stands there, eyes sweeping the room until they land on me. He hesitates. That alone almost unravels me.

I wonder if he's going to bolt. If I should say something first. But then he takes a step inside—cautious, unreadable—and I know this is it. My moment. My pulse is a steady drumbeat against my ribs, and I force myself to stay still. To speak before the panic wins.

The room settles into a heavy silence, the kind that crushes your ribs and makes breathing impossible. Or maybe that's just me. I know I have to speak before I lose my nerve, but my mouth is so dry it might as well be filled with sand. This is what he does to me, what he's always done to me—rendered me mute and incapable, like I'm anything other than the best and most brilliant version of myself. I can't let it stop me now.

I step forward, and the movement feels like a declaration all on its own. I meet his eyes across the room, a thousand unsaid words finally taking shape. "I used to think professionalism meant distance," I start, my voice barely above a whisper. But it's enough. It's enough to crack the silence wide open.

Noah's expression shifts. I have his attention.

My words tumble out, unsteady but determined. "That feelings were dangerous. That if you let them in, they'd drown you. And maybe that's true, but what I've learned working with you—Noah—is that connection isn't a liability." I pause, my gaze locked on his. It feels like standing on a cliff's edge, the air sharp and cold and exhilarating.

The room seems to fade, the other people turning into shadowy outlines of support. Of hope. But I can't look away from him. I won't.

'The thing that makes us better," I start, the tremor in my voice evening out. "Better doctors. Better people."

Noah's face is a study in contrasts. He's trying to stay guarded, to keep up the walls he thinks he needs. But I can see past them, past the practiced indifference to the part of him that still believes in us.

So I keep going. "I wanted to say this in front of people," I admit, forcing myself to breathe, to feel each word. "Because I didn't say it when it mattered most." The admission costs me, but it also frees me. I'm doing it. I'm saying what he needs to hear.

"I don't want you to go."

It hangs there, exposed and raw. Everyone in the room hears it, but it's meant for him alone.

I take a step forward, and something changes inside me, a shift I didn't know I was capable of. "But if you do," I say, my voice gaining strength, "I needed you to know that I'm not afraid anymore."

His eyes are wide, shock mingling with something that looks a lot like hope. It fuels me, gives me the courage to let him see everything I am, without the armor I've always worn.

I stand straighter, my hands at my sides, palms open. This is the most honest I've ever been. The most exposed. But also the most real.

Colleagues glance at each other, then back at us, the room charged with the weight of what's happening. Maria beams, practically glowing with triumph. Ethan shifts, an awkward but supportive presence at her side. Marcus looks genuinely impressed.

But none of it matters as much as what's between me and Noah.

I see him take a breath, his composure slipping just enough to show the impact of my words. He's silent, but I can feel the reply building in him.

The seconds stretch, and for once, I don't fill them with anything other than the truth of this moment. The truth of me.

A soft murmur spreads through the room. Someone whispers, "Wow." Another says, "Didn't see that coming." But the comments are distant, an echo behind the intensity of what I've just done.

The speech, if you can even call it that, is over. Or maybe it's just begun.

I meet his gaze, and for the first time since he walked away, I see something break open in him too.

The room buzzes back to life, but I stand firm, letting the vulnerability settle into a new kind of strength.

Silence fills the space again, but this time it's different. This time, it's full of possibility, not fear.

And when I take another breath, it's deeper than any I've taken before.

TWENTY-FOUR

NOAH

I'm cemented to the floor of the conference room, my heart in my throat, my pulse like thunder, my breath some place far away. Lily stands before me, her eyes dark and wild and terrified. My mouth won't work. My legs won't work. I might not be breathing. All I know is I have to get to her.

Around us, people pretend to resume conversation, but there's no missing the hushed whispers or the not-so-subtle stares. Colleagues I barely know are suddenly invested in the latest medical drama starring Dr. Noah Carter and Dr. Lily Harper. Someone from Peds glances over, eyes darting between us like she's expecting a declaration of marriage or a murder-suicide pact. Even Marcus is watching, his face an odd mix of surprise and smugness, like he knew this was coming all along. He's not the only one. But nobody expected it like this.

Especially not me.

Lily is still waiting, her confession hanging between us like a live wire. She doesn't flinch under the weight of everyone's attention, but I can see the rawness in her face, the way her usual armor has completely shattered. The badass surgeon exposed, more human and more breakable than I've ever seen her.

My heart is a jackhammer, trying to tear through my ribs, and I think, maybe I've forgotten how to do this—how to say the words back. How to be what she's asking me to be. How not to screw it all up.

Because holy shit, she actually said it. The thing I've been waiting months to hear and never thought I would.

My feet are moving before I give them permission. It feels like miles between us. Like I'll never reach her in time. And for a wild second, I wonder if this is what falling feels like. Falling, and having no idea if there's anything to catch me. I break through the invisible wall of spectators and keep walking, not because everyone is watching, but because I physically can't stop.

Lily stands completely still, like if she moves, the whole moment might break. She looks at me like I'm the last question on the hardest test, and she's terrified of getting it wrong. I stop in front of her and meet her eyes. They're impossibly dark.

"You could've just said you missed the snacks," I say, the words tumbling out awkwardly, like I've never used them before.

The room holds its breath, and for one awful second I think she might walk away.

But then she laughs. Soft, breathless, and so completely Lily, that I almost laugh with her. The tension snaps, something unwinds in my chest, and holy shit, that laugh feels like a victory.

I want to kiss her. I want to take her hand and drag her out of this conference room and run down the hallway like the idiots in love we may be, possibly, probably are. Instead, I let the moment hang, watching her face light up with something close to relief. I don't think I've ever seen her look so beautiful.

"I should've known," she says, a trace of her usual sarcasm creeping back in. "You only stay for the food."

The heat between us is like the middle of July, and I wonder if she can hear my heart thundering as loudly as I can. I try to say something back, but I'm suddenly aware of the hundred pairs of eyes still glued to us, the room that's gone from deafening silence to awkward coughs and shuffled feet.

Dr. Norton from Oncology clears his throat and turns away, dragging a confused intern with him. Marcus elbows the Peds doc, who quickly averts her gaze. It's like watching a car crash in reverse, the wreckage slowly righting itself and moving on like nothing happened.

I've never been so grateful to be surrounded by a bunch of emotionally stunted surgeons. They don't know if they should clap or sedate us. They pretend not to care, but I know by tomorrow, every department will be buzzing. Part of me wants to tell them to mind their own business. The rest of me wants to yell at the top of my lungs.

Lily hasn't moved, hasn't looked away, and the vulnerability in her eyes makes everything shift inside me. It changes what I thought this moment would be. It changes what I thought I would be. I never imagined I'd be standing here with all of Seattle watching, on the verge of losing everything I didn't know I wanted.

It's crazy, but my terrible joke is the bravest thing I could've said. It's not just humor, it's a shield—something to hide behind while I figure out how to be brave enough to say the rest. I look at Lily, and I'm not so scared anymore. Because she didn't walk away. She stayed.

And so did I.

"Are you coming?" I ask, aware of the ridiculousness of the question. As if she'd leave now, after she basically handed me her heart on a silver platter. But this is Lily Harper, and even after all this, she's the most unpredictable woman I've ever met.

She steps closer, her expression shifting from terrified to determined, in the space of a breath. "Do I have to give you a detailed surgical plan?"

I grin, relief pouring through me like a goddamn tidal wave. "A flowchart wouldn't hurt."

It feels like we're the only two people in the room, and I almost forget the rest of them are still standing there, mouths half-open, brains struggling to process what just happened. When I finally look around, I meet Marcus's eye across the room. He gives a little nod, and I can almost hear him say "about time."

The truth is, I didn't think this time would ever come. I didn't think she'd say it, or that I'd be able to say anything back. But here we are, and it's everything I've been too scared to admit I wanted.

Lily's waiting for me to move, to do anything other than stand here like an idiot, and I have no intention of screwing this up. Not now. I reach for her hand, feeling the rush of adrenaline as her fingers brush mine, and lead her through the stunned crowd.

I didn't even know what staying really meant until now. Until this. Until her.

We're almost at the door when I stop.

It's not the crowd. It's not the whispers or the heat of every pair of eyes burning into our backs. It's her hand in mine—solid, warm, real—and the surge of emotion flooding my chest like someone cracked it open and let the truth pour in. Months of friction. Banter. Bad timing. Missed chances. All of it comes crashing together in one singular, searing thought.

I turn to her.

And then—

I kiss her.

It's not tentative. It's not careful. It's not remotely professional. It's months of tension detonating between us like a goddamn supernova. Her mouth meets mine with a certainty that makes everything else fall away—the conference room, the onlookers, the rules. She grabs the front of my shirt and pulls me closer like we're already past the point of no return, like she's just as hungry for this as I am.

Someone gasps. Someone definitely drops a clipboard.

This isn't the kind of kiss that belongs in a hospital. It doesn't belong anywhere that has policies or HR departments or fluorescent lighting. It belongs in a movie. Or a thunderstorm. Or a locked call room after hours with the blinds drawn and a very good excuse.

But it's happening here. Now.

And neither of us gives a damn.

I break away just long enough to breathe, to look at her. Her cheeks are flushed, eyes blazing, lips parted like she wants to argue—but only if it ends with me kissing her again.

I grin. "You still think this is a bad idea?"

She exhales shakily, touching her forehead to mine. "Oh, it's an absolutely catastrophic idea."

Then she kisses me.

Harder this time.

Around us, the world keeps turning. But in this moment, it finally feels like we're exactly where we're meant to be.

Together.

TWENTY-FIVE

LILY

There's a moment right after you bare your soul when time stops and you think, this is it, this is the part where it all falls apart. I watch Noah for any sign, any movement, any flicker of hope. It doesn't come. Not for seconds that feel like hours.

Maria elbows Ethan so hard he almost topples over. Colleagues shift, murmur, speculate. The room feels too big, the silence too deep, the hope too dangerous.

And then Noah kisses me. And I kiss him back and it's everything I imagined and more.

The tears flow, unstoppable. But for once, I don't care who sees. Relief and disbelief crash over me, and I realize that hope isn't as dangerous as I thought.

The room exhales with us, a collective release of tension and anticipation.

"Oh my God, I knew it," Maria squeals, grabbing Ethan's arm with triumphant enthusiasm. He winces but doesn't pull away, probably afraid of losing a limb.

Marcus smirks, crossing his arms with the smug satisfaction of someone who had money on this exact outcome. "And they say surgeons have no heart," he quips.

Noah grins, finally, and it's like the sun breaking through a storm. "Was this your plan all along?" he asks, taking my hand in front of everyone, unashamed.

"Maria's plan," I admit, voice shaky but happy, so ridiculously happy. "I just... went along with it."

His fingers tighten around mine, and the gesture says more than any words. That he's not leaving. That I've done the impossible. That I'm not alone in this.

"Looks like you were wrong about one thing," he teases, leaning closer so only I can hear.

"Just one?" I shoot back, the old banter returning with ease with warmth, with promise.

His smile softens. "About having to do it all yourself."

I nod, blinking away tears that are more joy than anything else. "Guess I'm learning."

The room is still abuzz, colleagues exchanging looks and whispers, some genuinely surprised, others smugly claiming they saw it coming.

"It's like watching a soap opera," someone says, somewhere in the background.

"Better," comes another voice. "No bad acting."

But all I really hear is him, the way he laughs as he pulls me closer, the sound an anchor that grounds me, saves me, makes everything real.

Maria rushes over, dragging Ethan with her. She looks ecstatic, and also annoyingly validated. "You're crying," she points out, as if it's the most exciting medical condition she's ever seen.

"Am not," I lie, sniffing conspicuously.

She hugs me anyway, squeezing the breath out of my lungs but filling them with something more important. "I'm so proud of you," she whispers, and this time, I believe it.

Ethan pats Noah on the back. "Welcome to the club," he says, offering a lopsided grin. "We should've warned you it's contagious."

Marcus joins us, a satisfied glint in his eye. "You know there's no turning back now, right?"

"I'm counting on it," Noah replies, his hand still wrapped firmly around mine.

I've spent so long terrified of what this would mean, what it would cost, how it might break me. But standing here, surrounded by people who see me in ways I never let them before, I realize how wrong I was.

The professional world I clung to, the fortress of self-reliance, fades into the background. What's left is so much messier, so much riskier, so much more...

Us.

It's personal. It's imperfect. It's everything I was too afraid to want.

"I guess we know who said it first," Ethan murmurs to Maria.

She nods, eyes bright and knowing. "Told you it'd be her."

The chaos of the room dissolves, leaving only the two of us and a new kind of certainty.

He stays, I stay, we stay. And it's all the grand gesture I'll ever need.

TWENTY-SIX

NOAH

Lily walks beside me, and I can feel the shift in the air, the change in how people see us. A third-year resident from Plastics nudges someone from Cardiology, who nods toward us with a look that's half surprise, half vindication.

The earlier tension has vanished, replaced by a weird sort of celebration. Nobody seems to care that I just torched a job offer in one of the best hospitals in the country, or that Lily actually asked me to stay. They're just thrilled that something happened. That we finally happened.

Lily stays uncharacteristically quiet, letting me handle the spectacle. I should feel exposed, like I've been flayed open for the whole hospital to see. But I don't. Not even a little.

"We're gonna need more gummy worms," I announce, piling snacks onto my plate. The group laughs, and just like that, the tension that's been building for months dissolves in a single beat of shared relief.

The change in everyone's interaction is almost palpable. Norton from Oncology gives us an approving nod, and even the new intern, who probably doesn't know our names yet, looks a little starstruck. I half-expect balloons to drop from the ceiling or a flash mob to start up in celebration of our relationship status.

It's amazing how quickly a bunch of surgeons can shift from skeptical and aloof to celebratory and smug. And maybe it's because I don't care anymore—or because I do—but it all feels different now. The scrutiny doesn't bother me like it used to.

"Any more surprises?" Marcus asks, and it's only half a joke.

Lily cuts in before I can answer. "You mean other than this?" She gestures between us, a wry smile on her lips.

Marcus raises his glass in mock salute. "About damn time."

I catch Lily's eye, and for a moment it's just the two of us again, wrapped in our own impossible reality. The world keeps moving around us, the buzz of conversation and the clink of glasses, but it all fades into the background noise. It's nothing like when we first stood here, awkward and uncertain and full of the fear of what might happen. This time, I know exactly what happens next.

The playful banter between us now is effortless, a signal of what's changed and how much hasn't. It's relief and laughter and the joy of finally being on the same page, of finally being the same people we were before, but more.

The conference room hums with the satisfaction of an ending everyone was rooting for, an ending that doesn't feel like one at all. It's the start of something none of them expected, something I didn't expect until the second she said the words and I felt the ground drop out from under me.

I wouldn't have it any other way.

Lily nudges me with her elbow, a question in her eyes. *Are we okay? Can this last? Do you really mean it?* And my answer is simple, just three stupid words that change everything.

"I'm still here."

We break into the hallway, adrenaline buzzing in our veins, and all I can think is, *Holy shit, did that just happen?* I half-expect the world to reset, to snap back to its usual shape where Dr. Lily Harper doesn't ask someone like me to stay. But here we are, and it feels like stepping into an alternate universe.

The hum of the conference room fades behind us, and the quiet wraps around us like a force field. I'm suddenly aware of the distance between us, how it shrinks and grows with every breath, and I realize I'm still holding onto her hand. I let it go reluctantly, leaning back against the wall and exhaling the air I've been keeping prisoner.

I glance at her, waiting for the next impossible thing to happen. She's still standing there, exposed and maybe just as stunned as I am. *"I thought asking would make it harder when they left."* Her words replay in my mind, this new version of Lily throwing me off balance.

"I thought you didn't ask people to stay," I say, breaking the silence before it smothers us both.

She doesn't move, doesn't look away. There's something raw in her expression, a fragile honesty I'm not used to seeing. "I thought asking would make it harder when they left," she repeats, her voice so quiet I almost miss it.

I take in the sight of her, committing every detail to memory like I might need it to survive the next few minutes. She's still Lily—the control freak, the impossible surgeon, the woman who drives me insane—but everything feels different now. And in this moment, the newness isn't terrifying; it's electric.

"Was it?" I ask, my voice coming out rougher than I intend.

Lily hesitates, like she's picking her way through a mine-field of emotions she doesn't have names for. "It is," she says finally, her voice barely above a whisper.

We've spent months dancing around each other, trapped in our own rules, convinced this conversation would break us apart. But now, here, in this bubble of quiet and truth, I finally let myself hope.

The hallway feels intimate, a cocoon just for us. The hum of the lights, the distant noise of the hospital, the lack of judg-mental eyes—it all makes this moment seem impossible and perfect. My shoulders relax, and I realize how tense I've been. Not just tonight, but the whole goddamn year.

Lily is watching me, something tender and determined in her expression. It's a look that might have scared the hell out of me before, but now it just makes me want to close the gap between us.

I push off the wall and take a step toward her, testing the ground beneath us, making sure it'll hold. She doesn't retreat, and I swear the relief is so intense it makes me dizzy.

"So what now?" she asks, and there's a vulnerability in her voice that makes my heart trip over itself.

"Now," I say, the words coming easier than they have in a long time, "we figure it out."

I'm close enough to touch her, and it takes every ounce of willpower I have not to. I can't stop smiling, and from the way she's looking at me, she might be catching it like a contagious disease.

I let out a breath I didn't know I was holding, and it feels like I'm breathing for the first time. "Together," I add, making sure she hears me.

"Together," she echoes, like she's testing the word. Her smile is small but genuine, and it feels like an anchor, grounding me in this new, impossible reality.

The hallway stretches ahead of us. Not a divide, but a

promise. We're still us—Lily, who needs a detailed surgical plan, and Noah, who never follows them—but the old rules don't matter anymore.

They don't have to. We're writing our own.

In the parking lot under the evening sky, it feels like a different world—a place where I can almost believe we didn't screw everything up. Where I can almost believe Lily meant what she said. The distant hum of Seattle, the cool air against my skin, the lights of Emerald Bay blinking like lazy stars—it's all strangely quiet, especially after the chaos inside.

It's just the two of us now, and I don't think it's ever felt this real. We've left the conference room behind, along with the specter of an unfinished life, and now it's just us, the night, and a thousand words hanging unspoken between us. It's terrifying, the way this might actually work. Terrifying and surreal and... *Holy shit, do I hope it's real.*

We stand there, the silence so heavy it's almost solid. Lily's beside me, looking up at the sky like it's got the answers to the hardest questions. Maybe it does. Or maybe she does. Either way, I'm holding my breath again.

"So," I say, testing the waters, testing us. "There's something you should probably know."

Lily turns to me, and I half-expect the old version of her to reappear, the one who eats uncertainty for breakfast and doesn't have time for all this mess. But her expression stays open, a careful mix of curiosity and fear that I might ruin everything by opening my mouth.

"That job in San Francisco?" I continue, feeling the words push and pull at each other. "It's still technically on the table."

She blinks, and I can't quite tell if she's shocked, disappointed, or just processing the impossible idea that I didn't send the paperwork back. "But I thought—"

"I declined the offer," I interrupt, needing to get it all out before I lose my nerve. "I was going to take it, but I didn't. But you? This? I didn't want to leave it unfinished."

"But you resigned. I thought—"

"I was going to look for something local. If there was a chance for us, it had to be more than just because we work together."

"And if it didn't work?"

"Then at least I wouldn't be torturing myself every day, walking past you in the corridor."

The surprise on her face shifts into something softer, something I think I recognize as hope. It makes my heart trip over itself. "Unfinished?" she echoes, testing the word like she's not sure it belongs in her vocabulary.

"Yeah," I say, suddenly finding it hard to keep my cool. "I wasn't ready to give up on it. On us."

Lily stares at me like she's trying to memorize this version of me, the one who doesn't make jokes or deflect with sarcasm. The one who means it, every stupid word. I didn't think I could surprise her like this. Didn't think I could surprise myself like this.

We're both quiet for a moment, the gravity of what I've just said settling around us like a net. It feels dangerous and freeing at the same time.

"So what now?" she asks, the words carrying more weight than anything we've said all night.

It's the question we've been avoiding, the one that means we might actually have to figure this out, the one that terrifies me because I want so badly to answer it right.

"Now we figure it out," I tell her, letting a smile break through.

Her laugh is bright and unexpected, and it's like flipping

on a light switch. Everything seems clearer, less like a dream. The tension that's been riding my shoulders all night, all year, maybe forever, finally starts to ease.

She shakes her head slightly, still smiling, but I see it—right there in her eyes—the shift. The moment she lets her guard down completely.

And I move.

Not fast, not sudden. Just sure.

I close the space between us and kiss her again, slower this time, deliberate. Not a victory lap. Not a stolen moment in front of our colleagues.

But a choice.

Hers.

Mine.

Ours.

She meets me with the same energy, her hands catching my coat, pulling me just that inch closer, like we've both waited far too long. The kiss deepens, breathes, finds a rhythm that says we're here. We're doing this.

When we finally pull apart, her eyes search mine—not for confirmation, but for something more grounded. Something she already knows.

And I nod. Just once.

She exhales, like she's been holding that breath since the day we met.

The parking lot feels like a whole new world. It's not just that the weight's been lifted—it's the way she looks at me now, the way her eyes stay on mine and don't drift away like they used to. I never thought it would be like this. Never thought it could be.

Lily steps closer, and the air between us is alive, buzzing with possibilities I didn't dare believe in until now. She watches me carefully, like she's still expecting the other shoe to drop, like she still can't quite trust this is happening. But she will. I'm sure of it. As sure as I am about anything right now.

"So that's it?" she says, a teasing edge to her voice. "No surgical plan? No detailed instructions?"

I shake my head, the grin spreading wide and impossible. "Think you can handle it?" I challenge, not really asking.

She gives me a look that says she can handle anything, especially me. "Guess we'll find out," she replies, and it sounds like a promise.

The parking lot's lights cast long shadows as we stand together, side by side, a world apart from everything that's come before. The city stretches around us, open and endless, and for the first time, it feels like ours.

This is nothing like I thought it would be.

It's so much better.

On the street, under the night sky, everything feels new. The lights of Seattle flicker like a thousand possibilities, and for once, neither of us is rushing to be anywhere else. There's a calmness in the air, a soft chill that seems to hold the world in place, and I'm not sure I've ever felt this still.

We walk out into the open, the cool air wrapping around us, and it feels like stepping into another version of our lives— one where everything we didn't say is finally out there, breathing with us. It's all so strange and perfect, and I wonder how long this newness will last before it becomes something real and familiar.

Lily's hand brushes mine, not quite intentional, but not an accident either. She lets it hang there, in the space between us, and when I take it, there's no hesitation. It's easy and natural and right, like it's always been this way instead of just minutes.

We stand together, the city a sprawling expanse around us,

but nothing seems as important as the few inches between our bodies. I expect her to let go, to pull away because it's all so much, so fast, so completely opposite of who she is and who we are. But she doesn't.

She's still here.

It's quiet, and the silence is full of everything that's changed. It should be awkward. But it's not. It's comfortable and real, a bubble around us where nothing feels impossible.

I glance at her, my pulse an echo of hers, and for once, it's in perfect sync.

The night stretches ahead, long and open and promising. The distant sounds of the hospital fade, replaced by the steady thrum of my heart finally knowing its own beat. This is everything I didn't know I was waiting for.

Everything I was afraid to want.

We haven't said much, but there's nothing left to say. The weight I've been carrying for months is gone, lifted with a single conversation and a laugh I didn't deserve to hear. I finally know where I stand.

Next to her.

Lily watches me, her eyes dark and searching, and I wonder if she can see the change in me as clearly as I see it in her. The tension she always wore like a badge of honor is gone, replaced by something softer and more human. Something I never thought I'd see.

I squeeze her hand, needing to feel the connection, needing to know this isn't just some beautiful, fragile illusion. She squeezes back, and it tells me more than any of the words we've said all night. More than any of the ones we didn't say.

This is real. We're real.

"You're stuck with me now."

She rolls her eyes, a soft, affectionate gesture that I'm going to hold on to for a long, long time. "Finally," she murmurs, and it sounds like the most beautiful word in the world.

The lights of the city twinkle around us, and for once, we're not rushing to be somewhere else. We're not running toward anything or away from it. We're just here, together, with our fingers intertwined like it's been years instead of minutes.

It feels new and old and like everything I want.

It feels like forever.

TWENTY-SEVEN

♥

LILY

"Are you going to say something, or should I call it?" Noah asks, not unkindly. His voice is quieter than usual. He isn't making eye contact, which I both appreciate and resent.

"I'm thinking." I fold my arms tight, less for warmth than to keep my hands from betraying me.

He nods, as if this is a perfectly reasonable answer. He's never needed to fill silences. He just waits, patient as gravity, confident that eventually everything will fall into place.

I both hate and love that about him.

"Back there, in the conference room. I wanted to say something else. I just—couldn't."

He shrugs, but there's a twist to his mouth that suggests he already knows. "You don't have to."

"I do." I swallow, and it feels like passing a scalpel blade. "I was scared. Not of you. Just—scared." I exhale, a tremor running through me. My hands are shaking, so I jam them deeper into my pockets.

He doesn't move, but there's a shift in the air between us. He's listening. Really listening.

"I kept telling myself it was better to not need anything. Or anyone. To just do the work and ignore the rest." I stare at my reflection in the window of a nearby car—a ghost with dark hair and a surgeon's posture. "But I was wrong."

Noah makes a small noise—agreement, maybe, or just an acknowledgement of receipt.

I want to stop there. I want to let the words dangle in the air, suspended and unspecific, and pretend that counts as honesty. But I know it doesn't. I know it's not enough.

"I'm not good at this," I say. "You probably guessed that."

"Not a shocker," Noah says, and for the first time tonight, he looks directly at me. There's nothing cruel about it. Just... expectation.

I could leave it here. Let the awkwardness pass over us, like the weather. He'd let me. But for once, I want something more.

"I want you to know," I say, "that I wasn't lying. When I said I didn't want things to change. I meant it. But I didn't mean—" My brain sprints ahead, tripping over the words, "—I didn't mean I wanted you to disappear."

He turns toward me, hands out of his pockets now, like he's resisting the urge to reach for something. Or someone.

"You said it yourself, Lily. I'm hard to get rid of."

I force myself to laugh, but it comes out strangled. "Yeah, you're basically a barnacle. Or a tapeworm."

"High praise from the hospital's star resident." He tries for a smirk, but there's rawness underneath.

The silence grows, dense and magnetic, as if every molecule in the parking lot is contracting around us. I can feel my pulse everywhere—in my wrists, my neck, my tongue.

"I don't want to go back to how it was," I say, quieter now, each word knifing through layers of scar tissue. "Not pretending. Not hiding. Not from you."

Noah lets out a slow breath. His posture is open, relaxed, but his eyes are sharp, catching every flicker of my resolve.

"You know you don't have to be perfect with me," he says.

I want to argue. I want to say that's not possible, that the requirement for flawlessness is coded into my DNA, that any deviation is a personal failing of catastrophic proportions. Instead, I just nod. I don't trust my voice not to betray me.

Another car door slams somewhere down the row. I flinch, then recover, pretending I was only shifting my weight.

Noah waits. He could make this easy. He could fill the space with a joke, or a story about the world's worst night shift, or some useless trivia about sea otters. But he just lets me sit in it, lets me choose.

"I thought I'd lost you forever by not speaking up. Not telling you how I felt. I'm not going to keep the truth from you ever again," I say, and it's not a promise, but it's as close as I've ever come. "Unless you do something incredibly stupid, which is, frankly, a statistical inevitability."

He laughs, and the tension in my chest loosens a millimeter.

"Do you have a contingency plan?" he asks. "For when I inevitably screw up?"

"I'm a surgeon. I always have a backup."

He smiles at that, and I almost think I've said enough. But there's one more thing, and I need it out before I lose my nerve.

"I wanted you," I admit. "All those weeks. Months really. More than I thought was possible."

His face softens, just for a heartbeat. He steps a fraction closer, the toe of his shoe nearly grazing mine.

"I wanted you too, Harper. All of you."

I look away, but he doesn't let me. He reaches out, slow

and deliberate, and catches my chin with two fingers. Gently, like he's worried I'll break.

He waits. I nod, almost imperceptibly.

He leans in, but not so fast it's a foregone conclusion. There's a long, trembling half-second where I could step back, could duck away and pretend none of this happened. But I don't. I tilt my chin up and meet him halfway, stubborn to the end.

His mouth is gentle, not pushy or hungry, but careful—like he's touching a bruise. The heat of his hands bleeds through my skin, settling the jitter in my veins. My pulse, which has been in V-tach since the moment I spotted him in the conference room, slows to something approaching human rhythm.

I let myself notice every detail: the rough scrape of stubble, the smell of rain and laundry detergent, the quiet way his chest rises and falls in sync with mine. There's no grandstanding. No tongue, no teeth. Just the deliberate, patient pressure of someone who is absolutely sure of what he wants, but willing to wait for me to catch up.

When he pulls back, it's only far enough to look at me. His thumb brushes along my cheekbone, erasing the possibility that any of this is a mistake.

For once, I don't have a comeback. The world could end in this street and I wouldn't care.

"I'm still going to mess up," he says quietly. "Probably a lot."

"Me too." I say it without thinking, and immediately regret the softness in my voice.

"Good." He grins, and the seriousness evaporates, replaced by the familiar mischief. "Keeps things interesting."

The spell isn't broken, but it changes. We stand there, grinning like idiots, while the rest of the world goes about its business.

I can still taste him, and I want more, but I also want to

savor the feeling of not needing anything more than this. It's new. It's terrifying.

It's perfect.

He shoves his hands back in his coat pockets and rocks on his heels. "So, your place or mine, or is that against the rules?"

I arch a brow. "Since when do you care about rules?"

"I don't. But you do."

He has me there. I look at my feet, then at him. "I wouldn't hate the company."

"Then let's go," he says.

We walk. There's no plan, just the two of us drifting down a half-lit sidewalk with no destination except, I guess, my place. Seattle after midnight is a different city—emptied out, the usual stampede of commuters replaced by the gentle squish of shoes on wet concrete and the persistent, ambient hum of rain.

Our shoulders bump every few steps. The first time it happens, we both stiffen, like neither of us knows if we're allowed this much proximity. The second time, Noah laughs softly and bumps back, on purpose.

I could analyze this for hours—what it means, what the consequences might be—but I'm tired, and there's a warmth under my ribs that makes all the hypotheticals seem less important than usual.

The quiet is easy, not forced. For someone who never shuts up during rounds, Noah is remarkably content to let the silence stretch. The city does most of the talking: a cat skitters under a car, a bus huffs past on the far end of the block, somewhere a couple argues quietly about whose turn it is to walk the dog.

When I reach for his hand, it's because the urge is so strong I can't ignore it. I do it without looking, and there's a half-second where I expect resistance, a subtle tensing or a joke about hand-holding being unsanitary. Instead, Noah's fingers slot into mine like we've been practicing for weeks.

His grip is steady. Confident. I'd hate him for it, if I didn't find it so reassuring.

"You know," I say after a while, "people are going to talk."

"About what?" he deadpans. "Our tragic taste in footwear?"

"About this." I squeeze his hand for emphasis, then regret it. "About us."

He shrugs, unconcerned. "They already do. You're the golden girl. I'm the ER's cautionary tale. It's a classic."

I snort. "You really need to stop referring to yourself as a cautionary tale. You're giving the nursing staff ideas for your next Secret Santa."

He grins, and the neon sign from the 24-hour diner paints his teeth blue. "There are worse fates than free socks."

We pass a mural that's been slowly decomposing for years —what was once a heroic tableau of Mount Rainier is now a runny blur of grays and greens, but I still like it.

Noah is the first to break the spell of silence. "So. Think it's legal to list my car as a primary residence?"

I glance over. "That depends. Does it have Wi-Fi?"

"Only if I park near the hospital."

"How convenient," I say. "Do you want me to knit you a doormat that says, 'Welcome to Rock Bottom?'"

Noah nods, solemn. "That, and maybe a throw pillow. Something understated. Like 'This is Fine' in aggressive cross-stitch."

"You're handling both your joblessness and homelessness with real dignity."

"I try."

We walk on, and I don't kiss him again—but I think about it, and judging by the look on his face, he knows.

The walk resumes, slower now, like neither of us is in a hurry to reach the end.

I'm not used to this. The ease, the quiet certainty that someone actually wants to be here. It's not dramatic. It's not ever especially romantic, unless you count the smell of rain and the shared contempt for hospital politics. But it's good.

By the time we get to my building, my cheeks hurt from smiling.

I could get used to this.

I've never brought anyone back to my apartment. Not for dinner, not for sex, not for anything that couldn't be handled in a coffee shop or a dark bar with a clear path to the exit.

Standing outside my door, I feel the weight of the key in my hand and the pressure of Noah's presence at my back. The hallway smells like lemon cleaner and ancient carpet, and the silence is different here—thicker, somehow, the kind that amplifies my pulse until it's a drumline behind my eardrums.

"Moment of truth?" Noah asks.

I hesitate a beat too long, then unlock the door. I open it wide enough for both of us to enter, but not so wide he can see inside right away.

Noah steps past me, not rushing, not prowling. He pauses on the threshold, taking it all in with one of his slow, comprehensive looks.

He whistles, low and impressed. "Jesus, Harper. Is this place staged for a photo shoot?"

I want to laugh, but I'm suddenly defensive. "It's just... organized."

"That's one word for it." He steps farther in, careful not to touch anything. His shoes squeak softly on the polished wood floor.

The apartment is small—one bedroom, a galley kitchen, a living room with a thrift store couch and a wall of books so neatly alphabetized and stacked, it borders on pathological. The surfaces are all gleaming, the couch is arranged at a perfectly geometric angle to the coffee table, and there's not a single stray item in sight.

"You could perform surgery in here," Noah says, peering into the kitchen. "Actually, I think you have. Is that an autoclave?"

"Very funny." I slip off my shoes and line them up with the others in the rack, then hang my coat onto the designated hook.

Noah's coat, on the other hand, gets thrown over the arm of the couch. He kicks off his sneakers and leaves them slightly askew by the door.

He grins at me, like he's daring me to care.

I should. I don't.

He wanders the room, hands in his pockets, eyes scanning the shelves. "So this is where the magic happens."

"Define magic."

He lifts a book off the shelf, reads the spine—Robbins Basic Pathology—and puts it back exactly where it was. "Do you ever relax, or is that against the Harper Code of Conduct?"

I arch an eyebrow. "I've been known to relax. Once. In 2017."

He laughs, the sound bouncing off the tile. Then his eyes fall on the kitchen counter, where a stack of files sits in a neat pile. My stomach drops.

He crosses to them, lifts the top file, and reads the label: "'Trauma Protocol Revisions.' Rebel."

I want to make a joke, but nothing comes out. Instead, I just watch him, waiting for the punchline.

But there isn't one. He looks up at me, something unreadable in his expression.

"You left space for something unexpected," he says.

I blink. "I guess I did."

He sets the file back down, more carefully than he picked it up "You want a drink?" he asks. "Or is that a next-date privilege?"

The word next-date sits heavy in the air, but not unpleasantly so.

I nod. "Kitchen's fully stocked."

He investigates the fridge. "Jesus. You weren't kidding about the Tupperware. Are you prepping for a siege?"

"Meal prep is efficient."

He pulls out two bottles of water and passes one to me. Our fingers touch, and I feel the same electric hum as before, but now it's colored with something softer. The quiet, sustained current of being seen.

Noah plops down on my couch, spreading out like he owns the place. I hover, unsure if I should join him or keep standing at parade rest in my own living room.

He pats the seat next to him. "You're allowed to sit, you know."

I try to look exasperated, but the effort is half-hearted. I sit, close but not touching, and he immediately closes the distance, draping his arm across the back of the couch in a way that would annoy me coming from literally anyone else.

We don't talk for a while. We don't need to.

I look at my apartment, really look, and for the first time, it feels less like a fortress and more like a home. Maybe that's what happens when you let someone in.

I lean into him, just a little. He doesn't move, but I can feel his smile.

It's subtle, but it's enough.

I rest against his shoulder, just enough to feel the shape of him beneath the fabric. Not enough to mean anything. Except it does.

Noah's voice breaks the stillness. "You're sure about this?"

He's not teasing. There's no smug curve to the question. Just warmth. Just care.

I turn to him, our faces closer than I remembered them being. Close enough that I can see the gold flecks in his eyes, and the tension at the corner of his mouth. Like he's holding himself back on my behalf.

"I wouldn't have let you in if I wasn't," I say, barely above a whisper.

He studies me a second longer—like he's giving me one last chance to bolt—then leans in. His kiss is soft, tentative, not a claim but a question. My answer is in how I move toward him. In the way my hand finds his collar, then his jaw.

The kiss deepens—heat slowly building under skin that suddenly feels too thin. My chest tightens with something I can't name and don't want to control.

His hand skims my waist. Pauses. Gives me the space to draw a line.

Instead, I breathe, "Don't stop."

Noah stills, just for a moment. Then nods—just once—and kisses me again.

This time, nothing about it is tentative.

We move without speaking. Not frantically—not like the world is ending—but like we've both been circling this moment for so long, we don't need instructions. Just intent.

He lets me lead the way to the bedroom. It feels surreal to have someone follow me here—into this private, controlled, unshared space. I don't think I've ever been so aware of every object I own. The tucked corners of the bed. The neatly folded blanket on the chair. The candle on the nightstand I've never once lit.

Noah stands just inside the doorway. "Still time to kick me out," he says.

I shake my head. "Not unless you start rearranging my bookshelf."

He smiles—that slow, warm smile that disarms me faster than I'd like—and steps closer.

We undress each other gently, deliberately. My hands reach for the hem of his shirt, and he raises his arms to let it slide free. His chest is warm and solid under my palms. He kisses my temple. My jaw. My collarbone.

When he peels my shirt over my head, he does it slowly, like every inch of newly exposed skin is something he wants to learn, not just see. I should feel self-conscious—I usually do. But right now, I feel... here. Present. Unhidden.

His fingertips trail along the line of my ribs. "You don't have to be perfect with me," he murmurs.

I blink, and something in me stutters. "I've never let anyone see me like this."

He doesn't say anything. Just cups my cheek and presses his lips to the corner of my mouth in a way that feels like a vow. My breath catches in my throat. I don't look away.

When we finally fall back onto the mattress, it's not graceful. We laugh—just for a moment—our limbs tangling, sheets twisting under us.

"So much for surgical precision," I mutter, trying to find the rhythm of this new territory.

Noah grins, brushing my hair from my face. "We're doctors, Harper. Not gymnasts."

And just like that, the air shifts again—light, electric, absolutely real.

His hands find mine on the pillow. Our fingers thread together.

This isn't about performance. It's about presence.

And I've never been more present in my life.

There's no music, no candlelight, no dramatic sweep of silk

sheets. Just us. Breath, skin, nerves. Laughter caught in the throat.

The first few minutes are awkward—knees bump, angles misalign, my elbow somehow ends up in his armpit. We fumble through it, smiling against each other's mouths.

But it's not awkward-bad. It's awkward-true.

Every moment is discovery. Not just of bodies, but of how we are together—how I hold tension in my spine and how he senses it, kisses the space between my shoulder blades until it melts. How he's more patient than I expected. How I let him be.

At some point, my hand lands on the curve of his back and stays there. His eyes find mine, and we just look—like the moment requires confirmation. Like we both need to be sure this isn't just heat, but something built on something steadier.

It is.

When we finally move together, everything else falls away —my rules, his jokes, the hospital walls. There's just his mouth at my ear, the soft rasp of my name, and the way I lose all sense of the things I used to protect.

There's no rush. No crescendo. Just a steady, slow unfolding—like we're unwrapping something breakable.

When I reach for him, it's not out of urgency. It's out of want. Of choice. Of knowing.

And when I say his name—not sharp, not teasing, just Noah—he answers with his whole body.

Afterward, we lie tangled in silence, the world blurred at the edges.

I rest my head against his chest. I can feel his heartbeat, steady and solid beneath my cheek.

He traces his thumb lazily over the back of my hand, not demanding anything. Just being there.

"I thought I'd feel exposed," I murmur.

He kisses the top of my head, barely a brush. "You don't?"

"No," I say, eyes closed. "I feel... here."

And that, more than anything, terrifies me.

And I think—maybe that means it's real.

The room is quiet. Dim.

We haven't moved much. My leg is hooked over his. One of his arms is tucked behind his head, the other still resting across my back like he forgot to let go. Or didn't want to.

Neither do I.

Outside, somewhere down the street, a siren wails, fading into the distance. It reminds me of who we are—what we do. But in here, it's just two people breathing, slowly reassembling.

Noah speaks first, his voice low and unguarded. "That was..."

I lift my head. "Careful."

He nods. "And a little terrible."

I laugh into his chest. "Definitely the least efficient thing I've done all week."

"Top ten on my list, easy."

I shift so I can see him. He's smiling, but it's the soft kind—not smug, not cocky. Just present. Real.

"Are you okay?" he asks, quietly. Not as a reflex. As a check-in.

I nod. "I'm... better than okay."

And I mean it.

I reach for the blanket and pull it over us. It smells like laundry detergent and now, faintly, like him. He tucks it around me without being asked.

We lie like that for a long time. No rush. No obligations. Just the hum of skin against skin, our breath syncing slowly.

I think about the rules I used to live by. About control and containment. About how I made a fortress out of solitude and called it strength.

But this?

This stillness, this safety, this deliberate closeness—

It doesn't feel like weakness. It feels like living.

I wake to the smell of coffee. Real coffee, not the scorched-hair-and-despair blend they serve in the hospital cafeteria.

For a moment I think I've hallucinated it. Then I remember—last night, Noah, the couch, his arm around my shoulder and the slow, strange comfort of drifting off with someone else breathing beside me.

I never sleep past six, but today it's seven-thirty and my body feels... different. Not well-rested, exactly, but reset. Like the reboot button finally worked.

My feet hit the cold floor and I do a quick inventory—no catastrophic emotional fallout, no regret. Just a tightness in my chest that feels almost pleasant.

I shower, run a comb through my hair, and throw on sweats. I expect Noah to be gone, or at least hovering awkwardly in the entryway, but he's in my kitchen, barefoot, flipping through my protocol notes like it's the morning paper.

He's wearing one of my old oversized college T-shirts. I don't know when he stole it, but it fits him better than it ever fit me. His hair is even more of a disaster than usual, sticking up in all directions.

He looks up and grins, unrepentant. "Didn't mean to snoop. I got bored."

"You read trauma protocols for fun?"

He shrugs, unconcerned. "I like knowing what keeps you up at night."

There's a mug waiting for me—my favorite one, the only one with a crack in the handle—and he hands it over without ceremony. Our fingers touch, and for a second, everything else in the room goes soft focus.

"You realize this makes you officially unprofessional," I say, trying for stern but failing.

Noah leans against the counter, arms crossed. "I plan to be completely inappropriate over breakfast. I'm thinking pancakes. Or we could just eat your weirdly obsessive granola."

"It's not obsessive, it's optimized." I sip the coffee, letting the burn anchor me. "And you're not supposed to be here, you know. I never let anyone in."

"Yeah," he says, quiet but certain. "But you did."

I glance away, embarrassed at the heat creeping up my neck. "Don't get used to it."

He doesn't push. Just sets the files down and steps closer, resting his hands on my hips like it's the most natural thing in the world.

"Too late," he says, and kisses me once, soft and brief, before pulling away to raid the fridge.

I watch him move through my space, at home in a way I've never seen in anyone before. He fits, not because I made room, but because he found the gap I didn't know existed.

For once, I don't mind the mess. Not the paperwork, not the tousled hair, not even the fact that we'll be late for work.

We'll deal with it. Together.

I finish my coffee and smile, already looking forward to the next morning.

Maybe, if I'm very lucky, it'll always be this easy.

TWENTY-EIGHT

NOAH

The thing about hospital admin offices is they're more antiseptic than the actual ER, just without the charm of near-death adrenaline.

I sit in a plastic chair that's trying too hard to look like real leather, flipping through an HR brochure on "Work-Life Synergy." The overheads are the unflattering kind of fluorescent—designed to illuminate every pore and existential dread. There are three motivational posters, all different shades of blue, and a ficus in the corner that's survived on passive aggression and recycled air since 2007.

Across the room, a clock ticks with the efficiency only found in bureaucratic machinery. I check my phone. Eight a.m. On the dot, the door swings open and a woman in a sensible pantsuit—Ms. Norris, HR Specialist, per her nametag—steps out.

"Dr. Carter?" She's got a voice like a smile with no teeth.

I stand, offer a handshake that's neither limp nor crushing. "That's me."

She waves me into her office, which is somehow even more sterile than the waiting room. Desk wiped clean, save for a branded notepad and a pen that looks like it's never been used for anything riskier than a Post-it. No photos, no clutter. *She probably laminates her personal thoughts when no one's looking.*

She gestures at the guest chair. I take it, slouch just enough to convey that I'm not here to negotiate the Cuban Missile Crisis.

Ms. Norris sits. Folds her hands. Doesn't smile.

"Am I right in my understanding that you wish to rescind your resignation, Dr. Carter?"

"That's correct."

She pauses. No nod of acknowledgment. Just taps one manicured finger on the pristine surface of her desk, like she's trying to summon the ghost of a rulebook.

"You're turning down a remarkable opportunity," she says. "Competitive salary, a robust research endowment, relocation stipend—"

"I am," I say, and let the silence do its job.

She lets it stretch this time. Longer than expected. Ms. Norris is not easily rattled, but something shifts behind her eyes. Calculation, maybe.

"Was there anything about the San Francisco offer that gave you pause?" she asks.

The easy answer: It's not about the money.

The less-easy answer: I was ready to leave until I realized what—and who—I'd actually be leaving.

Instead, I go for a third answer.

"It's a great job," I say. "But I already found something better here."

She tilts her head. There's a flicker of interest. "That 'something better' wouldn't happen to work in cardiothoracics, would it?"

I smile, almost despite myself. "That's a separate form, I think."

Her mouth twitches, almost a smile, but not quite. Then she straightens the papers on her desk with a precision that's usually reserved for autopsies.

"Dr. Carter, I wouldn't say there are black marks on your file... but there are certainly a few muddy footprints." She flips a page. "Two formal warnings—"

"One was a misunderstanding."

"—three complaints, two scheduling violations, and a disciplinary note related to an incident involving a vending machine and a rogue tracheotomy kit."

"In my defence, I didn't harm the vending machine."

Ms. Norris doesn't laugh. Of course she doesn't.

"The truth is," she says, levelling her gaze at me, "your resignation saved us a difficult conversation. And now you're asking us to undo that clean break."

For the first time, I feel the air thin out in the room. My chest tightens. Maybe they don't want me back. Maybe I burned the bridge and then asked to borrow a bucket of water.

But then she picks up a folder—manila, well-thumbed—and opens it like she's cracking open a verdict.

"However," she says, flipping a page with deliberate care, "Dr. Patel submitted a formal statement on your behalf. As did Dr. Winston and Dr. Grant. All spoke to your growth this past year, your surgical outcomes, and your... let's say, unorthodox bedside manner."

I blink. "They wrote letters?"

She nods. "In Patel's case, a very strongly worded one."

"Did it contain threats?"

"Not overtly."

She slides a form across the desk.

"Emerald Bay will be happy to retain you," she says, voice

even but with the faintest rise at the end—as if this decision surprised even her.

I pick up the pen. Sign. A single black stroke in the endless paperwork of adulthood.

Ms. Norris stands. Offers her hand. "We're glad you're staying, Noah.

I give her a real smile this time, not the one they taught in orientation. "Thanks for understanding."

"Don't thank me," she says. "Thank your fan club."

I leave the office with my hands in my pockets, shoulders loose for the first time in months. There's a lightness under my ribs—like maybe, for once, I didn't sabotage my own future.

Not completely, anyway.

You can tell a lot about an ER shift by the first ten seconds of walking onto the floor. If it sounds like a beehive that's just been kicked, you're in for a long day. Today, the vibe is one step up from absolute chaos, but two notches below "call in the National Guard." Which, for Emerald Bay, is basically a slow morning.

I fall in step with Lily as she rounds the corner from the ICU. She's deep in the chart, eyes scanning the printout with her mouth set in a line that says either "I haven't had coffee" or "I'm mentally composing your eulogy." It's never easy to tell.

"Status update?" I ask, not bothering with hello.

She doesn't glance up. "Patient in 307's hemoglobin is tanking. He's got the GI bleed from last night."

I nod, already matching her pace. "Has Patel seen it?"

"He's busy with the codes from 309. Paging him is like trying to reach the Pope."

"We talking fresh frozen plasma or just a desperate plea to the gods of hematology?"

She flicks a look sideways, the ghost of a smile playing at the edge of her mouth. "Both."

The hallway is a funnel of gurneys, surgical techs, and the unmistakable scent of industrial-strength sanitizer. We side-step an incoming trauma cart—two paramedics bickering over who gets the last Clif Bar—and Lily doesn't miss a beat in her chart review.

"Anything else in the pipeline?" I ask.

"Burn unit's getting a transfer from Spokane, ETA ten minutes. And the orthopedic guy is still MIA."

I check my watch. "Three-to-one odds he's hung over."

She doesn't argue. She knows I'm probably right.

We slip into the 307 curtain, and for five seconds, we are pure professionalism. Vitals, history, assessment—it's a ballet, and we know all the moves.

Lily checks the IV, quick and competent. "You want to push another unit before the lab draw?"

"Why not live dangerously?"

She smirks. "That's your brand, isn't it?"

I reach across her to grab a flush from the tray, and for a millisecond, our shoulders touch. She doesn't flinch. Neither do I. If anything, it feels like a challenge.

Out in the hall, Nurse Patty gives us the side-eye over her glasses. "I see the Dream Team's back at it."

I wink at her, and Lily just shakes her head, but I catch the twitch of her lips.

We move down the row, triaging one disaster after another. It's a rhythm now: she does the hard math, I talk the families off the ledge, we reconvene at the whiteboard and argue about who gets first crack at the next train wreck.

Halfway through the shift, we're flagged down by Marcus, who's pretending not to watch us from the nurse's station.

He leans in, stage-whispering to Patty. "Told you they'd

end up working together again. Should I pay up now or wait for the engagement announcement?"

Fatty doesn't miss a beat. "I'll take cash or Venmo, honey."

Marcus catches my eye and smirks, like he knows exactly how last night ended. I give him a lazy salute, then drag Lily toward the break room.

We hit the supply closet for fresh gloves, and as I reach for the top shelf, Lily stands on tiptoe next to me. Our hands brush. Neither of us pulls away.

I say, "We're excellent at subtle."

She snorts, low and derisive. "You're excellent at being smug."

I grin. "It's a gift."

We stock up in silence, but it's a comfortable one—the kind that feels less like an absence of noise and more like a promise.

Back in the main corridor, we tackle the burn transfer together. The patient is a teenage kid with second-degree burns across his arm and chest. Lily assesses while I talk to the parents, answering questions and deflecting panic like it's part of the wound care.

We debrief outside the room, shoulder to shoulder against the wall. The chart between us, the air heavy with that faint, singed-plastic smell.

"Nice work in there," Lily says.

I shrug, but she can tell it means something. "You too."

There's a pause, but it doesn't linger. Emergencies wait for no one, and neither of us is interested in a big moment. We push off the wall at the same time, and for once, the world feels less like it's about to explode.

I catch her looking at me. She holds my gaze for a half second, then glances away, but not before I see the real smile.

I file it away for later, like a lucky charm in the pocket of a lab coat.

Hospital conference rooms all smell the same: marker fumes, recycled air, and a faint undertone of cold, damp fear.

Today it's packed. Dr. Patel at the head of the table, Chief Resident to his right, a handful of attendings orbiting like wary satellites. Someone brought a box of doughnuts, already down to crumbs and napkins. The main event is on the whiteboard: Lily's flowcharts, color-coded to the micron, with sticky notes in a grid so precise it might qualify as an art installation.

I claim the chair next to Lily. She barely registers me, eyes locked on her laptop as she reviews the slides for the fifth— maybe sixth—time.

"You're going to burn a hole through the screen," I murmur.

She doesn't look up. "Not possible. This thing is from the Bush era."

"W," I say. "Or H?"

That earns the tiniest twitch of a smile.

Patel calls us to order, his reading glasses perched at the end of his nose. "Let's hear the trauma protocol update, Dr. Harper."

Lily's in her element: brisk, unfazed by the weight of all the eyes in the room. She walks everyone through the algorithm—initial assessment, rapid triage, streamlined communication with the blood bank. Every time someone interrupts, she answers before the question finishes, like she's speedrunning the Socratic method.

I'm supposed to be here for moral support, but she barely needs it. Still, I throw in a nod or "exactly" when the moment calls for it, and once, when she blanks on a new policy code, I fill it in before she has to ask.

We're a tag team now. She does the hard math, I keep the room's pulse. Even Patel notices.

He stops us partway through. "So, Dr. Harper, you're suggesting a twenty percent cut to the in-room assessment time. You think that's feasible?"

She's ready. "I know it is. We've tested the workflow over the past three weeks."

Patel pivots to me. "You agree with this?"

"Only if I get to call the paramedics when the residents start dropping from exhaustion," I say. "But yeah. The data's solid."

Laughter—real laughter—ripples around the table. Even the Chief Resident cracks a smile.

We plow through the rest of the protocol. Lily has every slide down cold, but when a debate gets heated—old guard versus new school, tradition versus efficiency—I back her up, reframing the pushback with a joke or an anecdote. At one point, she glances over with a look that is equal parts exasperation and gratitude. I'm pretty sure I'll be hearing about it later.

Patel wraps up, removing his glasses and pinching the bridge of his nose. "All right. That was the clearest presentation I've seen all year. Any final comments?"

The Chief pipes up. "No one's going to say it, so I will. This is the first time our protocols have made sense in five years."

Lily blinks, surprised. For the first time all morning, she seems caught off guard.

Patel nods. "I expect a rollout plan by next week. Well done, both of you."

He dismisses the meeting, but not before locking eyes with me and tilting his head toward the hallway.

I trail him out, expecting a lecture. Instead, he stops and lowers his voice. "You know I'll be watching, right?"

I smile, easy. "You and half the hospital."

He grunts, but I catch the almost-smile. "Don't screw it up, Carter."

"Wouldn't dream of it," I say, and mean it for once.

Patel disappears into his office, and I double back to the conference room. Lily is packing up, her hands moving fast, but there's a flush in her cheeks she can't hide.

I lean against the door. "Nice save on the lab workflow question."

"You bailed me out on the ICD code."

"Teamwork," I say. "Or something."

We walk out, side-by-side. Staffers step aside without thinking, like we're a unit.

In the elevator, I nudge her shoulder with mine. "You want to celebrate?"

She arches an eyebrow. "Define 'celebrate.'"

"Dinner. Drinks. A victory lap through the med supply closet."

She snorts. "Two out of three."

The doors open to a blur of staff and gurneys, but for a moment, it's just us. No arguments. No old wounds. Just two people who finally—finally—figured out how to win, together.

If my entire existence could be distilled to a single hour, it would be this: six p.m., the muted hum of city traffic outside, Lily's kitchen lit up like a crime scene, and us trying—and failing spectacularly—to make dinner.

Her apartment—which is now *our* apartment— is still all sharp lines and surgical neatness, but I'm slowly making inroads. My jacket's on the back of a chair, my ancient running shoes by the door. There's a half-empty bag of off-brand tortilla chips on her pristine counter, and she hasn't binned them yet. Progress.

We're supposed to be making tacos. This devolves into a debate about the best way to cut an onion.

"You're going to give it a concussion," Lily says, eyeing my technique.

"Onions don't have nervous systems," I counter.

She looks up, deadpan. "Neither do you before your first coffee, but you're still sensitive."

I bow. "Touché."

The whole process is chaos. I try to freestyle the seasoning; she insists on measuring every spice. When I reach for the cumin, she swaps it for chili powder behind my back, just to see if I notice.

I notice. We argue, then laugh, then argue again. We bump hips at the stove, and at one point I flick a stray piece of onion at her and she retaliates by smearing salsa on my wrist.

We're both covered in food by the time the taco filling is done. The tortillas are charred in places. The guac is aggressively lime-forward, which I love and she pretends to hate. When we finally sit to eat, we're still in our scrubs—her jacket unzipped halfway to reveal a faded MIT T-shirt, mine dusted with flour and whatever dignity I had left.

We eat on the couch, plates balanced on our knees, reruns of *Grey's Anatomy* muted on the TV. I make a game of pointing out every gross medical inaccuracy.

"They just resuscitated someone with, what, a single chest compression?" I scoff.

Lily chews thoughtfully. "I once saw you restart a guy's heart by yelling at him."

"It worked."

She tips her head. "You have a powerful voice."

I grin, and she bumps my foot with hers.

Halfway through dinner, she grabs the remote and unmutes the show. We watch in silence for a while. I lean back, legs stretched out, and she ends up propped against my chest, head on my shoulder.

It's unremarkable and absolutely perfect.

I don't know when I started craving this—normal nights, bad TV, food that doesn't come from a vending machine. Maybe it's just the shock of not running for once, of staying put and letting myself be happy.

Lily glances up, catches me staring, and says, "What?"

"Nothing," I respond, even though it's everything.

She narrows her eyes, but lets it go. She rests her hand on my knee, fingers splayed, claiming space.

We finish dinner. I offer to do dishes and she doesn't object, just leans in the doorway and watches while I clean up. Every now and then she corrects my stacking. I let her.

When the kitchen is back to its textbook order, we migrate to the couch again. This time, she pulls a throw blanket over both of us. Our legs tangle together. Neither of us moves.

On TV, a surgeon saves the day with a risky, improbable procedure.

Lily rolls her eyes and scoffs, "No one would ever actually do that."

I nudge her shoulder. "Says the woman who rewrote the hospital's trauma protocol in a week."

She shrugs, like it's no big deal, but her smile lingers.

Later, we sit in the quiet, the only sound the low rumble of distant thunder and the soft click of the heating system. I let my hand rest on her waist, palm flat and easy.

She doesn't say anything, but she moves just a little closer.

I think about all the things I could say. How I didn't know I wanted this. How every day with her feels new and familiar at the same time. How, for the first time in my life, I don't need to look for the exit.

But I don't say any of it. I don't have to.

Instead, I just hold on, and let the night settle around us.

The best part of Emerald Bay is the view from the roof, especially after midnight, and now, when our schedules allow, I get to share it with Lily.

Up here, the city is a luminous sprawl, all neon veins and lit-up windows. The sounds of sirens and car horns and humanity are muffled, replaced by the quieter background of wind and distant waves. We're six stories above the trauma bay, but it might as well be another planet.

Lily sits next to me on the concrete ledge, her knees pulled up, the collar of her coat turned against the cold. Between us is a battered thermos of hospital coffee. She takes a sip and winces, but says nothing. I let the silence linger, because for once, it feels comfortable.

"You know we could get in trouble for this," she says, staring at the skyline.

"Define 'trouble,'" I counter. "Is it a misdemeanor if the coffee is technically from the cafeteria?"

She nudges my foot with hers. "You're impossible."

"And yet, here you are."

She shakes her head, but she's smiling. The wind pushes a strand of hair across her face, and I resist the urge to tuck it behind her ear. Barely.

We watch the traffic together. I wonder how many people down there are running from something, or toward something, or just trying to survive the night.

After a while, I say, "Do you ever think about leaving? Just... starting over somewhere else?"

She doesn't answer right away. "No. Not anymore."

I nod, take a swig of coffee. It tastes awful. "Me neither."

We fall quiet again. She shivers, just a little, and I drape an arm over her shoulders. She doesn't stiffen. Instead, she leans in, tucking herself against my side like it's the most natural thing in the world.

I tilt the thermos toward her. "You want the last sip?"

She glances up, eyes dark and sharp. "I thought chivalry was dead."

"I'm just afraid you'll stab me if I take it."

"Fair."

Despite our better judgement, we trade the cup back and forth until it's empty. I set it on the ledge, fingers brushing against hers. This time, she lets my hand linger.

"So," I say, quieter now. "What do we call this?"

She looks at me, mouth twitching. "What, the coffee? Or..." She gestures between us.

"Or."

She considers, then deadpans, "A tragic codependency."

I laugh. "Maybe. I was hoping for something with fewer DSM codes."

She's silent for a beat, then says, "I call it surviving."

I squeeze her hand, thumb tracing the ridge of her knuckles. "I call it staying. Showing up. Every damn day."

She studies me, like she's cataloging every cell in my face. "Then let's call it that."

We sit in the cold, the city buzzing beneath our feet, and for the first time, it feels like enough.

No emergencies, no high drama. Just us. Just this.

She tucks her head against my shoulder. "You know," she says, "if you ever start acting like a normal person, I reserve the right to break up with you."

I grin. "Deal. But you'll have to catch me first."

She doesn't reply, but her hand squeezes mine, and I know she means it.

We stay until the thermos is cold, until the wind picks up, until the lights in the admin building start winking out one by one.

Then we head down together, side by side, into the noise and the light and the rest of our lives.

TWENTY-NINE

LILY

The thing about going out to dinner as a couple—an actual, capital-C Couple—is that the whole world seems to be in on the joke before you are. Every restaurant in Capitol Hill has a waitlist. Every server greets you with a knowing arch of the eyebrow, the kind reserved for birthdays, anniversaries, and first dates that are clearly not going well.

Tonight, our chosen venue is two blocks from the hospital, but you'd think we were entering a parallel universe, one lit entirely by candles and the soft glow of other people's expectations.

Noah and I walk side by side, our paces mismatched but somehow always finding equilibrium. He holds the door for me—a move that would have made me break out in hives this time last year.

Tonight, I just smirk and mutter, "The patriarchy called, they want their gesture back," and he grins as if I've paid him a compliment.

The hostess beams at us with the brittle enthusiasm of

someone who's trained for both food service and hostage negotiation.

"Table for four, Dr. Harper?" Her voice is syrupy, her smile weaponized. She's already keyed in on us. Maybe it's the hospital badges still clipped to our coats, or maybe it's the way we smell faintly of antiseptic and poorly hidden stress.

We follow her through a corridor of booths upholstered in dark green velvet, past rows of couples in various stages of romance and ruin. Each table is its own biosphere: newlyweds playing footsie under the table, an older pair reading their menus in perfect, resigned silence, a group of off-duty nurses already two margaritas deep and getting louder by the syllable.

Maria and Ethan are waiting for us in the back, tucked into a corner booth that somehow makes their heads lean closer together. Maria's hair is out of its usual ponytail, dark waves framing her face, and Ethan looks like he's trying not to combust with happiness. They're both laughing at something —probably a joke Ethan told, because Maria's hand is on his arm and he looks like he's just discovered oxygen for the first time.

I would have rolled my eyes at this, once. I would have called it "the honeymoon phase" and mentally tabulated the odds of a breakup before dessert. Now, I just feel a weird sense of pride, like watching your mentee win an award.

Maria spots us first. Her face lights up, and she waves with both hands as if we might miss her otherwise. Ethan stands, which is a new development—he's either trying to impress Noah, or he's picked up some residual chivalry from somewhere.

Noah nudges me gently forward, hand at the small of my back. He does it casually, as if it's the most obvious thing in the world, but it still short-circuits my spine for half a second.

"Look at them," I say out of the corner of my mouth as we

approach. "Ten bucks says they're already talking joint finances."

Noah's eyes flick to the booth, then back to me. "You say that like it's a bad thing."

"It's a documented risk factor for homicide," I deadpan.

He laughs—a real one, not the polite chuckle he saves for patients. "I'll take that bet."

Maria is practically vibrating with anticipation as we reach the table. "You made it!" she says, as if we've just returned from the dead.

Ethan's smile is steadier, but there's something in his eyes —a calculation, maybe, or the comfort of finally being seen as a unit.

"Of course we made it," Noah says, sliding into the booth and somehow managing to take up more space than physics should allow.

I slide in beside him, my shoulder brushing his. Maria and Ethan are close on the other side, already an organism with a shared nervous system.

The table is set with mismatched candles in glass holders, the kind you find at estate sales and funerals.

"So," Maria says, barely containing her excitement. "Is this a double date, or are we still pretending we're just colleagues?"

"Can't it be both?" Ethan asks. He looks at me for backup, and I realize I don't have an answer ready.

Noah saves me. "Depends on who's paying," he says. "If it's a date, I'm expensing it as a morale-building exercise."

"Technically," I add, "it's a team meeting. The subject is resilience in the face of hospital bureaucracy."

Ethan laughs, which surprises me. He's not usually the first to break.

Maria leans forward, dropping her voice to a conspiratorial whisper. "You know, you two are a lot less intimidating outside the hospital."

I blink, unsure if this is a compliment or a warning.

Noah grins at her. "That's because we don't have access to scalpels here."

The server arrives and takes our drink orders with the practiced indifference of someone who's already seen three other tables crash and burn tonight. I order a gin and tonic. Noah gets whiskey, neat. Maria and Ethan both order the same IPA, in perfect unison, and then laugh about it for a solid five seconds.

I take a moment to observe them—really observe them. Maria's hand is never far from Ethan's. Every time he talks, she leans in, not just for the words but for the vibration of them. They mirror each other's body language without even thinking.

I look at Noah. He's watching me, not the couple across the table. He raises his glass in a silent toast.

"To us?" he offers.

I clink his glass, the sound sharp in the dark. "To us," I say, and it doesn't sound nearly as ridiculous as I thought it would.

The night is just getting started, and I have no idea how it's going to end. For once, that feels less like a threat and more like a promise.

The gin and tonic arrives first, beads of condensation already racing down the glass as if the ice is desperate to escape. Noah takes his whiskey in one swallow, then pretends he didn't, and when the server returns with IPAs for Maria and Ethan, they toast each other with embarrassing earnestness.

"To surviving another week," Maria says.

"To outliving the fridge in the residents' lounge," Ethan adds, raising his glass.

"To not being the subject of another HR PowerPoint," Noah offers.

I lift my glass, looking for a punchline, but all I can think of is, "To making it through dinner without a code blue."

The others raise their drinks, and for a second, it feels like we've all been doing this for years.

The conversation moves fast, buoyed by the way Maria and Ethan ping-pong off each other. They have that new-couple energy, still amazed that the other person exists. Their banter is a series of affectionate jabs, each one revealing a bit more about the weird, beautiful mess they've made together.

"Okay," Maria says, turning to us with the air of someone about to detonate a story she's been saving for the right audience. "You want to know how we almost got written up during our first week as interns?"

Ethan covers his face with one hand. "We agreed never to speak of this."

Maria ignores him. "So, he's supposed to file a progress report on a patient, right? Instead, he—"

"Accidentally," Ethan interrupts. "Accidentally."

"—puts the whole chart in the refrigerator. Not a copy, not a page. The entire binder." Maria pauses for effect. "Right next to a turkey sandwich."

Ethan's cheeks flush. "In my defense, it was four a.m. and nearing the end of a double shift."

Noah nods solemnly. "Classic mistake. Did you try microwaving it to see if the data still worked?"

"Unbelievably," Maria says, "it took them two hours to find it. Meanwhile, the entire med team is losing their minds thinking the chart's gone nuclear."

Ethan shrugs. "The turkey sandwich survived. That's the important part."

Maria leans over and kisses his cheek, which would have made me gag before, but now I just catalog it with mild amusement.

"My turn," Ethan says, emboldened by the attention. He

grins at Maria, who immediately goes on the defensive. "She once fell asleep standing up during rounds. Full-on narcolepsy. The team moved down the hall, and she stayed put like a statue for five minutes. When she woke up, she was still holding the chart, so she just sprinted after us."

Maria rolls her eyes but doesn't deny it. "It was the third day in a row without sleep. I'd do it again."

We trade stories for a while, the kind you only tell people who've seen you at your worst. There's a rhythm to it, a call-and-response of humiliations and triumphs, all leavened with just enough honesty to make it real.

Eventually, Maria and Ethan start in on hospital gossip— who's dating who, who got caught making out in the supply closet, which attending is most likely to be a robot. It's the usual, but tonight it feels less like surveillance and more like camaraderie.

At some point, I look up and catch Noah watching me. Not in the predatory, possessive way you see in romance movies, but in the way a scientist might observe a rare organism finally thriving in its native habitat.

"What?" I say, self-conscious.

He tilts his head. "You're different tonight."

"Not true," I protest, though I can't quite make it sound convincing.

He nudges my foot under the table. "You're not holding your fork like it's a surgical instrument."

I look down and realize he's right. I'm eating like a normal person, not attacking the food as if it insulted my family.

Maria and Ethan both notice the exchange. Maria gives me a look that says, *Go on, admit it, you're happy*.

I kick Noah back under the table. He just grins wider, utterly unrepentant.

The food arrives—a parade of small plates and mismatched utensils, everything meant to be shared. We reach across each other for bites, trade dishes, argue about who gets the last dumpling. There's no division of labor, no one keeping score.

At some point, someone tells a story about a surgeon who once performed a hernia repair in full clown makeup for a charity fundraiser. I lose it, laughing so hard my face hurts, and when I wipe my eyes, I see Maria smiling at me with genuine affection.

The restaurant is buzzing around us—silverware clinking, glassware chiming, strangers celebrating their own small victories. But at our table, it's as if we're in a soundproofed room, sealed off from the rest of the world.

I'm not used to this: the ease, the comfort, the complete absence of a need to be anywhere else.

For the first time in forever, I think I could get used to this.

Dessert is a chocolate cake so dense it threatens to collapse the table, and a crème brûlée with a shell so perfect I almost hesitate to break it. The table quiets for a minute, the four of us united in silent worship of sugar and butter. Maria snaps a picture. Ethan pretends not to care but immediately asks for it to be sent to his phone.

The first forkful of cake is so rich it makes my teeth ache. I push it toward Noah, who raises an eyebrow but takes the bait. We pass the plates around, trading bites and low-key insults. For once, I'm not cataloging every calorie or thinking about the gym session I'll need to atone for this later.

Noah's phone vibrates on the table, a low buzz that cuts through the candlelight. He glances at the screen, and I know before he says anything: trauma alert. He hesitates, thumb hovering over the notification.

I can see the tug-of-war on his face—professional obligation versus the lure of cake and company. Old Noah would have gone without a word. New Noah looks at me first.

"Go," I say before he can protest.

He frowns as if this is some kind of trick. "You sure?"

I lean over and kiss him, just a brush of lips, but enough to make Maria gasp and Ethan suddenly very interested in the tabletop's pattern.

"Go," I repeat. "I'll save your dessert. No promises it'll survive the night."

He laughs, relief flooding his posture. He shrugs on his coat, kisses the top of my head, and bolts, leaving behind a faint aura of aftershave and adrenaline.

Maria watches the exit, then turns to me with a look of awe. "Did you just let him leave in the middle of dessert?"

I fork a piece of chocolate cake and savor it slowly before answering. "I did. And if he plays his cards right, I'll even warm it up for him when he gets back."

Ethan laughs—a soft, genuine sound. Maria studies me for a second longer, as if recalibrating her mental image of me.

"I'm impressed," she says finally. "I would have thrown a fit."

"That's because you're a romantic," I say, not unkindly.

She grins. "And you're... What, exactly?"

I consider this, swirling the remnants of the crème brûlée. "Efficient," I say. "Maybe even sentimental, on a delay."

Maria seems satisfied by this, or at least amused. We settle back into the rhythm of the meal, Ethan and Maria taking turns ribbing each other, me playing referee but not really needing to. The absence of Noah is noticeable, but not painful. It's just... space, waiting to be filled.

We talk about nothing for a while—favorite movies, worst dates, the existential horror of medical billing. Maria tells a story about a disastrous Valentine's Day involving a goat, a helium balloon, and an unfortunate misunderstanding about lactose intolerance. I laugh, really laugh, and feel the sound echo all the way to my toes.

Every now and then, I glance at the door, half-expecting

Noah to materialize in a swirl of hospital-green, but I don't feel the old dread of waiting. If anything, I feel lighter. Like I've finally learned how to be present, even when the future is always one trauma call away.

We polish off the desserts, and Maria insists on ordering coffee for the table. The server brings it with a side of judgment, but we ignore her. We linger, the three of us, until the place starts flipping chairs onto tables and mopping around our feet.

As we gather our things, Maria gives me a hug—brief but fierce. Ethan offers a handshake, then switches to a shoulder squeeze at the last second. We leave the restaurant in a loose, meandering pack, the night air crisp and clean after the syrupy warmth inside.

I check my phone. No new messages. I tuck it away, oddly content.

Maybe I'm not just surviving, after all. Maybe I'm living.

Capitol Hill after midnight is basically the last level of a video game—quirky NPCs, unpredictable hazards, and a reward screen at the end if you make it to your apartment without tripping over a loose brick or being solicited by an amateur street poet.

Maria, Ethan, and I tumble out of the restaurant into air thick with ozone and streetlight. Maria's boxed up the leftover cake for Noah ("Protein for post-trauma recovery," she insists); Ethan has commandeered a stack of napkins and is currently using them to battle a chili oil spill on Maria's coat.

The walk toward the main drag is companionable and slow, no one in a hurry to be anywhere else. Maria and Ethan peel off at the light, headed for the parking lot and probably some unlicensed canoodling in the front seat of Ethan's Prius.

Maria pauses just long enough to hug me again, this time with less force, but more intent.

"You're coming to brunch next week," she says. "No excuses."

"Can't," I say. "I have a standing appointment with my couch and a history of bad Netflix decisions."

She snorts, undeterred. "Bring Noah. Or don't. Just show up."

I promise nothing, but we both know I'll be there.

They vanish into the crosswalk, and I'm left on the curb with a slightly lopsided box of cake and the luxury of my own company.

I savor it, this walk. The city is quieter than usual, the hum of distant traffic less frantic, the air less like a weapon and more like a promise. The crosswalks click and whir, lights changing for no one. I stroll past a tattoo shop still glowing neon at one a.m., a bakery prepping for the morning rush, a man in a raincoat walking a dog who looks older than some trees.

Halfway home, my phone buzzes. It's Noah:

Three traumas, one burrito, zero dessert. Send help.

On-call cupcakes in the freezer. Wake me when you're home.

He replies with a GIF of an exhausted sloth wrapped in a blanket. I save it to my camera roll, next to a photo of the two of us from earlier tonight. In it, we're both half-blinking, mid-laugh, unscripted and unguarded.

At a red light, I pause and look in the window of a vintage shop. My reflection stares back—hair windblown, makeup smudged, coat dusted with powdered sugar. I don't look efficient. I don't even look put together. I look... happy. Unfinished, but not broken.

And I'm okay with that.

I make it home in record time, unlock my apartment, and deposit the cake on the counter. The space is exactly as I left it: orderly, cold, maybe a little lonely. But it's my loneliness, on my terms. And it's only temporary.

I change into pajamas, check my phone again. Nothing new from Noah. I brush my teeth, debate texting him a goodnight, then decide against it. He'll be here soon enough.

I climb into bed, the sheets cool and smooth against my skin. I stare at the ceiling and listen to the quiet, cataloging the things that used to keep me up at night. The list is shorter than it's ever been.

Maybe this is what peace feels like. Maybe tomorrow will be a disaster, or maybe it'll be more of the same. Either way, I'll survive. Better yet, I'll live.

I close my eyes and drift off, cake in the kitchen, city outside my window, and the steady, certain knowledge that I am enough.

Hot Off
the Press

PRESS

THE
CHR

Breaking the news.
Breaking the rules.
Breaking each other's hearts.

alia smith

CHAPTER ONE

GRACE

I thread my way through what used to be the respectable half of *The Chronicle* newsroom, counting the number of new espresso machines and 'breakout areas' since the merger with *The Express.* Today, the open-plan is even more open than usual—whole banks of desks have been razed overnight, leaving tumbleweed clumps of Ethernet cable in their wake. Every face I pass is glued to a screen or a phone, but the air is thick with anticipation: something big is coming, and for once it isn't a police tip-off or a celebrity snorting coke in a pub toilet.

I clutch my coffee cup like it's a holy relic, thumb hooked through the handle, my last vestige of order in the chaos. The mug itself is a limited-edition *Chronicle Christmas* 2022, long since faded to a diseased grey. Some bastard has drawn a penis in Sharpie over the commemorative masthead. I don't even mind; it feels honest.

I skirt around a cluster of interns in slogan T-shirts, all of them speaking in that rising inflection that makes every statement sound like a question. Over the low privacy wall, the Crime desk is already breaking out the gin. Typical. There's *The Express* Features team, who moved into the office last week, glowering in their glass box like a pack of hungover wolves. You can tell the Broadsheet lot by their scarves and the way they look at everything with faint, cultivated disappointment.

My 'hot desk' for the day is in no-man's-land: the buffer zone between the dying world of print and the bloggy, viral, click-chasing disaster that is our digital future. I can see the wreckage of both from here.

I lower myself into a chair and do a quick visual sweep for hazards—spilled energy drink, errant Post-its, last week's newsprint ground into the carpet like ash. Satisfied, I open my laptop and spend two full minutes pretending to read my inbox while actually observing the movement patterns of my colleagues. From here, you can tell who's been called into the morning meeting already—everyone else walks like condemned prisoners, resigned but hoping for a last-minute stay.

A chirrupy ping from my phone: Dad, reminding me to "make the family proud." Because nothing screams pride like cross-checking the PM's decade-old expenses claim against a spreadsheet of sugar-baby subscription receipts. I text back a thumbs-up, then tuck my phone away with a sigh.

It's 09:29. The meeting is at 09:30. I glance at my reflection in the black screen of a powered-off monitor. Hair scraped back in an overworked ponytail, suit jacket aggressively navy, lipstick still (miraculously) present. I tug at my jacket, flatten the lapels, and pinch some colour into my cheeks. Mum would call it "polishing the armour." I call it survival.

The Editor makes her entrance at exactly 09:30: a middle-aged tornado in a trench coat, shoes sensible but eyes pure murder. She wields a novelty megaphone—another of her motivational gifts from management, I assume—and smacks it on the edge of a desk to get everyone's attention. A hush falls, broken only by the faint whirr of the Features team's coffee grinder.

"Right, listen up!" Her voice booms through the megaphone, setting off a minor panic in the sports corner. "As you all know, we're in the exciting, challenging, and frankly bloody terrifying first week of the new-improved *Chronicle* following our merger with *The Express*. Some of you have been here since we were using carbon paper and faxes. Some of you can barely spell your own names. Together, we're going to make this work, or die trying. Are we clear?"

A few mumbled affirmatives. The Features team, never ones to show weakness, merely arch their eyebrows and keep typing.

"Good!" The Editor grins, wolfish. "Now. One of the big changes is our cross-pollination of talent. That means all desks are hot desks, all stories are open for pitch, and you're all about to get very, very intimate with someone you may or may not like."

The room shifts, uncomfortable. I feel a low pulse in my throat, a kind of lizard-brain panic, but I keep my chin up and my gaze flat.

"Pairings will be announced now," the Editor continues, "and yes, it is random, and no, you can't swap unless there's an actual restraining order." She rattles a sheet of paper. "First: Anna and Jacek. Second: Monty and Prisha. Third: Grace Hampton and—" She pauses, and I already know, even before she says it. "Paul Callaghan."

I freeze, coffee cup halfway to my lips. Somewhere nearby, a stapler drops to the floor with a muted clatter. I count one, two, three heartbeats before I set the mug down, careful not to spill. Every muscle in my face has been trained for composure; only a tiny twitch in my jaw gives me away.

My vision narrows, a pinhole camera trained on the far side of the room. There he is. Black jeans, white shirt, sleeves rolled to the elbow, stubble a few days past respectable. Paul Callaghan leans back in his chair as if the last seven years have been one long, slow grudge. He meets my gaze and gives the tiniest shrug, as if to say: *Well, this should be fun.*

I manage a tight smile. Professional. Polished. And one-hundred percent fake.

My brain does a quick rerun of the past: Sheffield University, the student paper, the kind of late-night magic that burns too hot to last. The debates, the deadlines, the inside jokes that turned to arguments. And then the internship—mine, not his. A single decision that blew everything else to hell.

I thought the sting had dulled over time. But apparently, bitterness has a hell of a memory.

The Editor ploughs on, oblivious. "You'll be given a desk together and a weekly brief. Output will be monitored. If you can't work together, you'll both be fired and replaced with AI." She scans the room for questions. "No? Get on with it, then."

The meeting dissolves into murmurs. I stand, legs rubbery but serviceable, and feel the eyes of at least three people burning holes in my back. I manage to collect my laptop and the relic mug without looking at anyone, but as I pass the Features team, I hear them: "Is that *the* Grace Hampton?" "Didn't she used to be—?" "Yeah, with him. Drama."

I clamp my mouth shut, bite the inside of my cheek until I taste copper.

At the new desk—one of those ghastly modern things with a glass surface and no privacy—I arrange my things with surgical precision. Laptop exactly centre. Coffee to the right. Notepad to the left, pen uncapped and at attention. I focus on my breathing, force it to slow, force my hands not to shake.

Paul slides in opposite me with a nonchalance that is almost definitely rehearsed. He doesn't speak, just opens his laptop and begins typing as if the past seven years have been a mere prologue. He's as tall as ever, legs sprawled out under the desk, taking up more space than strictly necessary.

I sense, rather than see, a ripple of interest from the rest of the newsroom. Some people are here for the stories; others just want blood.

Paul looks up finally, and gives me that infuriating crooked smile. "Well," he says, "fancy seeing you here."

I smile back, tight and professional. "Small world, isn't it?"

He inclines his head. "Some would say inbred."

It's a test. I refuse to rise to it. Instead, I check my lipstick in the reflection of my screen and start drafting the day's column.

By noon, the first email arrives from HR: "Welcome to the new *Chronicle Express* Team!" There's a cartoon of a bee on it, in case we didn't get the cross-pollination metaphor.

I delete it unread.

By one p.m., I have typed and re-typed my opening paragraph twelve times, but can't get Paul's presence out of my peripheral vision. He hums while he works; a habit I'd forgotten and immediately resent. He writes fast, then stops, drums his fingers, and stares at the ceiling like a man searching for God in the air conditioning.

I get up to refill my coffee, and as I pass his side of the desk, I catch a glimpse of his screen: it's a spreadsheet of old *Chronicle* exposés, names highlighted in lurid yellow. There's a column headed "Untapped Stories." My own name sits at the top of one cell, right above the word "Skeletons?"

I don't break stride. I don't give him the satisfaction of looking back.

At the coffee machine, I steady my hands against the counter. They're shaking, just a little, but enough to make me hate myself for it.

It's not like we ever dated. Not really. What we had was

too quick, too bright, and burned out before either of us could claim it. But the anger—that's eternal. The memory of his hand on the small of my back as we ran to a student paper deadline; the way his eyes would go flat and cold when he was about to wound me, just for the sport of it.

I top up my mug, take a scalding gulp, and steel myself for the walk back.

At the desk, Paul is watching me. Not openly, but enough. I sit, log in, and fire off a pitch to the Editor: "The death of print journalism—report from the trenches." She replies in three seconds: "Love it. Pair up with Callaghan, see what you come up with."

Of course.

I paste the pitch into a shared Google Doc, and wait.

Paul types: "Nice opener. You've softened up since uni."

I reply: "You're just used to working with children."

He: "They're easier to train."

Me: "Less likely to stab you in the back, at any rate."

He doesn't answer, but I can see the twitch of his mouth, the way he's enjoying this. I refuse to give him more.

By five, we've drafted the column, edited each other's work, and managed not to murder one another. Barely. We've also hardly spoken, with communication limited to in-document comments. Bizarre. I gather my things, stand, and look him in the eye.

"See you tomorrow," I say, voice like ice chips.

He leans back, stretches, and says, "Looking forward to it."

I believe him.

As I leave, I can feel the newsroom watching, waiting for the first sign of blood. I give them nothing. My hands are steady, my mouth unsmiling, and my armour is back in place.

Tomorrow, I think, they'll have to try harder.

⚭

The next morning, Paul Callaghan makes his entrance as only he can: swagger dialled down to plausible deniability, sleeves rolled to broadcast a willingness for hard labour, but with that signature crooked smile to remind you that all of this is a game, and he's the reigning champion.

He pauses on the bullpen threshold, taking in the territory as if it's a wildlife documentary and he's sizing up the new alpha. The effect is immediate—conversations slow, screensaver glows multiply, and a heat-seeking wave of attention finds him, then rebounds to me, then back to him. A few desks down, the Sports desk starts a betting pool on how many days we'll last before HR gets involved.

He knows the room is watching. He plays to it, hands in pockets, chin up, eyes scanning the horizon before finally locking on me. Our gazes collide. My body betrays me with a full systems check: pulse up, shoulders back, jaw locked so tight I'll be massaging it for days.

He grins wider, lifts an eyebrow. Raises his hand in a lazy, ironic salute. The simple bastardry of it almost makes me laugh, but I force my expression into the granite calm I spent the whole bus ride perfecting.

He cuts through the desks with slow, measured steps, an assassin who wants everyone to see the knife. At three metres out, he stops to lean over the desk of a junior reporter—probably feeding them an obscene pun for the next day's headline. Two metres. One.

He stops in front of me, lingering just long enough to register the collective inhalation from the entire Features section. "Morning, Grace," he says, all politeness and mischief.

"Morning, Paul."

We stand there, old enemies, new partners, facing off with the polite grins of politicians before a televised debate.

The Features Editor, Sarah, summoned by some sixth sense for drama, swoops in with her arms already outstretched.

"Here we are!" she crows. "The Dream Team!" She says it with the same tone most people reserve for calling pest control.

She plants herself between us, radiating synthetic warmth. "Now, I know the last-minute desk arrangements are a shock, but think of it as an opportunity to, you know, build trust. Collaborate." She pauses for dramatic effect, her gaze bouncing between us. "Two of our best, together on one hot desk. The office is buzzing!"

Behind her, it is. Literally. At least five people are holding their phones in such a way that I'm ninety percent sure this is already being live-tweeted.

Sarah gestures to the pristine glass-topped desk directly under the big window—prime real estate, but with zero privacy and the least ergonomic chairs known to man. "This is you. Make it work. Keep filing your own pieces, but send your first joint column by Friday. Remember, the key theme: partnership." She claps her hands together, and the sharp sound lingers, a slap to the face.

She leans in, lowering her voice to what she probably thinks is a confidential volume. "I mean it, you two. The higher-ups want to see chemistry. Even if you have to fake it." Then she's gone, off to break up a minor insurrection at the News desk.

We're left staring at the glass slab, our own little island in a sea of anticipation.

Paul slides his messenger bag off his shoulder and drops it on the floor with a heavy thunk. "I hope you don't mind," he says, "but I took the liberty of booking us in for a brainstorm at the pub after work. Neutral ground."

Of course he did. I force a smile. "Not a chance. I wouldn't want to give the office pool an early payout."

He laughs, quick and sharp. "God forbid. I've got money on us holding on 'til Thursday."

I sit myself at the desk and begin the ritual of marking my

territory: notepad, pens, mug. Paul sets up directly opposite, mirroring every move with infuriating precision. We're so close that our knees nearly brush beneath the table.

He opens his laptop, the lid plastered with a sticker that reads: "Ask Me About My Data Breach." He makes a show of firing it up, drumming his fingers while the login screen loads. It's the same rhythm he used to tap on my thigh under the table at the Red Lion, the night we broke the story that made us both legends and, indirectly, mortal enemies.

"Do you want to write directly in the Google doc, or just shout over each other until something sticks?" he asks, voice pitched low so only I can hear.

"Whatever works for you. I'm flexible." I can hear the challenge in my own words and hate myself for it.

He tips his head, conceding the point. "I'll start with some research, then?"

"Perfect." I start typing, but every keystroke is haunted by the possibility that he's watching, judging, waiting for a mistake.

From the corner of my eye, I can see the newsroom's attention still locked on us. The Features team has a sweepstake grid going, red marker dotting our names in various cells labelled "fatalities," "romantic relapse," and "mutual destruction."

I decide not to dignify it with a reaction. Instead, I dig into the brief, determined to outpace him, out-write him, outlast him. I know how this will go: he'll try to charm, to provoke, to needle me into dropping my guard. But I'm older now, harder. I won't give him the satisfaction.

An hour passes like trench warfare—periods of tense silence, then sudden bursts of volleyed questions and passive-aggressive document edits.

At one point, he clears his throat and says, "You know, I've always admired your work ethic. Ruthless. I mean that as a compliment."

I keep my eyes on the screen. "And I've always admired your creativity. Even if it's mostly in service of self-preservation."

He leans in, folding his hands. "That's the only kind of creativity that matters, isn't it?"

I look up, let my gaze linger just a second too long. "Depends what you're trying to preserve."

He doesn't reply right away. He looks at me, really looks, and I feel my stomach lurch in a way I thought I'd trained out of myself.

A silence stretches between us, until the Editor's voice blares from across the room: "Grace! Callaghan! How's the new arrangement suiting you?"

Paul lifts his mug in a mock toast. "Seamless integration," he calls back.

I raise my own cup, chin up. "Like we were made for it."

Sarah beams. "That's the spirit!"

When she turns away, Paul drops his voice again, just for me. 'You're really going to make me work for this, aren't you?"

"You expect anything less?" I say.

Our knees bump under the desk, and neither of us moves away.

For the rest of the day, we play at truce. But everyone in the office knows it's only a matter of time before the first shot is fired.

And that, I realise, is what I've missed most of all.

CHAPTER TWO

♥

PAUL

The new office looks like an Apple store had a one-night stand with a WeWork, and now no one knows whose kid the bastard is. There's not a single soft edge in sight—everything is glass, chrome, and LED strip lighting set to a shade of "clinical optimism." I pause at the edge of the bullpen, two carrier bags weighing down my left hand, and take in the carnage. Even the air smells hostile, off-gassing from cheap furniture and management desperation.

My new desk for the day is front and centre, directly in the blast radius of the open-plan, and so transparent I can practically see my own shame reflecting back at me. There's Grace, already in place and radiating a weirdly tranquil aggression. Her jacket today is navy, sharp enough to be considered an offensive weapon, and she's arranged her notebook and phone in perfect parallel to the edge of the desk. There's not a single coffee ring or dog-eared Post-it in sight. Just like her to stake out territory before the ink is even dry on the seating plan.

I dump my carrier bags at my feet, making sure at least three people hear the thud. Someone in Features looks up, recognises me, and then ducks down again with a speed that suggests we're back in secondary school and I've just been let out of isolation. The rest of the room does a decent impression of working, but I can feel the low-frequency hum of rubber-necking. I know how this looks. The prodigal shit returns. The exiled son of tabloid hell, home to roost in the big leagues—if the big leagues now meant writing three listicles a week and dying a little more inside with every clickbait headline.

Grace doesn't look up, but she clocks me. Her eyes flick once, lightning-fast, then back to her laptop. I see the slight tension at her jaw—the tell she thinks nobody knows about, but is as obvious to me as a fire alarm. I almost smile. Instead, I press my palms flat against the glass and let the cold work up into my bones.

The ergonomic chair is set at a height appropriate for a toddler. I lower myself in, limbs unfolding like a deck chair that's lost the will to live. The upholstery squeaks. I make a mental note to sabotage it for maximum comic effect during a future staff meeting. For now, I just slide forward until my knees threaten to knock into Grace's. She doesn't shift. She wants me to know that this is her desk, her turf, her rules. She's *Chronicle* and I'm *Express*, and sharing a desk and even an office will never change that.

I oblige by making it a crime scene.

First, I open my battered laptop—the stickers on the lid have faded into a grey smear—and set it at an angle guaranteed to reflect sunlight directly into Grace's retinas. Then I extract my notebook, spine cracked, margins full of doodled gallows and anatomically improbable genitals. I place it on the desk with a soft slap, flipping open to a random page. For good measure, I flick at the surface, as if searching for invisible dust, and drag my fingers along the edge until the glass squeals in protest. Grace still doesn't react, but I see her hand tighten on her pen.

We sit like this for two full minutes, the world reduced to a two-square-metre theatre of war. My entire body itches. The shirt I picked up off my bedroom floor this morning is at least half polyester and refuses to behave—static clings it to my chest, rides up at the shoulders, snags at my elbows. I pull at it roughly, then look at Grace, who is (of course) dressed in a perfectly ironed blouse so starched it could stand up on its own.

She's changed, but not really. There's a new coat of polish —lipstick darker, hair more disciplined, makeup hiding the bags under her eyes—but beneath it, she's still the same. Hyper-competent. Incapable of half-arsing anything, except maybe her own happiness. The kind of person who'd get a gold star for dying if it were on the syllabus. Seven years and she still smells like ambition and posh perfume, with a hint of ink if you get close enough. I wonder if she still corrects grammar on street signs.

I don't get close. I know better.

Instead, I log in and start to work, or pretend to. My first action: Google "How to fake your own death and get away with it." My second: type up a list of all the stories I'll never get to write now that my days are numbered. I'm halfway through "25 Most Corrupt Council Leaders: Ranked!" when I feel her looking at me again. I meet her gaze dead-on, and give her the smallest nod. I can see the question in her eyes, clear as print: *Why are you really here?*

I'd ask myself the same thing, if I didn't already know the answer. It's simple. I lost a bet, a job, and my self-respect, in that order. Now I'm here so I can pay my rent, avoid Mum's phone calls, and pretend like I'm not one bad day away from joining the gig economy. I tell myself it's temporary. One week. One column. Then I can slip out the fire exit and never come back, telling everyone—including myself—that I gave the merger a go, but it just wasn't a good fit.

Grace breaks eye contact first, scribbles something in her notebook. Her handwriting hasn't changed—impossibly neat, borderline erotic in its regularity. I wonder if she ever writes angry. Probably not. Probably compartmentalises, bottles, files away under "To Be Processed When Convenient." I try to picture her screaming at someone in traffic, and can't.

My phone buzzes in my pocket. I check it under the desk, out of sight. Three missed calls from an *Express* colleague who was offered a settlement agreement the day after the merger was announced. A voicemail from my mum. A text from my bookie, who still thinks I'm on the inside at the *Express* and therefore have a hot tip for Premier League leaks. I delete them all, then flick the phone onto the glass so it skids to a halt, centimetres from Grace's perfectly aligned phone.

The office is louder now, with people moving purposefully and actually doing some work. Sarah, my new editor, is in her glass box, typing with two fingers and frowning at her screen like it's personally insulted her. I catch her glance in our direction, then away, then back. She's waiting for us to combust. Maybe she's rooting for it.

I allow myself a brief, ugly satisfaction in knowing that if anyone's going to break, it won't be me. I'm an old hand at public self-immolation. Grace, for all her control, still cares. That's her problem.

My hands are restless. I drum them on the desk, then run my thumbnail along the seam where the glass meets the metal frame. I flex my fingers. The office feels colder now, and I almost want to shiver, but don't. Instead, I glance at Grace, who is rereading her notes with a look of mild disgust.

I wait for her to say something, but she doesn't. So, I do.

"Thought you'd have switched careers by now," I say, voice pitched low enough that only she can hear.

She lifts her chin, eyes flat. "Why? The pay here is so competitive."

I snort, half a laugh, half a warning shot. "Could have gone into management. Or teaching. They love a control freak."

Her mouth twitches, just for a second. "And you could have gone into advertising. Or prison."

"Not too late," I say, and actually mean it.

There's a brief *détente*. We stare at each other, then away, then back again. The newsroom feels smaller, the glass walls closing in. Somewhere in the background, an intern is giggling into her sleeve. The Sports desk starts a slow clap, then stop when they realise we're not actually about to throw hands.

Grace picks up her mug and takes a long, deliberate sip. She never did like confrontation, but she's good at it when forced. I respect that, even as I make it my life's mission to force her into it as often as possible.

I watch her over the rim of my own mug, and for a moment, I remember what it was like to be on the same side of something. There was a time we could finish each other's sentences, and not always with a punchline. Now, we can barely stand to finish the same conversation.

"So." I clear my throat. "We going to pretend this is going to work, or are we just here to provide morale for the masses?"

She sets her mug down carefully, and smiles. "Why limit ourselves?"

I nod, conceding the point. "Always the overachiever."

There's a beat of silence, then Sarah's voice cuts through the noise: "Callaghan! Hampton! My office, now."

We stand at the same time, neither giving way, and collect our things with matching efficiency. As we pass through the bullpen, I feel the eyes on our backs, the betting pool updating live. I hope someone's smart enough to put money on the dark horse. If I have to go down, I'm taking at least three careers with me.

In the glass box, the Editor is waiting. She gestures us in, then closes the door behind us with a soft hiss. The walls are thin enough that if we shout, the whole office will hear.

I catch Grace's reflection in the glass. For the first time, she looks almost nervous.

I decide to enjoy it.

Sarah's glass box is more of a meeting room than an office. The big table has been set up like a breakfast bar, so tall my knees threaten to tangle with Grace's every time we shift in our seats. There are three glasses of water on the table, each poured to a different level, like some kind of psychological test. I claim the fullest, out of principle.

The Editor herself—Sarah, but always The Editor, even when off duty—perches on a stool and glances between us with a look usually reserved for bomb disposal. Her phone is glued to her palm, thumb twitching over the screen as if at any moment she might be called away to something more important, like a mass redundancy or a dog stuck in a drainpipe.

She clears her throat and puts on her best "fun boss" face. "Right. First of all, I want to say how thrilled I am that you two have been paired up. Truly." She nods at Grace, then at me, as if expecting us to catch contagious enthusiasm by eye contact alone. "You're two of our respective papers' most decorated writers. Your work speaks for itself."

Grace sits up straighter, pen poised. I slouch just enough to show I'm not buying it.

The Editor checks her phone again, then powers ahead. "I know this is a bit of a shock—merging the desks, the joint column. Management's really pushing for... integration." She grimaces, the word leaving a bad taste. "They want this to be smart but accessible. Hard-hitting but light-hearted. A bit of healthy back-and-forth." She gestures between us, like we're two sides of a novelty salt and pepper set. "You know, 'charmingly combative.'"

I make a note in my pad: "*Charmingly combative = punchable*." Then, for my own amusement, I doodle a hangman. The Editor watches my pen, jaw tensing.

Grace is all business, scribbling notes in handwriting so neat it could be a font. "Are we keeping the *Chronicle* style guide, or are we meant to dumb down for *Express* readers?"

The Editor blinks. "Oh, there's a brief. It's in the shared drive." She doesn't say whether she's read it. "But really, it's about chemistry. You two have history, right? I thought, why not use that to our advantage?"

I cough into my hand. "Not sure weaponising unresolved sexual tension is HR-compliant."

Grace's pen stops. She doesn't look at me, but her cheeks flush a shade darker.

The Editor ploughs on. "Right, well... think of it as an experiment. All the best columns have a bit of friction, don't they? The readers eat it up."

I say, "So you want us to bicker in print, and call it journalism."

She shrugs. "Worked for the *Telegraph* for years."

Grace jumps in before I can fire back. "Do you have a column title in mind?"

The Editor hesitates. "Well. Marketing has a few options, but I thought it might be better if it came from you. More authentic. Readers love authenticity."

She says "readers" the way politicians say "the people." I'm not convinced she's ever met one.

Grace nods, already listing options in her notebook. I can see her cogs turning—she's not above playing the game, as long as she gets to write the rules. I consider lighting a cigarette, just to see what would happen. Instead, I lean forward and drop my suggestion onto the table.

"He Said, She's Wrong."

The Editor blanches, eyes darting to Grace, who, to her credit, doesn't flinch.

Grace sets her pen down, aligns it with the edge of the notebook. "Or perhaps something less... inflammatory. 'Two Sides of the Story'?"

I grin at her. "Yours is more diplomatic. Mine will get the clicks."

"Mine won't get us sued."

The Editor exhales, a long slow leak of hope. "Why not brainstorm a few and send them over by end of day? I'll run them past legal, just in case." Her smile is now pure hostage video.

She slides two folders across the table, one for each of us. "Drop whatever you're working on. Your first topic is 'The Death of Truth.' Make it snappy. Maximum twelve hundred words, fifty-fifty split." She looks at Grace, then at me, then back to Grace, as if pleading for one of us to act like a grown-up. "You have seventy-two hours. There's a launch event Friday, so please try to have it in before then."

Grace opens the folder, already annotating. I glance at mine, then shove it into my bag unopened. I'll read it later, or never.

The Editor fiddles with her phone, then looks up. "Any questions?"

I ask, "Is this a test, or are we being punished for something?"

She laughs, but it sounds like a death rattle. "Bit of both, I suppose."

Grace smiles, professional to the end. "Thank you, Sarah. We won't let you down."

I nod, not quite agreeing. "Looking forward to it."

The Editor looks like she might vomit. "Right. Well. Off you go, then."

We stand, Grace gathering her things in perfect order, me knocking over my glass of water for effect. Grace doesn't comment, just hands me a tissue from her bag. I wipe the spill, but leave the glass right where it is, a half-moon of water spreading slowly toward the centre of the table.

Back in the bullpen, the tension has lifted. The Sports desk is arguing about something unrelated, the interns are playing games on their phones, and the Features lot has returned to their natural state of brooding. I follow Grace back to the desk, and for a moment, we walk in step, as if we've always done it.

She sits, then looks up at me. "We should meet after work. Actually brainstorm, if you're capable."

"I did offer a night in the pub."

She sighs. "Fine. But I pick the place."

"Deal. Nine?"

She hesitates, then nods. "Nine."

I watch her re-arrange her workspace, making small, invisible corrections until everything lines up. I wonder if she does the same with her life—endless, tiny adjustments, hoping that one day everything will just click.

It won't. Not with me here to fuck it up.

I flip open my notebook and start my draft, underlining the words: "*Death of Truth.*" I resist the urge to draw a tombstone.

Instead, I imagine what it would be like if we actually won. If we write the column, become legends again, and prove everyone wrong. The thought is so alien I almost laugh.

I look across at Grace. She's typing already, face set, jaw tight, like she's bracing for an earthquake.

I think, *I could do worse for a sparring partner.*

Probably will.

Keep reading:

https://mybook.to/HotOffThePress

SUBSCRIBE TO ALIA'S MAILING LIST
&
RECEIVE YOUR FREE NOVELLA

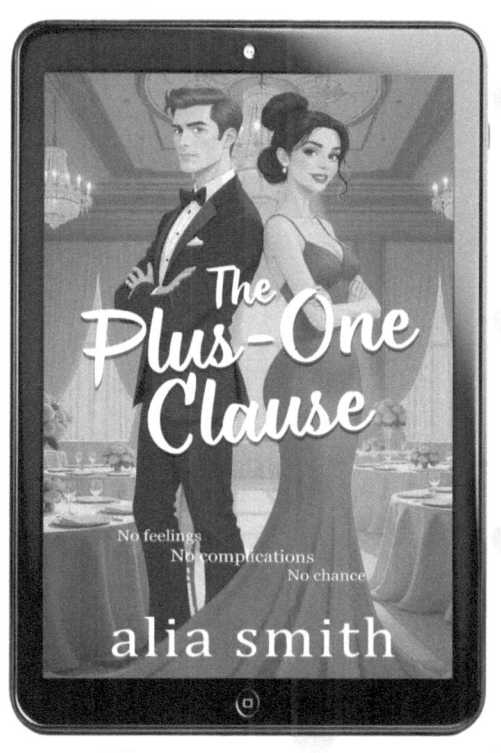

www.aliasmithbooks.com

ABOUT THE AUTHOR

Alia Smith writes heart-warming romantic comedies filled with wit, charm, and just the right amount of chaos.

When she's not crafting love stories, she can usually be found curled up with a book, getting emotionally invested in reality TV, or attempting to keep Galaxy—her cat and chief muse—from sitting on her keyboard.

She lives in a cosy Oxfordshire home, where she firmly believes that every great romance starts with a good cup of tea.

www.aliasmithbooks.com

instagram.com/aliasmithbooks

amazon.com/author/aliasmith

AUTHOR'S NOTE

Hi,

Thanks so much for reading *The Midnight Meet-Up*!

It was a lot of fun to write. I truly hope it was an entertaining read.

If you enjoyed it I would be incredibly grateful if you'd be so kind as to leave a review.

Reviews really help authors for a number of reasons, not least, providing feedback on what readers like and improving visibility of the book on online retail sites.

Thanks in advance and I look forward to reading your thoughts.

Alia xx

BINGE THE SERIES

BALKON media

www.ingramcontent.com/pod-product-compliance
Lightning Source LLC
Chambersburg PA
CBHW050550190726
48283CB00007B/2089